"The Highlands come alive... An extremely realistic historical that will keep you glued to each page."

—*Night Owl Reviews* Top Pick, 5 stars

"Wine delights readers as she creates an incredible marriage-of-convenience romance with excellent pacing, depth of emotion, sensuality, and grand storytelling. Wine always gets the heart of the history, atmosphere, and traditions of the Highlands, drawing her fans straight into her wondrous tale."

—*RT Book Reviews*, 4 Stars

"Highly entertaining...packed with sensuality... energy and passion leap from the pages... Mary Wine gives us a tantalizing read!!! A true win of a romance!!"

—*Addicted to Romance*

"Wine's attention to historical detail breathes life into this captivating tale."

—*Publishers Weekly*

"One heck of a page-turner... Mary Wine writes a great story with fascinating characters, lush scenery, hot scenes, and just the right dash of conflict... Ailis is everything I love in a heroine and so much more."

—*The Reading Cafe*

Also by Mary Wine

HIGHLAND WEDDINGS
Highland Spitfire

HOT HIGHLANDERS
To Conquer a Highlander
Highland Hellcat
Highland Heat

THE SUTHERLANDS
The Highlander's Prize
The Trouble with Highlanders
How to Handle a Highlander
The Highlander's Bride Trouble

COURTLY LOVE
A Sword for His Lady

STEAM GUARDIAN
A Lady Can Never Be Too Curious
A Captain and a Corset

HIGHLAND VIXEN

MARY WINE

Sourcebooks and the colophon are registered trademarks of
Sourcebooks, Inc.

Published by Sourcebooks Casablanca, an imprint of Sourcebooks,
Inc.
P.O. Box 4410, Naperville, Illinois 60567-4410
(630) 961-3900
Fax: (630) 961-2168
www.sourcebooks.com

Printed and bound in Canada.
MBP 10 9 8 7 6 5 4 3 2 1

One

1572

SHE WAS NOT AFRAID OF HIM.

At least, Helen had told herself so a hundred times over, and had even made certain to tell Marcus MacPherson the same when he was glowering down at her.

Yet, the truth was, she was running from him, and that bit of truth left her cheeks warm from temper. She snorted, finally pleased with some part of her circumstances. Standing in the rain, looking out over a deserted moor, she needed any way to warm herself, even being disgruntled. Her fingers were frozen, and beggars couldn't be choosers, after all.

"Having second thoughts, Helen?"

Helen turned to look at Brenda Grant. "No, simply enjoying a view that does no' include MacPherson Castle."

"Ye were there a long time." Brenda spoke softly, her tone hinting that she wasn't convinced by Helen's answer. "Long enough to consider it home."

Helen shook her head. "It is no' me home—that's why I left with ye." She felt something tugging at her heart but was determined to resist naming it. She'd made the choice to leave, so there would be no dwelling on anything left behind.

One of the Grant retainers burst out laughing. He was sitting with his comrades farther up the hillside from them in front of a fire. The men had built a crude shelter for the women before withdrawing to what was likely thought to be a respectable distance to preserve their good names. In the middle of the wilderness, it seemed ridiculous.

Brenda let out a sigh. "No' that I am one to offer advice on men. Me own circumstances are a mess, to be sure."

She patted the length of wool next to her. "Sit down, Helen, I am nae yer mistress. Share the shelter with me."

"I've no quarrel with me circumstances," Helen responded. "I am grateful."

Brenda's face contorted with disgust. "Oh aye, we are both reduced to being grateful for having to run like a pair of rabbits from the places that should have been our homes. Men have no kindness in them."

Helen settled down next to Brenda.

"Do ye think they know we're gone?" Brenda asked.

"I hope no'. The longer they think we're in the chamber with Ailis, the better."

Brenda looked at her. "Ye think Marcus will come after ye?"

"Nay, he has too much pride. The man is War Chief of the MacPhersons," Helen answered. "I worry they will come after ye, because returning ye to Grant land would gain them good favor."

Brenda was the niece of the current laird of the Grants, and she was a rare beauty. Laird Grant had arranged a second marriage for her, and she'd run before being forced to the altar.

"That is all we are to men in the end. A tool to be utilized," Brenda said. "Ailis is fortunate to have Bhaic's love."

"She is," Helen agreed as the rain increased and they both drew their feet up.

Brenda's words were haunting. Helen heard them well into the dark hours of the night, likely because the fairies and other night creatures enjoyed tormenting her by reminding her of her lot. Her simple life had shattered the moment she met Marcus MacPherson. He'd plucked her from her happy home as easily as he might a flower.

But she would not be broken, would not wither. No, she was going to find a way to regain control of her fate. So she'd left MacPherson Castle dressed as Brenda's serving woman. For sure, many would tell her it was reckless to venture out with so few men, but her alternative was to remain inside the castle and wait for Marcus to force a marriage on her.

She shifted in her sleep, the memory rising in full color. Marcus had lined up his men and offered her as a bride to them. To settle her into her life, he'd said. Well, she'd have none of it. Nor was she going to think about the way the man had decided to fight over her before one and all, as though he'd offered her even a single kind word that might have made her inclined to accept him. Damn him. He was her captor. She wouldn't be forgetting that.

Ever.

❧

MacPherson Castle was huge. It needed to be, because there were over three hundred retainers alone. When supper was laid out on the tables, their conversation echoed through the stone corridors. But that didn't stop a woman's scream from penetrating the chatter. Men came off their benches, their kilts flipping aside as they started toward the back stairwell where the sound had come from.

What stopped them was their War Chief, Marcus MacPherson, coming through the wide arched passageway. He had a woman with him who wasn't pleased to be his captive.

"What are ye doing?" Shamus MacPherson demanded from his seat at the high table.

"Uncovering a deception," Marcus replied to his father and laird. He set the woman in front of the MacPherson laird. "Helen and Brenda are no longer in this keep. Ailis has kept to her chamber to deceive us all into thinking Helen and Brenda were there with her. While this one"—he pointed at the girl—"has made sure no one saw her face to notice the game."

Shamus dropped his knife and looked at the girl. Her eyes widened. "I did as I was told by me mistress." She lowered herself awkwardly.

He snorted at her in reprimand. "Allowing her to act foolishly and leave the protection of this stronghold is no' to be commended, girl. Ye lack the sense to be a personal servant to me daughter-by-marriage."

The girl paled, shaking like a dried-out leaf in a windstorm.

Shamus grunted and waved her away before turning to his other son. "Best ye go discover what yer wife has been about this last week."

Bhaic MacPherson was already pushing his chair back. There was a grim set to his jaw as he moved behind the other chairs and down the steps to where his half brother was glowering at him.

"With child or no', that wife of yers needs a reckoning," Marcus growled.

Bhaic stopped in the passageway, just out of sight of the rest of the clan. "She is with child, so ye'll manage yer temper or no' be seeing her."

Marcus crossed his arms over his chest and grinned at his brother. Bhaic grunted, recognizing the promise in the expression. No one liked a fight better than Marcus, except perhaps Bhaic.

"I mean to have words with her, Brother," Marcus warned Bhaic. "And they will nae be kind."

"If ye truly want to frighten Ailis, speak nicely to her."

Marcus grunted and took to the stairs. Bhaic reached up and pulled him back by the shoulder.

"Helen may well be in the hands of the Gordons, thanks to this deception. Ye killed Lye Rob, and they would take great delight in paying us back in blood."

Marcus shot back at his brother. "Brenda and Helen could no' have more than half a dozen men with them."

Bhaic's face tightened. "I know ye're right to be

angry, Brother." He passed Marcus and took to the stairs. He offered his wife a single rap on the door of their chamber before he pushed it in and Marcus followed him.

Ailis Robertson was waiting for them. She stood in the center of the receiving room, ready to face them. Damn, but Marcus loved her spirit, even when it was at odds with what he thought she should be doing with all that strength of character.

"Ailis…" Bhaic began.

"I've deceived ye," she stated. "I've been pretending to be more ill than I am, so the women could stay with me and no' be seen."

"Ye know very well how the Gordons treat their captives." Marcus pointed at her. "Did ye no' think of what might happen to Helen and Brenda if they tried to ride across the Highlands with naught but a handful of men?"

She paled. Bhaic reached forward and gripped her forearm, but she sucked in a breath and steadied herself.

Marcus snorted at her. "How long have they been gone?"

"Four days."

Marcus gripped his sleeves so tightly his knuckles popped. "Where did they go?"

"To court, to seek shelter from Brenda's kin."

"Court." Marcus spat the word out like a curse. "Right into the hands of the Earl of Morton. Ye might recall how that man treats women he thinks can be of use."

Ailis stiffened. "I do."

Marcus grunted at her before he purposefully

turned on his heel and left the chamber, the longer pleats of his kilt flaring out behind him.

❧

"Ailis."

Bhaic MacPherson adored his wife, but his tone made it clear that he was less than pleased with her.

Ailis turned to face her husband. "I had to help Helen. Surely ye can see why."

"I was worried about ye," Bhaic informed her. "Abundantly so."

Ailis felt the nip of guilt. "I am sorry for that, truly."

Bhaic considered her for a long moment before he grunted. "Ye twist me, madam, and it is no' kind of ye to lord such a skill over me."

"It was nae for naught," Ailis defended herself. "Helen needed to escape before she was forced to wed a man whose only interest in her was pleasing his laird."

"Are ye blind, woman?" Bhaic demanded. "Marcus is smitten with her. He's been waiting for that serving woman to pop her head out of this chamber so he might have words with her because he thought she was Helen. *Waiting.* Marcus does nae wait on anyone except our father."

Ailis slowly smiled. "And yet, Marcus has no' said a single word about claiming her, only shown her to his men."

Bhaic was brought up short, forced to admit his wife was correct. "Marcus is a man of few words."

"As ye said, the only man in MacPherson Castle more stubborn than ye is yer brother."

Bhaic's eyes narrowed, but then he chuckled quietly.

"Aye, I said so and it's a solid truth. But he fought for her. When Symon was here, and ye know Symon had to offer to take her home since she was his kin and he is going to be the next laird. Ye know, Ailis."

"Aye, I do," Ailis agreed with a flush staining her cheeks. "That does nae mean I agree with the way yer brother locked Helen away the first time Symon was here."

"Because"—Bhaic held up a finger—"he is smitten with her."

"Yet he did nae declare himself."

Bhaic let out a long, frustrated breath. "He fought to keep her."

"After offering her to his men."

"He wanted to see if she'd take one of them. Marcus can no' afford to appear weak. He is the War Chief. The woman he takes to wife must crave only him."

Ailis offered her husband a small shrug. "He will have to decide if his pride is more important than admitting that to her."

Bhaic chuckled. "That will be an epic battle indeed."

Ailis moved closer, needing his touch, since she'd been going without it for most of the week. "Am I forgiven?"

Bhaic closed his arms around her, inhaling the scent of her hair. "Nay. Marcus is correct. It is dangerous to ride without proper escort." He lifted her chin so their gazes locked. "Ye know it full well."

"I do, and yet ye and I both know what it is to be forced into a union. Fate has been kind to us, yet that is not what happened to Brenda. Her husband was a harsh man."

"Aye," Bhaic admitted. "I see why they felt the need to run, but life is often hard, Ailis."

She knew that. It was such an undeniable fact that she stretched up and kissed the man she loved, taking solace in the way he brought her body to life and touched her heart. As for Brenda and Helen, she'd done all she could for them.

Helen was in the hands of Fate now.

❧

"Marcus."

There was only one man who could have stopped him in his tracks at that moment: his father. Shamus MacPherson still had moments when he sounded every bit as strong as he had been in his youth. But his hair was gray now and his body frail from the years he'd lived. Still, he sent his voice booming across the hall, so Marcus turned and moved toward him.

"They've gone to court," he informed his father.

Shamus made a soft noise in the back of his throat. Marcus ground his teeth together—he'd wanted to avoid discussing this with his sire. Shamus wasn't just his father; he was his laird. His word was law.

"Well now, they should have spoken to me on the matter," Shamus began. His captains were seated at the high table next to him, listening intently. "The Earl of Morton sent me a message, demanding details of how yer brother's union is faring. Bloody regent for the king, thinks his word is law—yet I suppose it is, for the time being."

His father seemed to lose track of what the point

had been. Marcus watched him put a chunk of cheese in his mouth and chew it.

"Were ye planning on sending a message back to the good regent?"

"Aye!" Shamus slapped the tabletop. "The man wanted yer brother and wife to come to him, but seeing as the lass is so ill with carrying the babe, I can nae agree to her traveling."

There was a gleam in his father's eyes that made Marcus relax just a bit. "It's the truth that she's been in her chamber for nearly a week."

"As we all know," Shamus continued. "And I can nae see sending Bhaic away, when it may well distress the lass further to have her new husband gone. Women are controlled by their soft hearts."

There were nods from the men listening.

"So then," Shamus said firmly, "I see no other course than to send ye along in their place. Since you're me only other son, the earl will have to be satisfied. Even if he is a Douglas."

Marcus reached up and tugged on the corner of his bonnet. He didn't trust himself to speak because everyone would have heard how much his father's orders pleased him.

They shouldn't have. He'd already spent far too much time thinking about Helen Grant. It might have been better if she'd been allowed to make her escape, for then he'd be able to get on with forgetting her.

Indeed, he'd told himself the same every day that he'd waited on the stairs for one of Ailis's waiting women to emerge from the chamber. He'd come so close to ripping the door open, and was slightly stunned that he'd managed to control the urge. Only his brother's assurances that his wife was ill had kept Marcus from the room.

He might be a bastard, but he wasn't coldhearted enough to risk scaring a woman while she was carrying a babe. Ailis was a formidable woman, but he knew what he was as well.

Feared.

There were times his reputation was helpful. Marcus stopped and wrestled with his frustration.

He needed to let her go. It would be better to have his father make a match for him with a bride who came to the union amenable.

Ha! More likely her knees would be knocking beneath her skirts!

"Going to be good to get out in the open air."

Marcus turned to find Finley coming up behind him. The retainer was wearing his customary grin, prompting Marcus to wonder for about the hundredth time just what the man found so enjoyable about life.

"Been inside for months now," Finley continued as he passed Marcus on his way out into the yard. He stopped and looked up before glancing back at Marcus. "Full moon, too."

"It will be that, all right," Marcus agreed.

Damn him for a fool.

He followed Finley, taking the fact that the moon would light their way as a sign he should go after Helen.

Indeed, fool. He could only hope he might come to his senses before he caught up with her. He was the War Chief of Clan MacPherson, a position he'd taken knowing full well he had to be suspicious, else he'd fail his clan. With a king on the throne who was only eight years old, it was best to look after his own kin, because that very same king's mother was intent on taking back the child and country she felt were hers. Elizabeth Tudor had done many in Scotland a favor by imprisoning Mary Stuart. The Earl of Morton, now regent for the king, was one of those.

Indeed, Marcus was suspicious by nature, and he suspected the earl would make good use of both women if they arrived at court. The earl had his own objectives, and they didn't include taking into account the feelings of those under his dictates. Brenda's uncle was laird of the Grants, so Morton wouldn't fail to see her use.

And Helen? Her father had a small, profitable estate in the Highlands with all the makings of a good place for Morton to position a spy.

The horses were already in the yard. Duana, his father's Head of House, came out of the passageway behind him with his personal belongings. Women were spilling out of the hall to bid their men farewell. Marcus lingered for a moment, watching them. But he snorted and tied his bundle to his saddle.

She ran from ye.

There was no reason for him to be thinking about having Helen to bid him sweet good-byes. Nay. He was going to perform his duty and nothing more.

He was not going to be dancing to love's tune.

And that was final.

✎❦

Court was not what Helen expected. Not one bit.

"Do nae stare." Brenda took her arm and steered her down one of the hallways. "I know they look a fright."

The ladies of the court had faces painted with white powder, red rouge, and lip color. Their hair was pushed up and over their heads to make it round. Their dresses were stunning silks and brocades that Helen would have enjoyed touching just to see what they felt like, but the dresses were huge and clearly supported by special undergarments of some sort. It was insanity to see how each lady held her hands perfectly in position due to the elaborateness of her costume. Some wore huge standing collars that went as high as their hair in the back. It was little wonder there was a small army of servants shadowing them.

"I have never seen anything so frivolous."

"Aye," Brenda agreed. "Fortunes are spent on those dresses, and for what? Ye must stand about all the day, hoping to be noticed for yer clothing alone. I was glad me husband sent me away from court." She drew in a deep breath. "It was the only thing he did that pleased me."

"I am sorry."

Brenda turned and considered her. "As if Fate has been any kinder to ye?"

"I believe it has," Helen admitted, realizing she was paying Marcus a compliment of sorts. "Ye were sent here to do yer duty, and I was taken for much the same reason. At least life among the MacPhersons did no' include someone having rights to me person."

Brenda's face tightened, memory taking hold of her. She shuddered and drew in a shaky breath. "Come, this way."

The women made their way deeper into the castle toward the rooms Brenda's kin had provided them. It was an older section of the castle, the stones dark and reeking.

"Court is no' so polished as ye hear in stories," Brenda said once they'd gone into their set of rooms and firmly closed the door. Inside, there was a receiving room that opened to a dressing chamber, and a bed was in the back. Only curtains separated the rooms.

"What a stench," Helen exclaimed. "Ye'd think those with finer blood than ours would know how to use a chamber pot."

"Ye'd think as much, no? I heard tell, Henry the Eighth forbid his courtiers to piss in the passageways, even had some of them lashed when they did nae obey because he was so a-feared his son Edward would catch disease." Brenda was pushing one of the windows open. A gust of cold air came in, but at least it carried away some of the stale air trapped in the chambers. It also disturbed the thick layer of dust coating everything. "Well, I suppose giving us these rooms is as warm a welcome as I am due."

"We're in the castle proper," Helen said as she looked around the rooms. "So we've no' come all this way for naught."

Helen began to pull the coverings off the table and chairs. Dust swirled in the air, but the furniture was sturdy and in good repair. Beyond an arched doorframe there was a bedchamber with a large bed that was hung with thick curtains.

"The difficulties will come with gaining enough coin for sundries," Brenda said. "Wood, food, drink, even water will have to be paid for. I'll need to go see me father's secretary and hope he has nae heard I've run away from the match me uncle made for me. It's still early enough in spring to think a letter has no' arrived here just yet."

A hope that was frail at best, but they would have to take what was at hand.

There was a pounding on the door. "Open in the name of the king!"

"The king?" Helen asked as she went to open the door. "The king is a lad of eight."

But there was an official-looking messenger standing in front of her. He wore the livery of the king and had a staff of office resting in his fingers.

"The Earl of Morton will see you both."

Helen felt a tingle shoot down her back. "We've only just come from the road."

"The regent will nae be kept waiting on yer vanity, woman. Ye'll come now as summoned."

There was no choice, really. Brenda knew it, coming across the receiving room. "Perhaps there will be supper," she whispered as they followed the messenger.

"Let us hope that is all there is," Helen whispered back. She knew full well what the Earl of Morton had pressed on Ailis Robertson. She would either wed Bhaic MacPherson or watch both their fathers be hanged because of the feud the two clans had been engaging in. Morton was determined to end such fighting and unify the Highlands. It sounded quite grand, until one considered that Morton was not above murdering to gain his will. He was not a man to be trusted, and Helen's belly knotted as she followed his messengers toward his receiving chambers. The doors they stopped in front of bore the royal seal of Scotland.

Indeed, she hoped the man would decide they were not worth his time, because if he took an interest in them, it would undoubtedly be for his benefit.

❧

James Douglas, the Earl of Morton, was a hard man. But what chilled Helen's blood was the gleam in his eyes that told her he believed in what he was doing. A greedy man might be controlled or influenced, but when one faced a man who had decided he was doing something for all of the right reasons, there would be no dissuading him from his course.

"Ye are the niece of Laird Grant?" he asked Brenda.

Brenda lowered herself. "Aye."

The earl's lips rose slightly. "And widowed?"

Brenda hesitated, earning a grunt from Morton. "Answer up, woman. Ye came to court seeking shelter. Well, I will be the one deciding on yer fate. Make no mistake."

"I am widowed. Me husband was a Campbell."

"I knew him," Morton said. "A petty bastard he was. And by the look of ye, it seems the rumors were true—the man preferred lads in his bed. Ye would get a monk's staff to rise. Ye are either barren, or the man did nae like women. Since he sent ye away so soon after yer wedding, I believe the latter."

Brenda was biting her lip and looking at the floor. Helen could see her battling the urge to speak her mind. The fact that she didn't sent a warning through Helen.

"Who are ye?"

Helen discovered herself under the cutting glare of the regent. Although she really should think of him as king, because that was how much power he wielded.

"Helen Grant." She lowered herself before him.

"Who is yer father?"

"No one of any importance," she answered.

Morton's lips curled just a bit. "I will be the judge of that."

"Me father has a small country home of his own and three sons."

"Hence she is me waiting woman," Brenda said.

The earl swept Helen from head to toe, taking in the modest clothing she wore. It was functional, made of serviceable wool.

He grunted. "Welcome to court. Ye are both me personal guests."

Brenda paled but sent the man a smile. "That is so very kind of ye. It seems my prayers have been answered."

"How so, madam?"

Brenda had regained her poise and offered the man a polished expression of serenity. "Me uncle, Laird Grant, is dying. He made a match for me with the Gordons. Such a match will serve only to unite the Gordons and Grants against the MacPhersons and Robertsons."

"Something I have little tolerance for."

"Yes," Brenda continued. "I heard of Bhaic and Ailis's wedding and surmised ye would no' be pleased with such a match."

"Ye think ye know me mind, woman?" the earl demanded.

Brenda lowered her body gracefully. "Only so far as I understand ye want an end to feuding, and such a match would have worked against that will."

The earl considered her for a long moment before he grunted. "Ye're intelligent enough, it would seem." He tapped the arm of the huge throne-like chair on which he sat. "Aye, well done."

The earl gave them a flip of his fingers, dismissing them. But four of his men followed them back to their chambers and took up position by the doors.

"Sweet Christ," Brenda breathed as she dropped into a chair. "I have brought ye to ruin, Helen. The Earl of Morton is a Douglas, and he's got his mind thinking about how to use both of us to his advantage. Damn all men and their ambitions. We are but lambs."

"Do nae say such," Helen admonished her. Brenda looked at her, uncertainty glittering in her eyes. "Ye heard me. We crossed the lonely moors with but a handful of men to find our own destiny, so do nae be giving up on that just yet. Yer kin will nae be able to force ye to wed one of the Gordons at the moment. That is what ye wanted, yes?"

"Aye," Brenda agreed as she stood. "It is. We'll take each day as it comes."

"Ye beguiled the earl well enough."

"Better to have him thinking I am his servant," Brenda remarked. "We might need his trust."

"For the moment," Helen said, "it would seem we have found a means of providing the sundries we need. If we are the man's guests, he can bloody well provide for us."

"I am more concerned about what he might decide we need beyond food."

So was Helen, but she didn't voice her concerns. She'd learned during her time at MacPherson Castle to keep her thoughts close and her mind working on ways to achieve her goals.

There was no way she was going to become submissive now.

❧

Morton's men were still at the door when Helen decided to venture out in search of supper.

Helen didn't let their presence disturb her. Instead, she focused on the fact that she was allowed out of the chambers. Guards might be lost in the crowded kitchens. She and Brenda had escaped Castle MacPherson, so all she needed to do was to discover a way out of court.

But she needed a place to go as well.

Why was life so difficult?

She made her way around the kitchens, simply another servant among many. There was a bustle near the cooking fires as the cook tried to decide where the best cuts of meat should go. Everyone was intent on making their way as best they might. Helen gathered up plenty of fresh food, telling the cook that she worked for a "personal guest" of Morton when the man thought to forbid her some rare oranges.

Helen was hurrying into the passageway, moving away from the kitchens, when someone stepped into her path. She started to go around, but he reached out and clasped her upper arm.

"Take yer hands—" Her tongue ended up stuck to the top of her mouth as she looked straight into the eyes of Marcus MacPherson.

And the man was furious with her.

"I've a mind to put them on yer backside, woman," he informed her under his breath as he pulled her out of the passageway and behind a door while she was still gathering her wits.

Realizing they were alone sobered her quickly. "Stand aside at once."

Marcus braced himself between her and the door. "If ye think to leave this chamber, ye'll go through me or no' at all, Helen. We need to have words."

The use of her first name sent a ripple of sensation through her. It was a familiarity he was using deliberately. "I can nae believe ye came after me."

"I did nae." He scoffed at her, his expression set in a hard mask. "I was summoned by the Earl of Morton. But that will not stop me from telling ye how foolish it was for ye to travel without a proper escort."

He hadn't come after her.

That knowledge shouldn't have stung, and yet it did. She felt as if a deep, burning mark were left across her emotions.

Shame.

She knew what it was called and couldn't truly shrug it from her shoulders because Marcus stood there, his eyes ringed by dark circles of fatigue because he *had* ridden hard after her. He'd worried about her welfare and she was sorry for that.

"Nae foolish, when ye made such a mockery of me good name by kissing me as if I were yer strumpet

in yer father's open hall before ye fought over me
and denied me the opportunity to return home with
Symon Grant." She drew in a deep breath but kept
her tone mindful of the concern she saw in his eyes.
"Any decent woman would have left such a situation.
I could not stay without declaring to one and all that
I belonged to ye."

Marcus's eyes narrowed, giving her the only hint
that she had affected him at all. Yet that failed to please
her. All it did was make her feel as if she were the most
unkind creature drawing breath.

"It was necessary to leave and so...I did." She
meant to brush around him, but Marcus didn't move.

"We're nae finished." He grasped her upper arms
the moment she came close enough. The food went
spilling onto the floor as she gasped, feeling his touch
as though his fingers were somehow on fire.

She'd convinced herself her memory was clouded
and she hadn't felt his grip so keenly during that kiss
at MacPherson Castle.

Now, she knew it was a solid truth that his touch
affected her, and she recoiled from it.

Marcus jerked her to a halt.

"Do nae," she warned softly. "Ye have yer position.
Do ye nae realize that me good name is all I have?"

"I did nae take ye from yer father's house without
thinking I had few other options."

It was the closest thing to an apology she'd ever
heard from him. She shifted because she was not
accustomed to being anything more than a hostage to
him. Apologies, well, those were given out to friends
and people that a person valued.

She had no idea what to make of it at all.

He was watching her intently, allowing her to be drawn into his topaz gaze. It was spellbinding, weaving some sort of magic over her that made her want to stand still and simply enjoy the moment.

"Marcus…" His name slipped through her lips while she was too caught up in the strange effect he had upon her.

"I like the sound of me name on yer lips." His attention slipped down to them. "But I believe I'll enjoy the taste even more."

She knew she would agree. Which was why she rebelled, lifting her knee and jamming it up toward his genitals. He shifted so she hit his thigh, but she was free and the door so very close. Helen grabbed it and scurried into the passageway as though her skirts were on fire.

Maybe they were—with hellfire, that was—because the temptation to kiss him was so strong that Helen suddenly didn't fear eternal damnation.

"I am sorry ye felt responsible enough to make certain I was safe." Back in the passageway, there were other servants about. Marcus stopped and crossed his arms over his chest when he realized they had witnesses.

"Gather yer things. I've business to attend to. Finley is in the stable with the horses. This is no fit place for ye or any decent woman."

He spoke the truth and was using her reasoning against her. She couldn't stop that thought from filling her mind. Marcus read it in her face, because he stepped closer, angling his head so he might look down on her from his greater height. How had she argued with him so freely? The man truly was huge. He could close his fingers all the way around her upper arm and lift her with ease, but she always seemed to forget that when he was close, saying whatever came to her mind. He set something loose inside her.

"I'll take ye back to the Highlands, lass."

"To what fate?" He really was the last person she should have thought to appeal to, but she couldn't seem to stop the words from crossing her lips. "One of yer men?"

"Castle MacPherson is a fine place to live," he answered her. "What will ye have here but a different union? One Morton makes the choice of. I doubt he'll be asking yer opinion on the matter."

He was right, but he was also the reason she could never go home. However, perhaps it was time to be bold enough to challenge him. "Let me go home. Lift the threat ye laid upon me when ye took me. Tell me ye will nae burn me father's house if I return to it. I will go with ye if ye do, and be grateful."

His jaw was tight, his neck corded. "And just what will yer kin do with ye? Do ye think I do nae know what their thinking is?" He shook his head. "They will wed ye to a Gordon, so they might think themselves safe from MacPherson reprisals when they take to thieving our cattle again."

"Me brothers were stealing back cattle that were taken," Helen said in defense.

Marcus scoffed at her. "If someone stole yer cattle, it was nae MacPherson men. Why do ye think I was riding on yer father's land? I was tracking our own missing heads. Yer brothers knew full well they were taking the easy way out by taking from MacPherson stock, thinking we have so much, no one would be the wiser. But we have more mouths to feed. The moment I fail to stop one family from stealing from me father is the beginning of everyone thinking they can thieve from us, and then I'll no' be able to feed me own kin. Ye have seen how many men expect supper in the hall. It's me duty to make sure they are provided for." He caught her arm when she tried to step back. "I took ye for yer own good, Helen. Yer brothers were playing a dangerous game, dabbling in dishonesty. Ye would nae have been safe from it."

She drew in a deep breath, trying to fend off hopelessness.

"It is long done now, and me brothers have learned ye will no' leave the matter be." She spoke firmly, fighting back against the truth of his words. She had to. Otherwise, the only course of action left was to submit to his will. "Lift yer promise."

"I will nae."

"Then I will nae go with ye," Helen told him softly. She pulled against his hold. He hesitated, but the curious looks being cast their way made him release her.

He let her go, and that stung far more than his grip had. "Perhaps me fate here is uncertain, but I will embrace it over being a prisoner of the MacPherson."

She turned her back on him and hurried away.

Beast.

She should hate him.

So why didn't she?

Oh, she knew it was in the way he'd come after her.

Her emotions were a tangled mess as she battled the urge to trust him while trying to recall that she couldn't do anything of the sort. The man had stolen her.

Yet he'd ridden after her.

Tangled.

And she very much feared that she was going to be strangled before she reasoned it all out.

❧

"MacPherson sent his bastard to see me?"

Morton growled but he wasn't really angry. No, anger only served one's enemies. He was thinking. Contemplating what he had to work with, which at that moment was Marcus MacPherson.

"Your plan to keep the MacPherson heir will not be realized," Morton's secretary said.

"That day will come," Morton warned in a low tone. "Have no doubt of it. The clans will come to respect the crown, and that can only be assured if their sons are raised here."

"Shall I dismiss the man?"

Morton held up a finger. "Nay. Marcus is MacPherson's War Chief."

The secretary nodded.

"I have a use for him that will send a stern message into the heart of the Highlands. Tell him I will summon him later today."

❧

The Earl of Morton was the fourth regent for James Stuart, and he knew that fact full well. He knew a few other things too, such as the fact that his predecessor had been poisoned. Of course, he had ordered the deed done.

He held out his hand for his cup. A burly retainer held it to ensure that Morton didn't suffer the same fate he'd given. Morton took a long sip and didn't allow guilt to settle on his shoulders. Scotland needed sacrifices. He'd done what needed doing to ensure that young James remained king and a Protestant. England's Queen Elizabeth could keep Mary Stuart as long as she liked, because if Mary ever came back to Scotland, Morton would happily kill her.

It really wasn't a matter of faith, choosing Protestant or Catholic. No, it was about unity. Morton wanted Scotland to rise up and become a respected nation. That would never happen if Scots fought Scots in a war that would only end when half the population was dead.

Which meant religion wasn't the only matter he needed to quell. Morton considered Marcus MacPherson, now before him. The man was pure Highlander and none too happy to have been kept waiting. Morton felt his pride rise as he considered the stance Marcus had taken in front of him. There wasn't a hint of fear in him, his feet braced at shoulder width, his arms crossed over his massive chest. The man had tugged on the corner of his knitted cap, but that was as courtly as Marcus was likely to get. Morton enjoyed that too. He didn't care for the feminine airs many of his courtiers had adopted from France and England. Scotland needed to unify, but her men should bloody well recall that they *were* men and leave the simpering and silk for women.

Marcus hadn't put on any velvet to impress him. No, the War Chief stood there in his kilt and wool doublet, with a leather jerkin. The only concession he'd made was to wipe the mud from his boots. Men such as Marcus would lead ranks of fighting Scots the rest of the world would have to reckon with. Which made it imperative that Morton bring the clans under control. He needed them to defend Scotland and keep her young king on the throne, not feud with one another.

"Yer father sent ye."

Marcus wasn't intimidated by the Earl of Morton's tone. "If ye do nae want to speak with me, I'll be on me way."

The earl smiled. "And no doubt consider the summons answered."

Marcus shrugged. "Well now, me brother, Bhaic, and his bride are expecting a child. That should assure ye they are doing their best to make the match ye insisted upon a good one."

"And the raids between Robertson and MacPherson have stopped," Morton cut in. "Aye, but now the bloody Gordons are making trouble."

"They are hardly the only ones, and old Laird Gordon is no' going to see the end of next winter," Marcus responded. "Lye Rob was a rat, and ye know it well. More important, the men of the Gordon clan knew it. They will nae have the heart to fight over his memory once their laird is gone to join his son. Better turn yer attention to Diocail. He'll be laird of the Gordons, and I do no' think him a fool."

Morton slowly grinned. "Ye're a worthy War Chief."

Marcus inclined his head. "I do me duty, and now that I've seen ye, I will be on me way. A War Chief belongs on his land, where he can attend to his duty."

"Let us discuss what I consider to be yer duty to Scotland."

Marcus stiffened. "Ye've already had yer way with me family in the matter of me brother's wedding. The feud between Robertson and MacPherson is put to rest. Keeping it there will take a great deal of me time, and I can nae attend to the matter while I'm standing here in the Lowlands."

"So do nae trespass upon yer patience?" Morton asked.

Marcus nodded once.

"Scotland needs all of her sons. The English queen is past her child-bearing years, and every nation in Europe is making ready to invade her realm."

"All the more reason for me to be grateful I was born Scots."

"Aye," Morton said. "Yet the world is nae as small as it once was. No' with ships sailing farther and discovering new lands. It is a fact that we share our island with England. War with England has cost Scotland greatly for centuries. Without an heir, our king is in line for the English throne."

"That will be a fine bit of justice, sure enough." Marcus chuckled. "Maybe settle a few ghosts down and give us some peace during the dark hours."

"Aye, justice at last," Morton agreed. "Our king will need strong alliances in place to support his reign."

Marcus wasn't slow-witted. His expression hardened. "What are ye getting at, man? I told ye that if ye want that feud to stay buried, I am the one who will make sure of it."

There was a clear warning in Marcus's voice. Morton wasn't offended, instead admiring the Highlander's strength.

"It shall require yer attention, of that I have no doubt," Morton said. "A marriage only begins the process. Highlanders do nae like to let their feuds go easily."

"Good to hear ye agree with me." Marcus reached up and tugged on his cap. "I will tell me father that ye considered the summons answered."

"Aye," Morton agreed.

Marcus was heading toward the door in the blink of an eye. Morton made a motion with his hand, and the men standing guard braced themselves in front of the door.

"Yet there is a service I require of ye, War Chief of the MacPhersons."

Marcus turned around slowly, clearly wrestling with his temper. "And what might that service be?"

Morton chuckled, letting out a crusty laugh as he hit the arm of his chair. "Ye are pure Highlander, man. Ye have no idea how it turns me stomach to walk through yon doors and witness good Scotsmen taking up the ways of the French court. That bitch Mary Stuart brought it here. Lace, perfume, men painting their faces like doxies. It is me pleasure to know her son will nae be raised by her."

"I'm Highlander enough to want to be finished with this summons. I belong on MacPherson land. Tell yer men to move aside before I lose me temper."

"The service I require of ye first."

Marcus faced off with him. "Keeping the feud between Robertson and MacPherson buried is going to take the next ten years of me life."

"Aye, and that is a service I appreciate, to be certain."

"Glad to hear we are in agreement." Marcus turned toward the door again.

"Yer father has raised a worthy son. I admire him for teaching ye duty before preference," Morton stated firmly. "I have a duty for ye."

∽

He didn't want to turn around.

No, Marcus would happily have chosen a fight with the men at the door, and that made him grind his teeth. The Earl of Morton had used such tactics before. The man was crafty, no doubt about it. Marcus had to think of his clan. The Earl of Morton was the regent, so there was no fighting his way out of the chamber.

Marcus turned and sent the man a hard look. "What is it ye want of me?"

"Since ye will be returning to MacPherson land and staying there," Morton said, "ye could help me establish a strong alliance with England by taking home an English bride."

"The fuck ye say."

The earl only smiled at his outburst, which pissed Marcus off.

"I thought ye wanted alliances. Tell some English lass she's to wed me, and she'll die on the spot the moment she gets a look at me. I do nae think that is the sort of alliance ye seek."

Morton started laughing.

"Enough," Marcus grunted. "Ye are toying with me."

The earl sobered. "I assure ye, I am no'."

All traces of amusement were gone from Morton's tone. Marcus suddenly understood in a very personal way just how his brother had been forced to wed. The man in front of him was ruthless to the core and intent on gaining his way. There was a cold, calculating gleam in his eyes that Marcus knew better than to discount.

The earl made a motion with his hand, and one of the doors was opened. There was a rustle as someone came in. Marcus prided himself on his strength, but he wanted to puke when he got a good look at the female Morton was presenting to him.

"She is a child," he spat in disgust.

"Fourteen."

Marcus stared at the girl in horror. She still had that slimness of limbs that went with an immature body. She blinked at him, her eyes large in her face. Two of Morton's men were pushing her forward. She shook her head and stepped farther into the room.

"Ye see? Katherine has a solid spine. She'll be a fine match for ye."

Marcus turned his attention toward Morton, but not before he caught the flash of fear in Katherine's eyes.

"Katherine Carew is the natural daughter of Francis Russell, the second Earl of Bedford. Bastard born, as ye are. Her father will soon sit on the Privy Council in England. It will be a fine alliance."

"Ye stole her." Marcus spoke quietly to mask his temper. "There is no way her sire would agree to an arrangement like this."

"Which is why I have selected ye for her groom,"

Morton explained. "Ye'll wed her tomorrow, stay one night so I can make certain the union is binding, and then take her to the Highlands until she gives ye a son. Her father will have no recourse after that."

Marcus actually took a step away from Katherine. "The hell I will." He growled at Morton. "She"—Marcus pointed at her—"is too young. For all that I am a bastard, and a mean one, I'll admit, I will no' be putting me hands on so tender a lass. 'Tis indecent."

"I am assured by the midwife that she has her woman's flow."

Katherine was pale. It was all Marcus could do to stand in place and try to think of a solution that did not include locking his hands around the Earl of Morton's neck. If it were only him, he would indulge his temper, but the lass standing there blinking at him and biting her lip to keep silent would only be given to another. Perhaps a man who valued Morton's approval more than his own decency. There were plenty of men who would sell their souls for the approval of the regent.

"A wedding and I will take her home, but there will be no bedding until she is grown fully to womanhood."

"Ye think me a fool?" the earl asked.

"To offer me a lass for wife, ye must be," Marcus answered pointedly. The earl's eyes narrowed with his displeasure.

"Take him."

The guards didn't hesitate once the order was given. Marcus turned on them, relieved to have an outlet for his disgust. But more men poured in from the side entrance, shoving Katherine aside. As he fought, he smiled when he noticed the lass grabbing her skirts and running toward the door that led to the court. She yanked it open and tried to escape while Marcus kicked one of Morton's guards through the door behind her.

Finley had been waiting on him. The retainer jumped into the fray as two guards grappled with Katherine. Morton had planned his attack well, making sure there were too many men for Marcus to defeat. They held him down by sheer numbers as he snarled at Morton.

"Ye'll wed her and bed her. Defy me, and yer clan will suffer. I swear that to ye," Morton hissed. "A night in chains will help ye see the wisdom of doing what I say. Take him away."

❧

"Helen, what is wrong?"

Brenda came toward her, cupping her shoulder to turn her around so she might get a better look at her face.

Helen stared, horrified by what she had to tell Brenda. "Marcus is here."

Brenda gasped. "He followed ye."

Helen scoffed. "The beast claimed he did not, that the earl summoned him."

She couldn't seem to stand still. She paced across the chamber and back as Brenda watched her.

"Of course. The earl is likely making certain Bhaic and Ailis are truly wed. Morton is a man who intends to have his way."

"Aye," Helen answered.

That was likely the way of it. She should be happy, but she wasn't.

No, she wasn't. Her heart ached, and that only frustrated her because she had set her mind to forget him, and yet she'd longed for that kiss, just as much as he had.

It would seem she had not escaped at all, and the only way to do so was to purge Marcus from her thoughts.

It was her poor luck to discover she had no idea how to accomplish that goal.

∽

It was hours later when Helen returned to the kitchens for more food. Servants were taking their ease, now that their masters had been served their suppers, and were enjoying their drink.

"Ye should have seen him…"

"He took on six men before they managed to capture him…"

There was a breathy female sigh. "A Highlander for sure. Such a shame he's to be wasted on so young a bride."

Helen slowed down, listening to the maids. They stopped when they caught her looking at them. It was rude. She should have looked down and been on her way, but their words were stuck in her mind.

"Are ye talking of Marcus MacPherson?" The words seemed to cross her lips before she decided to ask the question.

One of the maids smiled. "Saw him, did ye? Then again, he is no' a man that is easily missed."

Helen offered her a nod.

The maid looked around before she continued. "The regent wants him wed to an English chit that he's had locked away in one of the towers. I hear she's related to nobility."

The tray Helen held slipped from her grasp. The maids jumped as food went spilling onto the floor.

"Are ye daft?"

"Mind yer duties."

Helen stooped down to gather up the mess. "What happened to the MacPherson?"

"The earl had him tossed into chains, of course," one maid answered with a shrug. "The man is the regent. His will must be obeyed."

"Marcus MacPherson is the War Chief of the clan," Helen said. "He will not bend."

"Oh, he will," the maid informed her smugly. "There's a reason the Earl of Morton is the regent. The man is ruthless. That MacPherson will break."

"How?" Helen inquired in a hushed, horrified voice.

The maid was enjoying the moment. She smiled as she leaned closer to Helen, lowering her voice so it didn't carry through the stone passageways. "The earl is going to use the whip."

Helen cringed but her confidence returned. "Marcus will die first, and the earl will not want to have to explain to the MacPherson clan how such a thing happened."

"No, no, the whip will not be used on the War Chief," the maid explained. "The girl. Only a monster would fail to break when her tender back is bloodied."

"Helen?"

Brenda cupped her shoulders and pulled her completely into the chamber before shutting the doors.

"Tell me what has ye so horrified."

Helen snapped out of the shock she'd been in since leaving the kitchens. That left room for her temper to rise. "The Earl of Morton is a vile villain."

"Worse still, one who believes his cause is just," Brenda agreed. "Such makes him very dangerous, make no mistake. Now tell me what ye heard."

"The earl has Marcus in chains."

Brenda's face tightened, but Helen suspected it was because the other woman thought Helen was beset by tender feelings.

"And I would be angry if it were any innocent man put into chains," Helen informed her.

"We'll puzzle that another time," Brenda said, sweeping Helen's declaration aside smoothly. "Why is Marcus in chains?"

"The earl wants him matched with an English bride. Yet she is only fourteen."

Brenda recoiled in distaste. "It would seem Marcus is worthy of my good thoughts."

"Aye, worthy." And yet he was in chains. Helen paced across the chamber, desperate to discover a means to assist the man.

"Ye want to help him?" Brenda asked.

Helen turned back. "The earl plans to whip that girl until Marcus relents."

Brenda sucked in her breath. "He will have to, or Marcus is no' the man I believe him to be."

"She is fourteen, just barely so."

"I know full well what she faces." Brenda was standing, her fists tightened as she relived the nightmare of her marriage. "And I doubt the earl will leave the matter of consummation in question." Brenda's tone was tight. "This is court, so there will be witnesses to the bedding."

"That is disgusting."

"Aye." Brenda shook her head. "And no amount of tears will stop it. There are true villains here who enjoy the suffering of the innocent. It will be an entertainment enjoyed to the fullest by some."

"And they will no doubt enjoy seeing Marcus's honor break because they have none of their own." Helen felt her temper rise. Only this time, it was on Marcus's behalf. For certain, she found him overbearing, and he had wronged her. But she now recognized he had taken her for all the right reasons, and he deserved respect. Had earned it.

Brenda stared for a moment into the air, her mind lost to a memory. She shuddered before she drew herself together. "There is only one solution."

Helen moved closer.

"Marcus must wed tonight." Brenda shot her a determined look. "To ye."

Helen jumped back, but Brenda reached out and captured her hands. "It can nae be me, because I am widowed and no longer a maiden. The union might also be annulled on the grounds of the contract me uncle has made for me."

That was true. Young couples who ran away in the hope of being wed to their heart's choice often returned home to discover that their parents had such unions annulled because of contracts with others. "And we dare not leave Marcus unwed for Morton to utilize in his plans. Yet, Morton might annul the marriage in the morning."

Brenda nodded in agreement. "The earl has dismissed us as merely women. So, we must be cleverer."

Helen felt her lips curving in spite of the situation. "It is indeed an honor to be able to prove to that man that he does nae control all he sees."

"I will have to find a priest willing to defy the regent and some witnesses Morton will no' be able to intimidate. They will keep him from annulling the marriage."

"I will want it annulled," Helen exclaimed.

"What ye do once ye leave this castle does nae matter," Brenda replied. "Except ye shall have to gain Marcus's agreement for such an action."

"He'll give it," Helen answered. "For no other reason than we are saving him from Morton's plans. Marcus does nae bend well nor does he forget when a service is done for him."

Brenda nodded. For a moment she looked like she was going to argue, but she returned to her planning. "In the morning, I will change places with the girl so she can leave with ye."

"The earl will no' be letting ye leave, especially once he discovers we have ruined his plans for Marcus."

Brenda slowly smiled. "Leave that matter to me. There is something else I know about court, and that is where many people's dirty secrets are hidden. There are those who will help me keep Morton from making alliances with England, of that I am sure."

"But what of yer fate?" Helen asked. "Ye will be left here to face the earl's wrath."

"That can nae be helped, and I can no' return home. So, it must be me to stay and ye to go. For certain, I will face that man if it means he can nae force a girl to wed," Brenda said quickly. "Enough talk. We must away to church and find a willing priest."

"And the guards?"

Brenda rolled her eyes before she aimed a sad, pleading expression at Helen. "They will be no trouble at all."

Helen believed her but discovered her feet frozen to the floor. Brenda looked back at her. "It is the only way, unless ye prefer to leave him to his fate."

"Such would make me a monster."

But what would helping Marcus do?

Helen shuddered as she forced herself to move. Life often offered difficult choices. She sighed as they emerged into the hallway and discovered the guards away from their posts. They could hear the men down in the shadows of the passageway, several giggles telling them exactly what the men were about while they believed Helen and Brenda were eating.

Fools.

Or perhaps it was better to simply call them men, for males truly liked to think themselves smarter than women. Tonight, Helen would have to hope she was able to prove them wrong.

❧

Marcus MacPherson was chained like an animal.

She'd expected as much, since the only guards were at the entrance to the passageway leading to the cells.

Helen drew in a sharp breath when she stepped into the dungeon, sickened by the sight. Here there was more than the smell of human waste; there was also the overwhelming stench of vomit. It made the rest of the castle smell quite fresh by comparison. The lack of lighting completed the feeling of hopelessness the place was designed to instill.

It enraged her to see Marcus there.

"Here to see me in chains, mistress?" Marcus was watching the door, as was his habit. There was only a small pool of light near the door, but she could see him leaning against a rough stone wall, a thick collar locked around his neck and his ankles secured in irons.

"I hope ye enjoy the sight," he growled.

"I do nae."

Brenda gave her a little push to get her to move past the doorway.

"Ah, Brenda," Marcus remarked. "Another woman who will likely find joy in me plight."

"Stop it," Helen admonished him in a whisper. "We're here to help."

Marcus abandoned his lazy posture. "Go back the way ye came, Helen. Even if ye have somehow managed to steal the keys, I will nae leave ye here to answer for me escape."

Helen shook her head at the commanding tone he used. Part of her was overjoyed to hear him back in command, even if she wanted to label him a fool for refusing her aid. "I swear, ye would nae allow me to toss a bucket of water on ye if yer kilt was afire."

He flashed her a grin that she knew well and detested because it was so full of arrogance. "Ye should nae be so proud of yer stubborn nature, either."

And yet she enjoyed it full well because it proved that he was not broken.

"At least I am honest and admit me sins." There was an undertone to his words that heated her cheeks because she knew without a doubt his words were personal.

Brenda came into the cell, followed by the priest they'd found and a younger man who would act as witness.

"What are ye about?" Marcus demanded as Brenda shut the door firmly.

"I told ye." Helen gathered her courage. It was trying to drain out of her like a tankard with holes in the bottom. Even in chains, Marcus was formidable. "We are here to help ye. The servants are carrying the tale of what Morton wants ye to do. How do ye think we knew where to find ye?"

"I'll be helping meself," Marcus informed them all. "And I will no' be needing a priest. The earl might do a fair number of nasty things to me, but he'll no' put me life in danger. Let him whip me for refusing to wed. It will be a small price to pay for keeping me soul unblemished. He will not be breaking me to his will."

"Morton will make ye watch as he has that child bride lashed," Brenda informed him solemnly. "He knows yer weakness is the girl because she is innocent."

There was a long moment of silence as Marcus absorbed Brenda's words.

"Bloody fucking Christ," Marcus swore, his eyes closing as his lips curled back from his teeth in disgust.

Helen waited for him to open his eyes. She watched his jaw tighten as the horror sank in, his knuckles turning white because he was clenching his fists so tightly. She was clinging to some small sliver of hope that he'd see a way out of it, other than wedding her. But when he opened his eyes, she stared at something she'd never thought to see in his eyes. Need.

Helen took a deep breath, gathering her composure to say what she must. Marcus looked past her at the priest and the second man, and he cursed again.

"It's the only way, and ye know it." Brenda spoke up.

"I'll admit, it's clever, and a part of me would dearly love to see the look on Morton's face in the morning when he arrives and finds me a married man." Marcus let out a chuckle that was really more of a snarl. "But no. I will nae leave that child to his care. I could no' live with meself."

"Will ye be able to live with yerself when ye are forced to consummate the union with witnesses?" Brenda asked. "This is court. Such events are quite well attended, and I do assure ye, the guests will no' be polite enough to stay behind a wooden screen. They will stand right up at the bedside because they will be making wagers on how many thrusts it takes ye to penetrate her fully. There will be no soiling the sheet and pulling the wool over anyone's eyes. I know how it will go. Me father thought it a fine thing to have me wed here, in a place where the Campbells could no' send me back and keep me dowry by claiming the union was nae legally binding."

"Jesus, Brenda," Marcus exclaimed. "I knew yer father was a calculating man, but I never thought him such a cold bastard."

"The alliance was the only thing that mattered," Brenda explained in a hushed tone. "Morton is of the same way of thinking. He valued my sensibilities as much as he does yer sense of honor."

Helen found herself caught in Marcus's gaze again. He didn't like it. Well, they had that in common. There was no hiding that fact as they stared at one another, both of them wanting to refuse, yet neither of them willing to live with the consequences of doing so.

"So ye came to help me," Marcus said softy. There were others in the room but he was talking to her.

Only her.

"I cannot refuse to help that girl any more than ye can." It was not the kindest thing to say, but she felt too exposed. As though she were submitting to his will, calling him master, when she had spent the last year making sure she didn't bend to his demands. She could not lose herself to him. Better to have it thought they were united against an evil that needed preventing.

Even if there was a small part of her that enjoyed knowing she was the one to make the decision on who would wed whom. A small dose of humility would do him good.

"Her name is Katherine," Marcus supplied, his expression becoming unreadable. He looked past Helen at the priest.

"And she is newly fourteen this month, Father, so I would appreciate it if ye would stop edging toward the door. The women are correct. This is the only solution. Much as I would have it otherwise."

"At least for any decent person it is," Helen added to soothe the priest. Perhaps she was really trying to convince herself. She was having a great deal of trouble staying in the cell.

The priest started to say something, but seemed to be thinking the matter through. He nodded at last and looked toward Helen. "If ye would step over to yer groom's side."

Groom.

God help her.

But the stone walls around her seemed to be permeated with hopelessness. Likely absorbed from the countless unanswered prayers trapped inside the dank air.

No, she was going to have to do this. That was the only way God might work the matter out.

Helen wasn't sure her feet were going to respond to her will. There was a logical necessity, but that didn't seem to be calming the wave of panic washing through her. She felt like she was standing in a winter storm, the wind biting through her clothing as the very strength of the gusts threatened to blow her away.

But she lifted one foot and then the other. A few steps had never taken so long, the space seeming to grow as time slowed down and allowed her to notice every little detail about Marcus MacPherson. Tiny things, such as the way little lines appeared at the creases of his eyes when he was contemplating her. His lips were thin and pressed into a hard line that betrayed how much he did not want to wed her. That fact made her heart ache, because no matter how much she didn't want him for a groom, it hurt to know he rejected the idea of taking her to wife.

None of it made any sense. What she did comprehend was the sound of the priest beginning the prayers she knew by heart and had once dreamed of being a part of. Back when she was a girl and looked at a wedding as a day of happiness. Today would be no such thing.

For she was wedding her captor.

Two

SILENCE WAS DEAFENING AT TIMES.

The sound of the door closing bounced around inside Helen's skull, like thunder cracking just above her head. She knew the sound was harmless, but it was so intimidating that fighting off misgivings became nearly impossible.

Helen couldn't take the silence anymore. "It had to be me, because of Brenda's contract with the Gordons."

Marcus was leaning back against the stone wall, watching her. His eyes were blue like his father's and brother's, but in the darkness, she couldn't see them. Still, she felt his scrutiny and would have sworn he was peeling away the layers of her skin to get a look at her thoughts.

"Well, ye need no' glare at me," she admonished him. It was strange, to be sure, being in the position to reprimand him. Even though she sounded a bit more pleading than she liked.

Helen retreated to the far side of the cell. Not that the action afforded her any sort of real comfort. Marcus seemed to fill the place with his presence. Yet that had always been the way she perceived him: too large, too imposing. She stood up to him because to do otherwise felt like granting him her surrender.

He finally nodded and offered her a pursing of his lips. "Ye've caught me by surprise, madam. Enjoy the novelty of it. I promise ye, it does nae happen very often."

She ended up choking out a single laugh before she sat down with her back to him. "Best on to the matters at hand."

The darkness was welcome as she pulled her skirts up and pulled a small dagger from her boot.

"Do nae use yer thigh."

Her cheeks heated because the topic was so intimate, but she turned her head to look at him for an explanation. Marcus knew more strategy than she did.

"If Morton has ye inspected, the source of the blood will be clear. All yer effort will be for naught," he explained.

"I see…" That left her with the knife poised in the air as she debated the best location to cut herself.

"Better to use me, lass."

His tone was soft, and she recognized it well. It was the one he used when he was intent on getting his way and knew full well she wasn't going to like what he had to say. "What do ye mean?"

She really wanted to resist the urge to ask, but all of their effort was for naught if a midwife found a cut on her—and a midwife would strip her bare.

Marcus was grinning, that arrogant curve of his lips that made her grind her teeth so often. Oh yes, the man knew she wasn't going to like his suggestion, but he was also supremely confident that it was the only way.

Ye like that facet of his personality as well…

Fine. So she did. Strength in men was attractive; she wasn't the only woman who thought so.

"Me head is bleeding from the tussle I had with Morton's men."

Helen was suddenly up and moving toward him. "I should have thought to bring some things in case ye needed tending."

She rose onto her toes, pushing his hair aside to look for the wound.

"Helen."

She felt her body tighten. He was able to whisper right in her ear since she'd come so close.

"Let me put me head between yer thighs, and the matter will be done."

"I will no'!" She jumped back like a startled doe as Marcus choked on his laughter. He took a long moment to enjoy the way the words had formed into something that sounded scarlet. She blushed but ended up smiling because it was amusing.

"Stop toying with me," she responded.

He lifted one dark eyebrow in response. "Some women would consider having me head between their thighs a treat."

Her cheeks caught fire. "I am no' that sort."

He sobered, resuming his assessment of her. Something lit his eyes. It looked like respect. "I was no' accusing ye of being a lightskirt."

She nodded in acceptance of his apology. "Good."

"Which makes me want to try it on ye."

He was serious. She wanted to look away, but whispers rose from her mind, the sort of talk that a woman heard in the kitchens when the younger staff members had all gone to their beds and the women were discussing passion.

Some men applied more effort to their wives than others, and to hear them talk of it, bed sport was well worth the vows of submissiveness and obedience. Marcus was watching her, his lips curving up as he read her thoughts right off her face.

Her cheeks burned scarlet.

"Enough," she admonished him. Or perhaps it was more correct to say to herself, for it was her imagination running wild. "There will be none of that."

She honestly wasn't sure if she was telling him or herself.

His lips curled up as he flashed his teeth at her. "Why no'? Ye're me wife."

"And ye know why." She blinked at him, trying to recover her poise. Katherine. Yes. That was the reason for everything. "Katherine is the reason I am here. After we are away, we'll get an annulment…"

She had to avert her gaze to get her mind focused on the plan.

"After ye've convinced everyone that I had ye?" Marcus shook his head. "Ye came here to prevent a grave injustice, Helen. I'll no' be gaining me freedom by disgracing ye."

"Concern for my good name?" she inquired in surprise. "It is far too late for that. As ye said when ye lined yer men up before me," she said, "I've been away from home too long for anyone to consider me virtue still intact. At least this way, there is some purpose to everything that has befallen me."

And that meant she needed to take the last bit of action needed. Helen stiffened her spine and walked back toward him. She sat down and forced her stiff hands to pull up her skirts until only a bit of her chemise guarded her sex. She couldn't dwell on how exposed she felt. There was a rustle from the chain as Marcus moved. At least the sound of metal grating over stone renewed her sense of purpose.

But it still took a great deal of nerve to sit steady as he settled beside her.

He was everything men were expected to be. Marcus didn't shrink from his duty, and he was loyal to the core. Indeed, he was the sort of man she might have been very happy to have courting her. Of course, those girlhood dreams had long since vanished into the past.

"Use that dagger to open the wound a bit, so the blood flows."

Helen pulled the dagger again, only hesitating because sinking it into him wasn't holding the satisfaction she had sometimes dreamed it might. Instead, she bit her lower lip as she used the blade to reopen the wound on the back of his head.

He didn't make a sound until he'd rolled over and settled his head directly in the notch of her thighs. She was breathless, a crazy twist of excitement going through her.

"I should likely thank ye for no' cutting deeper."

She was suddenly tongue-tied. He was just as big and overwhelming as ever, yet his head was resting against her thighs, and she would be a liar if she didn't admit there was something she liked about having him so close. Maybe if they had met at a spring festival, she might have embraced the things he stirred in her. It would be an outright lie to say she did not want to know him better. And if she was not mistaken, he was teasing her. Beneath the gruff exterior, there were remnants of the boy he'd once been.

"I never wanted yer blood."

He choked on a chuckle. "So hitting me with that pitcher was….just a….what, lass?"

The memory made her smile. "A reminder. Of manners. Ye were acting like a whoremaster, lining yer men up like that and setting them on me."

"Ah." He made a low sound in the back of his throat. "Maybe I deserved it, at that."

"Ye disagree with me." She shrugged. "Men and women often do."

He nodded, the motion sending a soft sensation through her belly. She looked away, feeling like something very private had just been exposed to him.

"Ye've been serving in the kitchens."

It wasn't really a question, but it did give her something to sink her attention into that didn't allow her to feel uncertain. When it came to her circumstances at MacPherson Castle, she was very, very sure how she felt.

"Servants are paid." Helen leaned back against the stone wall and felt its rough edges against her scalp. "I assure ye, I was not."

His expression tightened, surprising her so that she returned her gaze to his.

"Ye should no' have hid from me. I would have righted yer circumstances if I'd known ye were being treated unfairly."

"I did nae hide." She pushed at him. "Get up."

Marcus didn't move for a moment, giving her a steady look that dared her to force him. Helen felt her eyes narrow. "Well then, ye want to play the part of me devoted suitor, completely at me beck and call…"

He made a rather male sound before he was twisting and sat up next to her. Which gave her the chance to laugh at his expense. "Ye have more than yer share of pride, and that's a fact."

"As do ye, Helen."

She shifted and stood, moving away from him. She'd only taken a quick glance at the blood staining her chemise. It would serve its purpose. That should have been what her thoughts settled on, but all she ended up doing was dwelling upon what he'd said and the way her sex felt so very sensitive. As though she was eager for him to touch her.

"I never saw ye in the hall. Little wonder ye did nae find the MacPhersons' castle to be a fine place. Ye did nae give it a chance. Me father makes sure there is fine music and good drink in the evenings. He is nae an overly stern laird. Ye should nae have stayed away, nursing yer pride." His tone was kinder than she'd heard from him before. It declared a level of sincerity that sent a little twist of excitement through her.

Yet it also needled her temper.

"Nursing me pride?" She turned on him. "I was working because I was nae a MacPherson, so was nae due any free time to indulge in comforts. I toiled more hours than there was sunlight, and if I made the mistake of resting me head on the table and was discovered, I got a taste of the rod being laid across me back. The blasted thing leaves welts. Ye brought me there, it was no' me place to go whining to ye."

She'd seen his disapproval before. Been the recipient time and again, but now she witnessed it crossing his face on her behalf. It unsettled her, leaving little seeds of doubt about just how guilty he was.

"Duana is more of a bitch than I seem to have noticed."

Helen scoffed at the Head of House's name. "She is hardly alone. What did ye expect when ye dropped me off the back of yer horse and swore ye'd burn me father's house to the ground if I strayed?"

"I certainly had nae thought she was working ye like a slave," he answered. "Ye have never had any difficulty speaking yer mind to me, Helen. Admit ye were holding on to yer pride."

His point was valid. He was the War Chief, his day full of pressing matters that affected many, and she was but one person.

"If I was, ye can nae fault me, seeing as it was the only thing I had left to call me own," she shot back. "Ye stole me in me house shoes. It was a mighty cold winter, I can tell ye."

And she didn't like thinking about it. Helen pulled her knees up and leaned against the stone wall, closing her eyes in some vain hope that sleep might arrive and still her thoughts. Was she expecting him to have a personal interest in her? Yes. She had to admit it was so. Still, she couldn't seem to reconcile herself to cooling her temper, in spite of knowing she was not making much sense.

Well, at least that brought her back to a place she knew very well. When it came to Marcus, she had more impulses than sense. Better to bite her lip and keep the shame of it to herself.

～

Marcus caught sight of one of her boots. They were fine ones that reached halfway up her calves to keep her warm when the snow drifted. They were also new, which meant Ailis had made sure Helen was provided for.

He should have seen to her.

But what did he know of the things a captive needed? Perhaps if she'd been a man… Well, he'd not have taken her if she were male. It was a harsh truth that he'd shouldered, because taking her had been the only solution to protect her from her kin.

"Your brothers are too inexperienced to know that the Gordons are trying to use them."

Helen resisted the urge to open her eyes and look at him. Marcus admitted to enjoying the way she tried to ignore him—and failed. He liked knowing he held her interest, could rouse her passion.

His eyes narrowed because he'd caught a whiff of her scent while he lay with his head in her lap. His cock was hard beneath his kilt.

And she was wet.

They were always nipping at each other, and he realized it was because there was a pull between them. Something they hadn't planned to discover in the other person, or could decide to cultivate. More than one arranged match had discovered that sad truth.

It made him want to dig into her anger, pull it apart so that they might find a resolution that would grant them the peace to allow other feelings to flourish. A woman had the right to be angry about being stolen. He would not begrudge her that.

"I needed to make certain ye would stay in the castle, Helen. A lone woman trying to cross the Highlands...it is no' safe," he offered softly. "I did nae want to bind ye, or lock ye in a cellar, or set someone on ye. So I made sure ye had nowhere to go." He grunted. "At least until Debra Grant arrived."

She let out a little huff. "I am no' senseless enough not to hear the truth in yer words." She didn't look at him, her admission coming out in a whisper that tugged on something inside him. Damned if he didn't want to fold her into his arms and soothe away what troubled her.

He was a War Chief, not a bloody poet.

Better to stick to what he knew.

"The Gordons were making trouble for all the estates along the borders, in the hope they might make the tenants doubt the MacPhersons."

She turned to look at him at last. "Fine, ye stole me for all the best reasons, and no, I would no' have preferred bloodshed or being chained."

His gaze went to the collar he was locked in. For a moment, he felt they had more in common than he'd ever imagined a woman and a man might. He'd been raised to think women settled into their circumstances. Now, he realized they were forced to that end and it grated on them as much as he hated the chains binding him at the moment. Morton had fine reasoning for his forced match as well.

"I was sick with the thought of what Morton wanted me to do with Katherine. Christ, Helen, she's but a child. I would have scared her to death. Ye have me gratitude."

Helen failed to control a smile that lifted the corners of her mouth. It lasted only a moment before she rolled her lips in to control her response.

He liked the fact that she struggled to do so.

"Ye are nae so fearsome."

"And yet, ye never came to me." He cut back to the matter that was his purpose. "Ye should have."

She narrowed her eyes at him.

"And ye label *me* stubborn, woman," he groused.

"Rightly so, when ye resist the solution Brenda and I bring ye." Helen had moved so she was facing him, leaning toward him to keep her voice low. "Do ye have any idea how hard it was to find two women willing to distract the guards so we might get that priest in here? We are newly arrived and have no coin between us."

"I wondered how ye managed that bit." Marcus dropped his voice, wanting to draw her closer. She was straining to hear him. "And there is another reason why the pair of ye should no' have left MacPherson land."

She offered him a smug look. "And just where would ye be if I was no' here?"

Marcus drew in a deep breath. "I told ye I'm grateful to ye."

It was clearly what she'd wanted him to say, but

the smugness dissipated from her face as she absorbed his words.

"Did that no' please ye as much as ye thought it should have?"

She offered him an honest look. "Nay. 'Tis the truth I am more angry on yer behalf. Ye are an honorable man, and this…is injustice."

"Yet in the name of peace."

They stared at one another for a long moment, caught in the grip of truth and its harsh edges.

"I should have made sure ye were treated better," he said as he started to chuckle. "Truth is, I've never encountered a woman who would no' complain. It never crossed me mind that ye'd bear up, just to prove to me that ye might."

She fluttered her eyelashes at the sarcastic twist of his compliment. "It made me strong." She was toying with the hem of her skirt to avoid looking at him, but realized what she was doing and lifted her chin so their gazes met once more. "It was past time for me to grow up."

Her anger was cooling, leaving her looking at him as though she had never really done so. The moment was so very odd. She had never thought to have a personal conversation with him. She'd simply never thought he might be interested.

"How old are ye?" he asked.

"Twenty-four." She was nearly past the age of being considered for marriage.

"Duana will learn the error of her ways," he said firmly.

"I do nae want yer protection," she muttered. "Only for ye to lift yer threat against me father's house."

"I am yer husband now."

She'd be wise to recall just how stubborn Marcus was when it came to doing what he thought best for her. "An annulment will be best for both of us. I certainly do nae need to trap ye into this union. Can ye just imagine the stories that will be told about how I took ye unawares?"

He chuckled, the sound menacing. "Careful, lass, the winter is long and I enjoy a good fight. Keep talking like that and I'll think ye're tempting me with the promise of entertainment while the snow flies."

"Ye would," she answered with a shake of her head. For a moment, they smiled at one another. Marcus was the one to return to a serious expression.

"Yer skirts are stained, lass."

Helen shook her head. "Everyone knows court is riddled with gossip." She shot him a look full of certainty. "Besides, ye were the one who told me my name was already beyond redemption. So it matters not."

"And ye think I would be willing to let ye shoulder the burden by yerself?" Her eyes widened at the tone of his voice. "Ye can be sure of one thing, Helen. It will no' happen while I have any choice in the matter."

"Well, ye did nae have any choice," Helen replied. "No' any real ones, that is. So we shall simply make the best of it."

"By getting an annulment?" he asked.

"Yes," she answered, trying to gauge his mood. The man wasn't making any sense with his probing questions. "Yer father will no' approve a match with me. Ye're a son of the laird, so he must have a dozen offers."

"I am bastard born."

"That makes little difference," she said. "Ye are also War Chief."

He chuckled at her. "Ye misunderstood me statement, lass." Marcus sent her a stern look. "I am born out of wedlock because me mother had an iron will and refused to wed unless me father converted."

"That must have raised a scandal."

"Aye," he confirmed. "And I have that same will, Helen. Be very certain of that. It is time for both of us to wed."

She felt something twist in her belly again. It was dangerously close to anticipation. Her mouth had gone dry as she battled the impulse to mince words with him. Half of winning a battle was picking the time to attack. While they were stuck in a cell was poor timing indeed to convince him of the logic in getting an annulment.

"Ye should think the matter through. An annulment would be best for yer father and brother."

His eyes narrowed, confirming she'd hit his single weak spot.

"The earl will be furious," Helen continued. "Better to send him word after ye are home that yer father made ye see reason. Ye have annulled the marriage, and ye are ever so repentant."

"While I stay on MacPherson land where the man can nae try his luck at forcing me to his will?"

Helen shrugged. "He is the regent. Yer brother realized it was necessary to keep in Morton's good graces."

Marcus set his jaw in disapproval. She knew the look well, having been the recipient of it more times than she might count.

"Ye'll see the wisdom of it," Helen offered softly. "In the morning, when the earl comes and finds what we have done."

And she would have her annulment. Helen was certain of that. Marcus was the War Chief of Clan MacPherson. He would do what was best for his clan, as he always had.

Satisfaction swept through her. There was a victory in knowing she'd been the one to save him, but it was overshadowed by how grateful she was to know that he would be free. Something inside her was strangling at the sight of him chained.

"And if I grant ye an annulment?" he asked her. "What will ye do? Go home and give yer kin the power to make a match for ye?"

"I have nae truly thought about it," she answered truthfully. "There is Ailis. I enjoy being her companion."

"As me wife, ye would have yer own waiting woman."

Helen snorted and rolled her eyes. "Try telling such to Duana. I am tempted to agree to remain yer wife, just to see her face when ye tell her."

He flashed her a cocky grin.

"Ye'd set yer entire castle on its ear, mark me words," she told him. "Ye might enjoy it, but the regent will no' be appeased, and yer clansmen will whisper about how ye should have recalled that as a son of the laird, ye needed to make a match that brought allegiances to the MacPherson. Better to have yer father send Morton a letter saying he has taken ye in hand, once ye are far enough away from this place. The fact that ye are bastard born offers yer father a way of smoothing matters over."

It was the logical thing to do. So why did it feel wrong? Helen shied away from thinking about it too deeply. What mattered was freeing him and Katherine.

All right, and being the one to decide what was going to happen for a change. She was enjoying that part very much.

"That would be a good way to smooth over the earl's temper, no doubt." Marcus agreed.

And that was that. The sharp edge of reality with which she was well acquainted.

Helen leaned her head against the wall and closed her eyes. This time sleep was much more sympathetic toward her. It swept her up and buffeted her against the storm of reality, granting her peace, at least for a few hours, so she might rest and regain her strength.

Lord knew, she'd need all she could muster to make Marcus see reason. He would. She felt more certain of that with each hour that passed. He might be stubborn and full of his own authority, but he was also dedicated to his clan. He would never hurt the MacPhersons. So he'd grant her the annulment.

And that would be that.

❧

"Helen. Wake up."

She opened her eyes instantly. Marcus was using a tone she recognized well as one that was full of authority. There was the faintest glow of light coming from under the door.

"Come here now." Marcus spoke softly and deeply. "Before ye are discovered over there, where I can nae have put me hands on ye."

She'd drifted down to lie on her back sometime during the dark hours of the night. The floor was hard beneath her back and as cold as a grave. Her muscles ached as she moved, turning and crawling toward him while she fought with her skirts.

"It's cold, sure enough," he offered once she was close to him. He clasped his hands around hers, making her gasp.

"Ye are nae chilled." No, his flesh was warm and welcoming. Maybe there were sound reasons why she should not huddle against him, but her mind was too locked in the grip of sleep to produce any of them. All that mattered was the comfort his body provided.

"No' as cold as ye," he said.

She'd never been so cold, or maybe she'd never enjoyed having warmth rubbed back into her hands so very much.

That wasn't it.

Helen blinked, the last of sleep's hold peeled away by Marcus's touch. He was stroking her hands, slowly using his warmth to melt the chill encasing her flesh.

"Does my touch truly shock ye so much?"

She realized she'd been staring at his hands as he stroked hers. Transfixed, really. "Nay," she sputtered as she looked up, but found his gaze just as unsettling. "I just realized it has been a long time since someone touched me."

It was a confession, an intimate one, and Marcus didn't miss it. "I shouldn't have said that." She tried to move away, but he stopped her.

"Be still. We're about to have company."

He was still stroking her, and she couldn't help but stretch her back as he drew his hand along her spine. Delicious sensation went washing through her, easing the ache the hard floor had left in her flesh. A little sound of bliss crossed her lips before she felt his hand close around her neck and he captured her lips in a kiss.

It was startling, but in the way that excitement was. As though something snapped through her body, awakening all sorts of cravings she never realized she'd been starving to satisfy.

She shifted, uncertain, overwhelmed, and he moved with her, controlling her neck as his mouth took hers in a motion that further captivated her. The reason was simple: He wasn't ravaging her this time. It was a slow meshing of their lips, as he teased her mouth, inviting her to kiss him back. For one magical moment, she did, mimicking the motion of his lips and learning the way as he guided her in an unhurried savoring of her mouth.

He increased the pressure as she responded and gained confidence in kissing him back. She had never fully comprehended how sensitive her mouth was. Marcus was showing her the true purpose of her lips, introducing her to the delight that came from having them stroked by his. It was the sweetest bliss, one she willingly gave herself over to.

But the door was shoved in and Marcus broke away from her.

"Ah…Morton." Marcus's voice boomed across the cell and echoed into the corridor behind it. "A fine morning it is."

The gentle stroking of her fingers had lulled her into a false sense of complicity. Marcus swept that aside as he rose. All of the strength she knew he possessed was there as he pulled her along with him, pushing her partially behind him. It was like a bucket of cold water hitting her, the bubble of bliss created by the kiss popping and dropping her back into cold reality.

"Enjoying your last night as an unwed man?" the earl asked mockingly. "Be very sure that I plan to make certain ye are up to yer wedding duties."

"I told ye, man. I will nae be bedding that child. No decent man would agree to put his hands on one so tender," Marcus stated clearly. Eight men were behind the earl, and Marcus made sure none of them missed his words.

"Ye'll do as told," Morton informed Marcus. "Scotland needs alliances."

"And just how do ye propose to bend me to yer will?" Marcus asked as smugly as if he'd been standing in the open Highlands with all of his clan behind him.

It was foolish, but Helen had to admit that she admired his bravado.

The earl's mouth curved, and there was nothing nice about it. Helen felt a chill go all the way down to her toes as she watched the way the Earl of Morton grinned at Marcus.

"Ye will agree to the wedding and the bedding, or I will have ye dragged out to the yard, where Katherine will suffer for yer disobedience to my will." He held out his hand, and one of his men placed a whip into it. The leather looked cold and shiny. The earl made it dance just a bit, the knotted ends of braided leather making a tapping sound against the stone floor. "Shall I send my captain for Katherine?"

~~

Brenda was risking a great deal.

And the truth was, she had never felt more alive.

She had to control the urge to smile, schooling her features to look smooth and calm. The castle came alive at first light. She'd been waiting for the horizon to turn pink, pacing across her chamber after she'd dressed in Helen's other dress. It was nearly a rag, with patches on top of patches at the hemline. The chemise was threadbare, while the stockings had more darned spots in them than fabric.

Helen's heart ached for her friend, but the clothing was exactly what she needed to make her way through the passageways so early in the morning. Court was a place of intrigue and night liaisons. The nobles slept while their servants began the task of making sure there would be a fine banquet supper that evening when their blue-blooded masters awoke.

The maid in front of her was nervous. She looked back and forth, casting numerous glances back at Brenda to make sure she was still following. At last, the girl stopped and pointed down a narrow section of passageway. They were in the oldest part of the castle now, the walls rough and lacking the smooth coat of plaster that had been applied to the newer sections. One could almost hear the echoes of the centuries here, and Brenda fought the impulse to cross herself.

She mustn't spook the maid. Brenda pulled a pearl from a pouch at her waist. It was one that she'd inherited from her mother, but she couldn't be bothered by the loss. Court servants worked long hours for masters who often mistreated them. One only entered such service for the income that might be earned. The maid's eyes brightened as she took the pearl and eyed it critically.

She finally nodded and slipped it into a pocket of her skirt. Many noble families were at court because they had lost their fortunes and intended to secure a new office from the regent to gain income. It wasn't uncommon for a servant to be paid in gems that had been in noble families for generations.

The maid held up a finger. Brenda pressed back against the wall as the maid went toward the man guarding the door ahead of them.

"It's so cold here…" the maid began. "Can ye no' spare a moment to come to the kitchen and warm yer hands?"

Brenda listened as the maid cajoled the man, finally succeeding in taking him by the arm and moving on down the passageway.

Once they were gone, Brenda hurried toward the door, opening it and going inside without knocking. Katherine bolted upright in her narrow bed, but she didn't scream. No, there was a look on her face that told Brenda the child knew there was no point in crying out for help that would not come.

"I am here to help ye escape."

Katherine might have been young, but she had sharp wits. She was out of the bedding in an instant, crossing over to Brenda with her face set with determination. "How?"

"I am Brenda Grant. Ye must wear this clothing."
Brenda was already yanking on the ties to open the
bodice. "And I must put on yers."

Katherine was only wearing a chemise. She turned
and scampered across the small chamber to where a
wardrobe stood. She opened it and pulled out the
pieces of a simple dress.

"Why are you helping me?"

Brenda looked into Katherine's eyes. "Because I
also was wed too young. Men are controlling beasts,
and we women must do what we can to outwit them
when possible."

The chamber was full of the sounds of rustling
cloth. If Brenda had had any doubts about the action
she was undertaking, the way Katherine held her questions and focused on getting into the servant's clothing
without a single protest stilled them. Katherine knew
too much about the harsh realities of life already, it
would seem.

"Me friend Helen wed Marcus MacPherson last
eve," Brenda explained.

Katherine was lacing up the front of her bodice but
raised wide eyes to stare at Brenda. "The Highlander?"

"Aye, he is that, but a decent man, make no mistake." Brenda finished dressing and reached out to cup
Katherine's frail shoulders. "Morton is a villain."

"Yes, a black-hearted one."

Brenda nodded. "If ye would be free of him, ye
must memorize how to get to the yard where Marcus's
men are. They will take ye away from Morton's reach."

"What will happen to you?" Katherine asked.

"I will stay in yer place, for the guard will surely

peek in to make sure no one is the wiser about him leaving his post. If he were to cry the alarm, the gates would be closed and ye discovered."

Katherine was thinking it through. "Morton will punish you. Severely so."

"Leave that matter to me," Brenda said. "I have kin here in Scotland. He will not find it so easy to mistreat me. Marcus will take ye to the Highlands. He is an honorable man. Remember that, because it will nae be a simple life for ye since ye are English."

"Better than what the earl would make of me today," Katherine answered quietly. She was older than her years, the innocence ripped out of her. "I will go and be grateful to you forever."

"Now listen carefully. Ye must do exactly as I say so that everyone believes ye are me, being taken home in shame to fulfill the contract me uncle has made for me."

෴

Finley wasn't a man given to dishonesty, but he enjoyed a good raid. Of course, most of the time, raiding happened under the cover of darkness. He looked up, noting the sun that was rising. It was full daylight, and the courtyard was alive with delivery wagons and those coming and going on business with the regent.

The Earl of Morton was truly king in every way except name. Parties of ambassadors were coming through the gates now that they were open. Men dressed in velvet and silk. Finley shook his head and busied himself with making sure the horse in front of him was bridled correctly.

"Men looking prettier than women," Skene remarked beside him. "It is nae for me."

"No' me either," Finley agreed. "The sooner we ride, the better, I say."

"Ye've faith in this scheme, then?" Skene asked.

Finley looked around before he shot his fellow retainer a hard look. "Best ye hope it succeeds. I do nae want to have to return and tell the laird that Marcus is chained or worse."

"Aye," Skene agreed. "For all the trouble I had wrapping me thoughts around the idea of ending the feud with the Robertsons, I find peace suits me well."

"Better to have the help of women than a war against our own king's regent."

❧

Brenda peeked out of the door, watching as Katherine made her way down the passageway. She'd told the girl to move at a steady pace, looking down, like a servant intent on a chore. Yet the girl seemed to move too slowly. Brenda felt her heart pounding while she watched Katherine get closer and closer to the end of the passageway and finally make the turn around it and disappear from sight.

She sighed in relief and decided to savor it while she might. Turning around, she surveyed the cell. It really wasn't much more than that. There was the narrow bed and the wardrobe. A stool sat on the floor near a tiny table. The only other thing in the room was a prayer bench. Brenda went toward it, because it allowed her to have her back fully to the door. She took a moment to pull up the soft neck wrap she wore so that it covered her head. The bench had a thin pillow that did little to protect her knees as she interlaced her fingers and adopted a position of prayer.

Not long after that, she heard the door open, the hinges grinding. Brenda didn't move, and a moment later, the guard closed the door, clearly pleased to discover his charge where he had left her.

She smiled in victory.

❧

"Ye can have yer captain unlock me," Marcus boldly informed the Earl of Morton. "It's past time I returned to MacPherson land to deal with keeping peace between Robertsons and MacPhersons. That's the alliance I am engaged with ensuring for Scotland."

"Remove the strumpet," the earl said. "It's time to get on with yer wedding."

The captain made a single step toward them before Marcus was standing all the way in front of her. "Helen is me wife."

The earl's face darkened. "Impossible."

"Nay," Marcus confirmed in a hard tone. "And me temper is near to the breaking point over having to wed her in this piss-stinking hole."

"Ye did nae have to wed her," the earl exploded. "Ye have defied me, man."

"A fact ye should thank me for," Marcus responded in disgust. "The last regent ended up poisoned because of some of his deeds. Best take heed."

The earl shifted his attention to her. "Perhaps I will just have ye widowed, MacPherson."

"Touch me wife, and ye'll need more alliances than ye can form."

The men behind the regent weren't sure what to make of Marcus. They shifted, uncertain if they should take action. But there were also a few looks of disgust in their eyes, looks aimed toward the Earl of Morton.

"Now unlock me and let me be on me way," Marcus continued. "Be very sure that we had witnesses, men ye do nae need knowing ye would press a child into wedlock with me."

"Better to hope I never learn their names," the earl hissed.

"No, man," Marcus countered. "Ye'd best pray they do nae tell their friends who have daughters what ye think is an appropriate age to wed. For all that I do nae have any children, I know that a man will fight to protect them. Marriage may be a business, but it is one conducted between adults."

The earl locked gazes with Marcus for a long moment. Helen could feel the tension filling the room. Both of their blood might end up spilled on the stone floor. After all, a man who could so easily decide to wed a child to Marcus might not care what was said.

He should be concerned. The earl was forgetting that Scots did not take well to men who were depraved.

"Go home," the earl finally said. "And make sure I do nae hear of unrest in the Highlands."

Morton turned and left. A captain stayed behind, a set of keys jingling as he lifted them to fit one of them into the lock that held the collar around Marcus's neck. Helen stepped aside, but her gaze was glued to the motion of the man's hands as he turned the key.

The sound of the lock grating was sweeter than any music she'd ever heard.

The thick band of the collar opened, allowing Marcus to pull it off his neck. He made a soft, growling sound that had the guard backing up.

"Here." Helen went after the man and took the keys from his hand. She turned and knelt to fit one into the leg irons. She turned the key on one leg iron and then the other.

The moment he was loose, Marcus reached down and hooked her arm. She'd forgotten how much bloody strength the man possessed. A gasp escaped her lips as he put her on her feet and pulled her along with him through the doorway and out into the passageway. It was a good thing her skirts were hemmed high, because the pace he set was so fast she nearly had to run to keep up.

And there was no question of not staying beside him. Marcus hadn't released her, his grip solid and unyielding. She was caught in a strange mixture of memory and reality. She clearly recalled being pulled along beside him, while his men held her brothers back with their drawn swords. Today, Marcus took her into the yard where once again his men waited with their horses.

She recoiled. It was simply a response that overrode all attempts at thinking. Marcus turned to look at her, his keen gaze feeling like it actually touched her. He came to some decision quickly.

"Skene."

It was a command his men seemed to understand. The burly retainer acted upon it, coming up beside her and blocking her way to freedom.

There was no safe haven behind her. She knew it, and still she looked at the horse in front of her as though it was the last place she wanted to go.

She wanted to scream with frustration and force her mind to function.

All she managed was to bite her lip as Marcus leaned over and cupped his hand. "Lift yer foot, Helen."

Later, she would likely recall why she detested him ordering her about, but at the moment, it was a relief to have him giving her direction. Her head was full of memories, and the ones from the night before were making everything very confusing. The haven she'd thought court to be was now more dangerous than returning to MacPherson land.

She was frozen as Marcus grabbed her ankle, pulling her foot off the ground, and then he straightened, lifting her up and onto the back of a horse.

She stared at him, their gazes meeting when he took the reins and handed them to her.

Who was he?

Why didn't she know the answer to that?

She did, and yet, at that moment, it seemed everything was changing. He made a harsh sound under his breath, and she realized she was just sitting there, staring at him. She took the reins, the feeling of them against her fingers more of a puzzle for her racing thoughts.

Marcus didn't grant her time to make sense of what she was doing, the wisdom of it, or even if she wanted to go with him. He mounted his stallion, his men following his lead, and a moment later, they were riding out of the gates of the castle.

It brought Helen relief and renewed apprehension. Having the castle falling behind them was pure delight because it meant the earl would not put Marcus back into chains.

But she also was staring at Marcus's back, and he was every inch the Highlander she'd met that day when he'd stolen her.

Today, there was a new set of sensations. He was just as powerful and commanding, but what struck her deepest was the beauty of seeing him free. It really made everything worth it, filling her with a sense of accomplishment that had been missing from her life.

No matter what she thought of the man, one thing was certain: Marcus MacPherson had touched off feelings inside her that she had never realized might go so deep. Was that something to cherish?

She simply had no idea.

❧

She felt Marcus watching her.

That was an oddity, because he'd never troubled himself with her before.

Helen felt the frustration that had kept her company for the last year and a half rising inside her. Honestly, when it came to Marcus, it was as if the tide came in every few hours, wave after wave of anger toward him and what he'd made of her life.

She wasn't sorry, either. Frustration was far better than pity. Better to spit in the eye of Fate than to cry in a broken heap where it had dropped her.

But she did twist her lips into a grimace as she forced herself to move. Every muscle she had protested the simple action of walking because Marcus had kept them riding the entire day, even past sundown. She knew the only reason they were stopped now was because the horses needed water.

Not that she could blame him. If someone had locked her in chains, she would likely not rest until she found her home either.

"Thank you."

Helen was so deep in her thoughts that Katherine's voice startled her. The girl blinked at the way Helen jumped before she offered up a shy smile.

"I am deeply in your debt."

Helen relaxed and returned the smile. "Ye should no' have to be. I did the only thing any decent person should have."

"Decency," Katherine said in a soft voice clearly laced with an English accent. "I have discovered men talk more about it than actually act upon it. They seem to think the Bible was written only for women to heed."

"Aye," Helen agreed. "It is a sad fact."

Katherine walked beside her for a moment. Marcus glanced back at them, but it was Skene who was assigned to safeguard them as they stretched their legs along the river's edge.

"So, are these men..." Katherine asked slowly, gauging whether or not Helen approved of her asking a question. Helen continued to smile, encouraging the girl. "Are they in fact Highlanders?"

Helen nodded. "Yes. A fine example of them, too. They are MacPhersons."

"I see," Katherine remarked as she silently surveyed Helen from head to toe.

"I was born a Grant," Helen offered.

"Is it a good match for you?" Katherine asked.

Helen choked on a snort. Katherine's eyes widened, shaming her. "Yes, I suppose it would be considered a fine match. Me father has no great name."

"Mine does," Katherine supplied. "It is a curse because men fight over me like a chest of gold."

"It can also be a curse having no recourse against men with more power."

Helen regretted her words. Katherine was young and shouldn't have to face life's harsher lessons just yet. The English girl surprised her by nodding, her eyes full of comprehension.

"No' that it matters," Helen continued. "The wedding was only for the Earl of Morton's benefit. We shall get an annulment."

Skene heard every word, his eyebrows lifting nearly to his hairline. But Helen quickly lost interest in the man because Marcus was standing behind him. Her new husband didn't care for what she'd said. His jaw was tight, and the knuckles on his hand where he was holding the pommel of his sword were white.

"Mount up," he ordered. "I won't rest easy until we get out of the Lowlands."

❧

The next few days passed in a blur. Helen spent most of it on the back of a horse. Marcus would call a halt and let them rest for short periods only. So when he stopped in front of a rough-looking inn, the place looked as welcoming as a castle.

In reality, it was a tavern that served basic meals to

those on the road. The bottom floor of the building was filled with long tables around which a plump woman bustled as she served up stew and the local ale.

Marcus had words with the owner of the place while Skene and Finley stood very close to Helen and Katherine. The rest of the MacPherson retainers moved to some of the tables, making it clear they expected the other travelers to make way for them. No one argued. The other travelers picked up their mugs and bowls and gladly sat across the room while casting suspicious looks toward the Highlanders. They were still in the middle lands, not yet truly in the Highlands. For all that every man in the tavern room was a Scot, there was a marked difference between them.

The MacPhersons were Highlanders. They gave allegiance to their clan and survived in harsh terrain. They clung to their traditions because there was strength in numbers. Katherine's predicament was certainly an example of this. Without her family, the girl's fate could be a dire one.

Well, the MacPhersons had interfered in that. At least insofar as stopping the Earl of Morton's plans for her. It came at a price, though. Brenda would have to face the earl when he learned of their deception. And Katherine? She was heading to a place where no decent English lady ever went. Her reputation would be stained forever.

Helen knew a great deal about a stained reputation. She shifted her attention to Marcus but didn't feel the rise of her temper. That was new, and it shook her a bit because he had been the target of her anger for so long. Oh, it was a sin to be so discontented. She'd often reminded herself of the merits of cultivating forgiveness, if for nothing other than the ease it would grant her.

Today, it seemed that was the case. She wouldn't go so far as to say she forgave Marcus. No, not while she was fairly certain her toes were still numb from a winter spent in house shoes. All Helen had to do was look at Katherine and see the patches upon patches on the clothing the girl wore to recall just how little forgiveness she owed Marcus.

And yet…

She frowned as she felt her conscience stirring. Guilt was needling her as she looked at Katherine. It would have been in Marcus's best interest to wed the girl. The Earl of Morton was not a man to cross lightly, and many in the room would have said not at all. Not only was the man regent, but he was a Douglas, and that clan had the numbers to make it very unwise to cross them. Even if his dictates fostered revulsion in many of his clansmen, they would listen to his reasoning and find it just. Or at least justifiable because of the good it would bring in the end.

Indeed, guilt was sitting solidly on Helen's shoulders now, urging her to improve her opinion of Marcus. Oh yes, he was arrogant and presumptuous. Yet he was also a decent, honorable man. Marcus finished his business by pressing silver into the palm of the innkeeper. He caught Helen looking at him, their eyes meeting. Something twisted inside her belly. Some recognition of him went deeper than the way she noticed the other men in room. Clearly, she should have dispensed with her anger at him sooner, because now she knew no way to think about the man other than intensely.

"This is no fit place for women," Marcus said once he was standing beside her. "I've rented a room above stairs for ye both."

Katherine made a soft sound of gratitude. The child looked worn out, with dark circles beneath her eyes. Marcus took her arm to steady her as they climbed the stairs. The wood creaked and dust tickled Helen's nose, but the promise of a bed shimmered like a treat.

Marcus went inside, looking around the chamber twice before he turned and caught Helen with a stern look. "Do ye still have that dagger tucked into the top of yer boot?"

"Of course," Helen answered.

Katherine's eyes widened. "What a fine idea." The English girl only smiled when both Helen and Marcus looked at her in shock. "Of course I was speaking of the boots." For all her youth, Katherine was very accomplished in the art of plying her innocence.

"Aye." Marcus's tone made it clear he didn't believe her.

"Here now." The woman who had been serving the tables hustled through the doorway, her arms full. Helen took the pitcher she was grasping with her right hand while the woman laid out the other items.

There was a large plate with supper for both her and Katherine. Bread, cheese, and some late-harvest fruit. Marcus waited until the woman finished and left.

"Bar the door," he instructed Helen before he went

back into the passageway. Marcus turned and pegged her with a solid look. "We'll be just below, but I can nae set a man here without insulting the landlord."

Which meant another night on the cold ground. Helen nodded, taking solace in the fact that Marcus didn't trust easily. He'd passed up a string of villages behind them because he didn't know the landlords of the taverns.

As he left, Marcus pulled the door shut with a solid sound.

Katherine was already sitting on one of the stools at the table. She was gripping handfuls of her skirt to keep from tearing into the food.

"Eat," Helen told her. "Ye need no' wait on me."

Katherine smiled before reaching for the round of bread and ripping it in half. She plunged it into one of the bowls of stew and sighed as she bit off some of it. Helen was more interested in washing off the grime from the road. She poured water into a bowl and dunked a length of linen into it.

The water was dingy by the time she finished, but her skin felt delightful. By then, Katherine was done with her meal and had stood up to go and make use of their washing facilities. Moments after she finished, the girl was lying in bed, exhaustion taking over.

Helen took longer to eat, but in the end, no matter how much she wanted to think, her body was too spent. She crawled into the bed next to Katherine and surrendered to sleep.

⁓

She smelled him.

Marcus, that was.

Helen shifted closer to that scent, a deep sense of enjoyment moving through her. She felt him stroking her again. Those large hands that held so much strength could be so very gentle against her skin. It was a marvel that surprised and delighted her.

Yes. He was smoothing his hand along her face and down her neck, then back up to her face and chin before he clamped his hand over her lips.

Helen came fully awake with a start, slamming into Marcus as she sat up, which felt very much like falling onto the floor. He held her against him, his hand cutting off the shriek that tried to escape her lips, but she heaved and lifted her body right off the bed. She must have surprised him because his body gave way, rolling back and away from the bed.

She tumbled down on top of him, her head knocking against his jaw. She heard him grunt before he turned them, rolling her beneath his larger body and locking her in place.

"Damn ye…vixen," he muttered.

"What are ye doing in here with me?" she demanded in a harsh whisper.

"Am I no' yer husband, woman?"

Helen gasped, bucking against his hold. He cursed in Gaelic and followed her as she rolled away from him. It must have been surprise that allowed her to break free, because a moment later she was able to get to her feet, backing out of the chamber. It seemed too small with Marcus sharing it.

"I did nae mean it like that," he said as he followed her out of the room and closed the door behind him.

"And ye'll be telling me now if any man under my command put his hands on ye."

"I'm no' sure what business it is of yers." Actually, she did understand. Fully so. Marcus had always taken his duty to heart. She sighed when he stiffened. "I should no' have said that. 'Twas scurrilous and unfair."

His expression had hardened. She watched him absorb her apology and relax a bit. "Ye did nae bar the door."

That snapped her completely out of slumber. "Oh…aye, ye did tell me to do that."

"For all the things I allowed ye to go without, protection was no' one of them, Helen."

She nodded, acknowledging the truth of his words. But her temper was still stirred. "Checking to see if the door was barred did no' have anything to do with ye putting yer hands on me."

"True." He tilted his head to the side, and she caught a flash of his teeth as he grinned.

That smile was trouble. A solid promise that the man was in the mood to press his will on her.

"When I opened the door and saw ye lying there, it was pure pleasure to know I have the right to touch ye."

Her breath got lodged in her throat for some reason.

"Ye should no' be thinking like that," she admonished him in a voice that was too breathless for her taste. They were just at the top of the stairs, which meant their words could bounce right down to the men sleeping in the tavern below. The last thing she needed was more than thirty witnesses to the fact that Marcus was declaring he'd put his hands on her. There would be no annulment if that happened.

"Ye're thinking about it too." He was watching her from his greater height, coming closer.

Helen felt him testing her nerve. Her heart was accelerating, her breathing increasing to keep pace, and all of it because he was close enough for her to catch the scent of his skin.

"I was reacting to it, ye gob." She kept her tone soft, trying to imply he was of little importance to her.

"We have that in common, lass." He cupped her elbows and had her upper arms clasped in his hands before she finished snarling at him. "I was drawn to ye as well."

Helen flattened her hands against his chest, but there was no stopping him. Marcus angled his head and pressed his mouth against hers. She jerked against his hold, but not because she thought to escape. No, it shamed her to realize she had no control whatsoever over her body. The second she felt his grasp on her arms, it was as if someone had set off a black-powder keg inside her. It blew right through the wall of decorum that stopped her from doing the things she wanted to do.

And the things she wanted to do with Marcus were definitely among the things she'd been warned against.

Now, with his mouth coaxing hers to respond in kind, she couldn't seem to recall why it was wrong to kiss him back.

It felt so very delicious.

So did the way his chest felt beneath her fingertips. Her intention to push him back melted beneath the sweet wave of sensation sweeping through her from his kiss, leaving her smoothing her hands along his chest and slowly, tentatively exploring the way he felt beneath her fingertips.

The kiss changed in response. Marcus pulled her closer, wrapping his arms around her and making it a true embrace. She wasn't his captive just then. No, there was a whole new feeling to the way he moved his hands along her back, rubbing her gently as he brought his hand up to her nape and threaded his fingers through her loose hair.

She shuddered, gasping at the intimacy. Somehow, she had never realized what that word truly meant. Now, it was a feeling, working its way through her flesh, layer by layer, seeping deeper than she had thought possible.

It was shocking and she craved more of it, but the sheer intensity of it all made her pull away. She only succeeded because he'd abandoned his hard grip on her. She ended up against the wall, her hands flat on the rough wood because she feared she'd reach out for him again.

She wanted to.

No, that wasn't exactly true. Part of her needed to put her hands on him. It was a craving, a hunger that grew with every passing second. His embrace made her feel complete for the first time since she had left her father's house.

She couldn't. The only thing she had left that was truly her own was her body.

He crossed his arms over his chest. She'd seen him standing that way too many times to count, his feet braced shoulder-width apart while he considered those around him with a keen gaze.

"Go back to bed, Helen. Before we wake that child."

Even whispered, she heard the command in his tone. Her temper arrived at last, balking at being told what to do.

Which only made her scoff at her own fickle emotions. Clearly she needed more sleep, because she was making no sense whatsoever. She stopped long enough to place the bar across the door and make sure it was pushed all the way down. The bed was warm and inviting, although she was still pondering why she could not control her responses to his kisses.

For the first time, she thought about what it would cost him to keep her as wife. The MacPhersons were a powerful clan to be sure, but one reason they were so was because of alliances. She brought none, and after the annulment, Marcus could wed another who would strengthen the clan.

So that was it. There was nothing more to consider. They would get an annulment.

And she was going to make sure she explained to him exactly why he wouldn't be kissing her ever again.

❧

Brenda had expected to be discovered sooner.

Not that she was unhappy, far from it. Nearly a week passed before Morton sent for her. There was no way to keep her face hidden from the guards, and they lost a great deal of their color when she turned to face them instead of Katherine. The door to her tiny cell was closed quickly before she heard one of them running down the passageway.

She tried not to think about being free from the

four walls because she would be foolish indeed to hope for good favor from the Earl of Morton. No, it would be the flash of his temper she felt, but it would be worth it. Marcus would be well away now, on his way back to the Highlands.

"Ye bitch."

Brenda lowered herself before the earl, and he backhanded her. She stumbled because of the strength he'd used, righting herself as pain went through her jaw.

"Where is Katherine?" the earl demanded.

"With Marcus MacPherson."

The earl was still breathing heavily from how quickly he had come to see the truth of his guard's words. His face was flushed, and it darkened as he absorbed her words.

"Ye bloody Highlanders," he raged. "The lot of ye will bend. Mark me words, ye will."

Ambition was an ugly thing, Brenda thought as she observed the earl. She didn't move, didn't speak. There was little reason to. A man who was in the grip of greed wasn't one to bargain with.

"I suppose ye agreed to this because of that girl's age?"

She hadn't expected him to ask any questions. After all, he was a man who believed his opinion was superior to everyone else's, especially a woman's.

"Katherine was a child still. Did ye no' think about the fact that having a babe might have killed her? What sort of alliance would that gain ye? The English do nae need new reasons to loathe us."

The earl grunted and swept his eyes over her from head to toe, making her shift uncomfortably as his gaze lingered on her breasts. "Ye are a woman, and a handsome one at that."

He wasn't paying her a compliment. No, the man was calculating his next move. A chill touched her nape as she witnessed the way he contemplated her the same way he might a mare.

"Widowed as well?" He waited for her to nod. "Is it true ye warmed Bhaic MacPherson's cock?"

The earl was being base on purpose. The man wanted to frighten her, and Brenda knew she had best save her true fear for later. Coarse language was hardly the worst a man such as he might press upon someone in her position.

"I was his lover for a short time."

The earl chuckled. "With that face, ye might serve as a fine whore for me when I need to hear what a man is saying while his cock is inside ye."

Brenda had expected vengeance from him, but she still felt the color drain from her face. He didn't miss it, chuckling at her horror.

"Aye, ye'll do as told, or I'll find a man to wed ye to who will make yer last husband look like a bloody saint."

He turned and left the cell. The guard shut it, and Brenda heard the lock turning. The sound actually pleased her, allowing her to collapse onto the stool and let her mouth drop open in repulsion. Indeed, she enjoyed knowing the door was locked because it meant she was forgotten.

The true fear would begin whenever Morton had her taken out of the cell.

Marcus MacPherson would have to be taught a lesson.

Morton returned to his receiving chambers and settled into the throne chair. Scotland hadn't had a king in almost a century—not a real one, anyway. Oh yes, there was always a whelp somewhere with the right royal blood, but the regents were the ones who ruled. Even Mary Stuart had been crowned as an infant and sent to France at the age of five. Her return had nearly pushed the country into civil war, but she'd managed to keep Scotland from becoming the property of France, and she had whelped another infant king who needed a regent.

Morton intended his regency to be long.

So the Highlands would have to be tamed and brought under royal rule. Marcus couldn't be allowed to slip through the plans Morton had made for him. It was simply a matter of the earl maintaining his position. No one obeyed a man they saw as weak.

So, Marcus MacPherson would have to be taught a harsh lesson. It was only a matter of deciding upon the means.

Three

"SKENE, MAN, EITHER SPIT IT OUT OR I'M GOING TO smash ye in the jaw."

Skene didn't take offense. No, the burly retainer flashed a grin that showed off his cracked front tooth before he nodded at Marcus.

"Well now, some of the lads were wondering if ye're wed or no'." Skene asked his question diplomatically.

"Amuses ye, does it?" Marcus asked.

Skene shrugged. "It's the truth that some of us can nae help but enjoy the similarities between yer brother's wedding and yer own." Skene was grinning like a man who had just walked in on two naked and eager women in his bed. "More than one of us has decided we'd be a great deal better off if we'd never crossed paths with the Earl of Morton."

Marcus couldn't help but snort in response. "He's more bastard than I am."

"What can ye expect from a Douglas?"

It was the sort of comment Marcus was accustomed to, but the earl had prompted one change that was not altogether bad by forcing Ailis Robertson on his brother, Bhaic. Morton had started to put an end to the feud between the Robertsons and MacPhersons. To be sure, Marcus had told the man the truth—it would take years to see the matter finished. Skene's easy acceptance of what everyone thought of the Douglases was proof of that.

"So we, the lads and I, were left wondering just what ye are thinking to do with that Grant woman."

Now there was a question. Marcus found himself looking toward Helen and considering her. He'd been doing his best to avoid looking straight at her because she was a handsome woman. It wasn't so much her features that drew him to her; he liked her brazen refusal to back down from him.

Skene let out a low whistle. Marcus snapped his attention back to the man, only to hear his retainer chuckle at his expense.

"Do nae be thinking ye know all that much about what I think," Marcus warned Skene.

Skene shrugged, continuing to move his hands slowly over his horse's flank. "What ye think? Nay. I do nae know much of that, but ye did fight Symon Grant, the laird's son, for her, sure enough. There's a bit I saw with me own eyes. Sure, some might argue ye done it to keep yer prize from being stolen, and no' many would question it. Still…ye kissed her."

He'd done that and more. Marcus couldn't help but recall how he'd kissed Helen before one and all in the hall. Indeed, his men were not fools, and still he felt a bit like the collar of his shirt had suddenly become too tight.

"So then." Skene refused to let the matter rest.

"What should I tell the lads? Ye understand, none of them want to be flirting with a woman ye are planning to keep."

"And if I say I am no' intent on seeing me marriage through?" Marcus growled.

Skene looked him straight in the eye. "In that case, ye would no' be such a hard bastard as to deny us the chance to win her favors while we are out here and away from the rest of the men." Skene sent him a very knowing look. "That woman is a vixen and worth the risk of being bitten to gain her."

"Well, ye can tell the *lads*…" Marcus stressed the last word. Skene actually looked disappointed, making Marcus clamp his teeth together in temper.

"Tell them what?" Skene pressed.

"That she's married to me."

It wasn't truly an answer. Marcus felt that bit of knowledge nipping at him as he finished with his own horse. He stomped away from the animal as he contemplated why he was riled. The answer was standing down at the river's edge, and he realized his pride was still wounded by the way she'd left him.

Vixen.

Skene had called her that justly, as well as making a fine point about how likely she was to bite any man who tried his hand at her.

Well, that wouldn't be any of his men.

Marcus was surprised by how quickly that thought crossed his mind. It was like a brand had been pressed onto him before he'd realized what was about to happen. Now it was sizzling as it cooled, the sting of it settling deep into his flesh.

Vixen, indeed. But she was going to be his.

❧

"How far is it to the Highlands?"

Katherine tried not to sound weary. The girl was forcing a serene smile that didn't quite reach her eyes. She
had midnight eyes so dark they seemed to have a flash of
blue in them, along with black hair to match. Coupled
with her fair skin, it made a striking combination.

"We've another few days before we cross onto
MacPherson land," Helen told her. "The pace should
ease once we do."

At least she hoped so, because her backside was
feeling the lack of time out of the saddle.

Are ye sure of that?

Helen didn't care for that idea. Once Marcus wasn't
focused on getting them back to his father's land, the
man might just turn his attention toward her.

She was looking across the camp toward him when
she realized Katherine was watching her. "We're on
McTavish land at the moment."

"Are the MacPhersons feuding with these
McTavishes?" Katherine asked.

Helen leaned over and wrung out the linen cloth
she'd been using to wash her face and neck. She
plunged it back into the river, ignoring the chill in the
water. It was worth the discomfort to be clean. Or, at
least, cleaner.

"No' officially feuding," Helen said. "However,
among Highlanders, a bit of toying with one another
can happen. If the McTavishes discover us, they may
take us unaware while we're on their land."

"Toying?" Katherine questioned.

Helen stood and took a last sweep around her neck with the cloth. "They might take some of the horses and demand a ransom."

"I see," Katherine answered. The girl wanted to ask something more—it was there in her eyes—and she finally gathered her courage. "Would they steal us? I heard the men talking about how Marcus stole you."

"That was an altogether different matter."

Katherine stared at her, likely trying to decide why Helen's voice was tense. Katherine suddenly smiled. "Perhaps it is best you are wed."

"Naught could be further from the truth," Helen informed the girl quickly.

There was a soft male chuckle behind her that Helen recognized all too well. In spite of knowing who it was, she jumped and tried to whirl around, but she was too close to the water's edge and the ground was soft. It gave beneath her feet, and she started to tumble backward.

Marcus leaped forward, moving like a streak of lightning to catch her forearms. He jerked her to a halt as she felt her skirts being tugged into the water behind her.

"Supper is ready, Katherine," he said without taking his eyes off Helen. "Up to camp with ye."

Katherine immediately started up the hill to where the men had set up camp, far enough from the water so they might hear anyone approaching. Helen realized she'd made a critical error in lingering over her vanity and allowing Marcus to use the sound of the rushing water to get close to her.

She had her footing now. "Thank ye," she said to Marcus.

He stepped back but blocked the path up to the camp. He was contemplating her, which made her cheeks heat with temper.

No, that wasn't it. Her eyes widened as she realized she was blushing.

That unsettled her completely and she stepped to the side, edging away from him because she was so keenly aware of him. Her heart was accelerating again, making a mockery of her firm decision to tell him why he mustn't kiss her again.

"Come here, Helen."

She'd been looking away from him, so the tone of his voice startled her. It was a request, not his usual command, and she had no idea how to deal with such a thing from Marcus MacPherson. He was her captor, not her suitor. Just thinking that word made her blush deepen because she recalled their conversation in the dungeon very well.

She'd enjoyed that private glimpse at his person. Enjoyed even more the idea that he wanted to know more about her. It was so strange to think they might be more than captor and hostage.

Yet she liked it very well.

He extended his hand in invitation. "Come here. Let us try to be easier in each other's company."

Something inside her leaped at that idea, excitement prickling across the surface of her skin. "That would be unwise."

He crossed his arms over his chest and took a slow step after her and then another. "Why do ye think so, lass? Ye kissed me back, and I enjoyed it full well. So did ye."

"And yet"—she opened her hands wide—"surely ye must see that an annulment is the only logical solution to this marriage."

But he hadn't agreed to an end to their union, and the realization made her stare at him in mounting horror. He'd kept her before; he might do so again.

Marcus's expression darkened, his jaw tightening, but he drew in a deep breath and extended his hand again. "I do nae agree. We are both at an age when a wedding is expected. We should be enjoying the fact that we were no' pressed to consummate our vows immediately and have been given time to come to terms with the arrangement. Come here and learn to be settled near me."

She was stunned, shock holding her in a tight grip as she blinked and waited for him to say something else. But the man was standing there, fully expecting her to put her hand into his.

Part of her wanted to.

And the other completely balked.

"I am no' a mare to be broken to ride."

He blew out a long, frustrated breath. "Can ye nae notice that I am trying to speak to ye sweetly, woman? I am War Chief. Wooing is no' a skill I have much practice at."

"Oh, I know that very well." She couldn't help but see the humor in that, as well as a bit of enjoyment for getting him to admit that he was not accomplished at something.

Marcus didn't miss it either. He grunted, the sound

betraying his frustration. "I suppose ye're due a bit of needling toward me."

"That is no' what I am doing," she answered. "I am speaking good, sound, logical facts. Ones ye would be wise to listen to."

"I'd rather try me hand at kissing ye," he replied.

He reached out and grasped a handful of her skirts. She'd expected him to reach for her upper arms, so he was pulling her against him and cupping her neck before she realized what he was about. He held her for a moment, so close their breaths mingled.

"No' that I am complaining, sweet wife. Kissing ye is something I find very pleasing."

He smothered her retort, controlling her attempts to push him away while he kissed her hard. His sweet kisses had slowly roused her before; now, the way he claimed her mouth sent her body into flames. The heat flared up, consuming everything she thought she knew and leaving her prey to the cravings that began to swirl inside her.

Marcus held her head and angled his face so he could fit his mouth against hers. It was savage, and yet there was a hint of control because he stopped short of bruising her lips. There was no denying him though, and she didn't want to. Her memory offered up a perfect recollection of what delight there was in his embrace, and she was hungry for more of it.

She reached for him, gripping his jerkin and frustrated that the stiff leather wouldn't allow her to get a good hold on him. It wasn't really necessary—he was holding her so fiercely she'd never fall—but she realized she didn't want to be his captive. She wanted to meet him and give him back as good as she got. So she opened her mouth wide, enjoying the male sound of enjoyment when he followed suit.

He was tasting her, slipping his lips along hers and using his tongue to tease hers. She shivered, sensation shooting down her spine. He rubbed her neck, gently reassuring her. And then he was stroking her again, running his hands along her body and boldly cupping the curves of her backside through the layers of her skirts. A twist of enjoyment went through her that touched off a soft throbbing at the front of her sex.

It was as if she were transparent to him, her needs and cravings something he could read like ink on parchment, and that was incredibly exciting. It was as if she had been asleep and had woken up in the middle of a festival. The delights for her senses were abundant and vibrant and so plentiful that she felt as though she was spinning around and around like a child in the middle of it all.

Pure bliss. That was the only way to describe it, and she wanted more.

But Marcus suddenly stiffened, his body going rigid before he slumped to the ground. Still dazed from his kiss, she watched him fall as though it were happening slowly. By the time she looked up to see what had felled Marcus, his attacker had his hand clamped around her mouth as he turned her and pulled her back against his body.

Helen still tried to scream, but the sound was smothered beneath the hard grip against her lips. Fear was burning through her, but she refused to let it paralyze her. She kicked her feet up and off the ground, taking her captor by surprise. For a moment, she felt his grip slacken, felt freedom within her reach. She surged forward with every bit of strength she had, only to feel something strike her across the back of the skull.

Time was still moving slowly, which allowed her to realize she was slipping into unconsciousness. She felt the blackness coming toward her, knew it was going to engulf her, and there was nothing she could do to stop it.

Nothing at all.

✤

Marcus awoke with a roar.

The camp erupted as his men surged to their feet. Partially eaten suppers went spilling into the dirt, and not a single man gave the food a second thought. They pulled out their swords and took positions that would give them the best chance to defend what was important. The horses, Katherine, and Marcus.

Finley and Skene met Marcus halfway down the slope to the river's bank.

"Where in the fuck were ye?" Marcus demanded.

The two MacPherson retainers offered him a half shrug. "We pulled back to give ye and the lass a bit of privacy."

"Seeing as ye are wed and the young English miss is no' old enough to be noticing what ye two might have been about," Skene finished up.

If he hadn't been so furious, Marcus would have laughed. Fate was a damned bitch, laughing at his expense while watching him dance to her tune. His skull felt like it had been split but his vision was fine, so he was going to live. But the way Skene started to turn purple because he was holding his breath to keep from laughing warned Marcus that he might prefer death.

"Helen was taken," he was forced to admit.

"Someone"—there was a choking sound—"snuck up…on…*ye*?"

Marcus grabbed a handful of Skene's jerkin and hauled him close. "That would no' have happened if ye had left camp where I told ye to make it."

Skene was still trying to hold back his amusement, making little snorting sounds like a pig wallowing in mud.

"Here now." Finley interrupted him with a hand on Marcus's shoulder. Marcus turned a deadly look on his man. Finley held up a strip of plaid and a parchment that had been stuck into a tree trunk with a dagger.

"The McTavish," Marcus snarled.

"They'll no' harm the lass," Finley said, trying to reassure him. "It's just a bit of ransom they are after."

"I know what the game is," Marcus shot back.

Oh, indeed, he knew it well. Had played it more than a time or two. This time was different. He felt his temper straining against his self-control, which almost never happened to him. He was a man who lived by his ability to make decisions without allowing his emotions to override his logic. A War Chief with a lack of self-discipline was one who would get his men killed out of folly, instead of making sure the fight was worth the blood it might cost to claim victory.

And tonight, he was furious.

Over a woman.

Admitting that only made him grind his teeth more. As soon as he got his hands on Helen, he would make sure the woman was just as twisted by what he made her feel as he was by her effect on him. He had no idea how that might come to pass, but he knew one thing for certain.

There was not going to be any annulment.

"Let's go get me wife."

As Marcus started up the slope, he passed several of his men who were there in the darkness. Most of them failed to control their grins, which tempted him to smash more than one of them in the jaw.

Well, he'd save his rage for whichever McTavish bastard had put his hands on Helen. In fact, he was going to enjoy hearing her tell him what she thought about him fighting over her again.

Because it would give him the chance to kiss her quiet again. And that was another thing he was sure of.

There was going to be a lot of kissing.

❧

She still had her dagger.

Helen dismissed the throbbing in her head and ordered herself to focus on gaining her freedom. Not that a dagger was going to be of much use inside a fortified castle. It might be handy for cutting the rope binding her wrists, but a huge stone tower was looming ahead of them and she was surrounded by McTavish retainers. Ones that were all enjoying having her in their midst.

"Awake at last?"

The man holding her in front of him on a horse had felt her rouse.

"Ye have made an error in taking me," Helen warned.

The large chest she was being held against rumbled. "I do nae think so, lass. Ye were kind enough to supply me with all the information I needed there on the riverbank. I heard ye clear as a church bell."

"If that is so," she answered, trying not to allow her voice to tighten as they moved closer and closer to that tower, "ye should have heard that I am no one of any importance."

"I heard ye are wed to Marcus MacPherson. That makes ye valuable—and in more than coin."

She stiffened because they were close enough for the men on the walls of the castle to begin ringing the bells. That told her she was riding with Laird McTavish's son; Rolfe was his name. The men she was riding amidst answered the bells by raising their voices in a cheer. The man holding her tightened his grip on her.

"Easy now, lady," he said. "Ye know the game we play. No one will harm ye, and I wager yer bridegroom will be along in short order to ransom ye."

"Ye would lose that bet," Helen hissed. "If ye were listening, ye should have heard clearly that our union is unconsummated. That is because the marriage was a necessary thing to prevent evil being done. I brought no dowry, so Marcus will likely thank ye for taking me off his hands."

They rode right under the portcullis, chilling her blood. Was it her fate to be imprisoned in every fortification in Scotland? Fate was a cruel mistress for certain. People were spilling out of the two main towers to see why the men were cheering. Women pointed at her while children tugged on their mothers' skirts, begging to be told what was happening. It chafed Helen's pride to notice the glee with which her plight was being explained.

The horse stopped as a retainer took its bridle. Another man came around and reached up to help Helen down. Her captor gave her a push, so there was no choice in the matter. She slipped down the side of the horse in a tangle of skirts and would have ended up on her backside if the retainer hadn't caught her by her upper arms.

There was a swish and flash of motion as the man responsible for her newest incarceration dismounted. Helen caught a glimpse of his thighs before the pleats of his kilt settled into place just above his knees. He was huge, just like Marcus, and every bit as suited to the rough Highlands. Yet he was younger, just becoming a man. His body might be grown, but there was still a hint of youth in his eyes that marked him as less experienced than Marcus.

"I'm Rolfe McTavish, and ye are me guest." He spread his arms in mock courtesy.

Helen smiled sweetly at him and fluttered her eyelashes. He burst out laughing, a good number of his men joining him.

"What ye are is a fool," she informed him when he'd sobered. "I will bring ye naught."

Rolfe's eyes were green, like a spring meadow. At that moment they were glittering with enjoyment.

"Mistress, ye have already brought me something that no amount of silver can buy." He hooked his hands into his belt, looking down at her from his greater height as his men pressed in to hear what was being said. "I took Marcus MacPherson, War Chief of the MacPhersons, by surprise!"

There was a moment of shocked silence before the entire yard erupted into hysteria. Rolfe leaned back and roared with mirth.

Helen had no idea why she chose to act. Only that ever since she'd wed Marcus, holding back her impulses had become impossible. One moment Rolfe was chuckling like a marauding Viking, straining her temper to the breaking point, and the next she was planting her foot right in his balls. Helen picked up her knee high enough so she could send her foot smashing toward his unprotected groin. She felt his balls depress beneath the sole of her boot and watched the way the man stiffened before he landed on his ass while sucking in his breath and fighting to keep his eyes from rolling up into his head.

"And now, I've taken ye by surprise," she informed him. "Trust me, Rolfe McTavish, I am more trouble than ye need."

❧

"Riders ahead."

Marcus had already heard the soft sound of approaching horses. He gave Skene a single nod and his men left the road, moving up into the trees. They pulled up the section of their plaids draped over their shoulders to help conceal them, most of them reaching down to run soothing hands along their mounts' necks to keep the horses quiet.

"MacPherson plaid," Finley called from his post farther ahead of them all.

There was a collective sigh of relief as they came back to the main road. The only set of eyes that remained wide was Katherine's. At least the girl sat on a horse well enough and kept her mouth shut. She was watching everything with the wonder that only a stranger could experience.

Marcus listened to the sound of the horses coming closer. He could see them now. A solid fifty men, and they were all riding hard. His brother, Bhaic, spotted him and lifted his hand to slow the pace of the men with him. Bhaic swept his eyes over them all, lingering for a moment on Katherine, his expression turning grim.

"That bastard had his way with ye?" It wasn't really a question. Bhaic was furious and only trying to keep his anger in check because of the way Katherine was watching them. "Bloody bleeding Christ, she's barely weaned."

"And no' me wife," Marcus told his brother. "How did ye know of Morton's plan?"

"Lyel and Kam nearly killed their horses riding back to tell me yer plight," Bhaic informed him. "They said Morton's men clamped ye in irons for refusing to wed."

"Aye, but I would have suffered that well enough," Marcus said. "Do nae tell me ye would have been foolish enough to ride back into that man's reach? Christ, man, after what he threatened ye with at yer wedding? The MacPhersons need ye."

"They need ye as well, and I know full well yer

nature and the earl's. Morton plans his traps well. Ye're damned right I was riding for court to make sure the earl knew we will no' be keeping silent while ye were being held," Bhaic replied. He bit back the next thing he was going to say, making a clear effort to swallow his temper. "So if ye did nae wed her, how did ye come to have her with ye?"

"Helen."

His brother waited for an explanation.

"Christ and brimstone," Marcus swore before he lifted his hand and ordered his men to dismount and water the horses. Bhaic did the same. Two of the men took their horses, leaving him facing his brother. Marcus told the tale, and to his credit, his brother clamped his lips together to keep from interrupting. By the time Marcus finished, Bhaic's lips were a white line, his blue eyes sparkling with amusement while he coughed to cover his laugh.

"I do nae need ye finding entertainment at me expense," Marcus warned his sibling.

Bhaic lifted an eyebrow. "Dearest Brother, there is no way ye are going to escape it. No' after the way ye ordered yer men to dog me heels while I was trying me hand at impressing me wife!"

He threw his head back and roared. Marcus had the urge to lunge at Bhaic and give him a good thrashing, but he muzzled that impulse because Helen was still out of his reach. He needed to keep his priorities straight.

"If ye're quite finished, could we get on with collecting me bride?"

Bhaic leveled a smirk at him. "Bride, is it?"

Marcus was fighting again to control his temper. "It is, and no' a bloody word about it."

Bhaic lifted his hands in mock surrender. "Wouldn't dream of it." But he choked on a new round of chuckles. "Now, me wife would, of that I am quite certain."

Marcus sent his brother a deadly look. Bhaic sobered, returning his attention to the matter that was most urgent. "Aye, aye. The McTavish. We'll need Symon Grant for this."

"The devil ye say," Marcus argued.

Bhaic shook his head. "Better to have a strong witness. With the union unconsummated and not contracted, the McTavishes could obtain an annulment through their own priest on the grounds that Helen has been compromised by being inside their castle. All it would take is a midwife doing an inspection to confirm she's a maiden still. They could keep her unless we make sure they realize they're angering more than just the MacPhersons."

It was a hard truth, as Marcus well knew. He had faced such realities before, but this time it was different—and his brother noticed.

"Ye want her back?"

Marcus sent him a hard look. "Helen is me wife, and the only way the McTavishes are keeping her is if she's me widow."

❧

"Finished hiding from me at last?"

Considering her circumstances, tartly greeting Rolfe McTavish wasn't the wisest choice Helen might have made. He raised one of his fair eyebrows at her while he came through the door of the chamber she'd been pacing for the better part of two days.

Helen turned and propped her hands on her hips. The man's lips twitched.

"Ye're Marcus MacPherson's match, and that's the truth," he said.

Helen rolled her eyes. "As if I care what ye think."

Rolfe leaned back against the door, but thought better of it and moved away so he'd have more space to maneuver if she made another attempt to wound him. Helen slowly smiled. "I do hope ye've had enough time to recover."

"Ye're a vixen," Rolfe remarked.

There was a touch of admiration in his tone that didn't please her at all. For all her bravado, she was very much the man's prisoner. "Came here just to tell me what ye think I am? Ye should nae have wasted yer time. I care not for yer opinion at all."

He flattened his hand over his chest. "Ye wound me again." His eyes glittered with enjoyment. "Vixen."

Helen offered him a bored look. At least she hoped that was what she managed. The truth was, she was very aware of her circumstances. That knowledge weighed on her shoulders, the uncertainty eating at her.

"He hasn't come," she said. "I told ye he would consider himself well rid of me."

"If Marcus were that great a fool, I would see it as my good fortune to take him unaware for a second time. Ye, madam, are worth keeping."

Helen lost her control over her emotions for a small moment, her eyes widening with horror before she looked away and gathered herself.

"Ye care for him."

Helen shook her head. "Not a bit. I wed him to prevent the Earl of Morton doing harm to a young English girl."

"And still," Rolfe replied softly, "I recall well what I heard the man saying to ye on that riverbank. He was intent on wooing ye."

"Perhaps," Helen agreed. "However, now that I am gone, he can return home and take a bride who will bring the MacPhersons a fat dowry. A woman he'll no' have to pay suit to."

Rolfe raked her from head to toe. "He'll have to search far and wide to find one who is yer equal."

"I have no dowry and no great name. The search will take him as far as his father's study, where there is no doubt a stack of offers waiting. He is War Chief of the clan, and such a position would make a strong alliance for any clan in the Highlands."

"His brother wed for those things," Rolfe continued. "Ye, madam, are the woman who will not shake in fear when he comes to share yer bed. The sons ye will birth to him will be worthy of their father's name, and the daughters will be no one's fools."

It was a tantalizing idea that beckoned with an allure she hadn't anticipated. Happiness. How long had it been since she'd contemplated having a life full of something as grand as that?

"Enough." Helen pulled away from her musings. "Ye are simply attempting to soothe yer injured ego, looking for confidence where there is none, because Marcus MacPherson has no' come to yer gates."

Rolfe was silent for a long moment, confirming

she had hit a weak spot. She could see him weighing her words.

"Ye might be correct."

Relief swept through her, granting her a much-needed rest from the worry that had been keeping her company in her confinement.

"And as I told ye, madam, I would consider his blindness to yer worth to be the same as taking the man from behind again. If he does nae come for ye, I'll keep ye for meself and the sons ye birth will be mine."

Her eyes widened, her temper straining once again. She reached out and grabbed the nearest item at hand, which happened to be an earthenware bowl sitting on a table. She sent it hurling at his head, and only quick action on his part kept him from harm. The bowl made solid impact with the door, breaking with a loud sound that had Rolfe's men wrenching the door open to defend their master.

"Easy, lads," Rolfe informed his men while he kept his attention on her. "Best get accustomed to her nature, as it seems we're to have this vixen with us for a while longer. I was just expressing to her how much I find that idea to me liking."

"Toad!" Helen grabbed another dish and sent it to join the bowl. Rolfe was halfway through the door and ended up diving into one of his men to avoid being hit. They tumbled to the floor in a tangle of legs and kilt pleats, pleasing her greatly.

But one of the retainers closed the door, and she heard the bar being lowered into place in the hallway beyond.

It was a harsh sound. One that chilled her blood. She moved over to one of the windows and peered out as she had countless times before, only to notice that she was too far above the ground to survive leaving the chamber through any means but the door.

They'd stripped the bed curtains from the bed when they brought her to the chamber, and it hadn't taken her long to deduce why. It was a fine chamber, grander than anywhere she'd laid her head for many years, but she was left wondering what her fate might be. Another fortress to be confined in among those where she had been called a captive.

Damn, but she hated Fate at the moment.

And she wasn't talking to God either. No, she needed her temper to cool before she unleashed any prayers that might be full of what she was really thinking.

Which left her sitting in a chamber with absolutely nothing to do except wait upon the whim of men.

Indeed, she wasn't talking to God, and that was final.

❧

"No time for that."

Willy Grant growled at his cousin as he pulled a giggling McTavish wench up and off his lap. He reached over and slapped her on her rump to get her moving. She snorted as she went.

"Damn yer hide, Leif. What do ye mean by ruining me fun?"

Willy looked around and then back at his cousin. "We've business to attend to."

Leif's interest perked up. "The sort that will put coin in our hands?"

"If we play the game right."

Leif started to reach for his whisky, but pushed it

away instead. They'd left their pitiful farms behind to make solid coin. But moving fleece was hard work. Leif was interested in something more profitable, for certain.

"Rolfe McTavish rode out today to arrange a ransom for that Grant woman he stole," Willy began.

"Aye." Leif nodded. "I saw him leave."

"Seems old Laird McTavish fancies seeing one of his daughters wed to the War Chief of the MacPhersons."

"Marcus is already wed," Leif said in disappointment.

"But the union is no' consummated," Willy continued. "I heard from one of the men who heard it straight from the Grant woman's mouth and also from Marcus MacPherson the night they stole her. There is also no contract. Seems the two wed to avoid a nasty bit of business planned by the Earl of Morton."

Leif spat on the floor. "Damned Protestant."

"Aye." Willy confirmed his own distaste. "Think on it, man. She's our cousin."

"She is?" Leif questioned.

Willy waved his hand in the air dismissively. "In some distant manner, I'm sure. No' that it matters all that much. If we were to go to old Laird McTavish and offer to take our little cousin home, that would leave the way open for his daughter to wed Marcus MacPherson."

"Where is the part where we earn coin for this?" Leif asked impatiently. "All I'm hearing is that we are getting saddled with a woman to escort. Besides, I hear the old laird is half out of his mind. That's why no one ever sees him anymore and his sons are running the clan."

"His secretary is intent on securing alliances, and he is in control of the man's signet ring and coin.

He's already told me he's interested in discussing the matter with us. I just needed to find ye to work out the particulars of the arrangement."

Leif weighed Willy's words for a long moment. "All right, then. I'll go with ye, but I'm warning ye, there had better be a good sum of silver involved, or I'll no' be dealing with that devil woman."

Laird McTavish was sitting in a huge chair that looked like a Viking throne. He wasn't the frail old man they expected to see. No, he was proud and burly, but one of his legs was missing from the knee down, and in its place was a wooden peg.

"Speak one word about me leg, and ye're dead men."

Leif and Willy immediately stopped staring at the missing limb. Laird McTavish grunted with approval.

"Highlanders do nae respect a man who is missing a leg," he said bitterly. "Even when it was lost defending his own land."

He was lost for a moment in anger, his face drawn tight as he clearly raged against the blow Fate had dealt him.

"Tell me what business ye seek to do with me."

Willy cleared his throat and began. "The Grant woman. See, she might have taken vows with Marcus MacPherson but there is no contract, and yer own son heard Marcus admitting the union is unconsummated. We also heard ye wish yer own daughter to wed Marcus."

"Continue," Laird McTavish instructed.

"She's our cousin, Helen Grant is," Willy informed

the man. "If ye were to speak to yer own priest about an annulment, on the grounds that her father never agreed to the match and might well have made another contract for her, we might escort her home while ye return one of yer daughters to Marcus in her place."

The chamber was silent for a long moment. McTavish made a low sound in his throat.

"It's true that I've a mind to see me daughter Joan wed to Marcus MacPherson," Laird McTavish declared. "Or Breana. It matters not which one. And your plan is a bold one that puts me daughter at risk."

The secretary moved forward. "Gain is earned through brazenness. If Marcus took her, without chaperone, we might press for a wedding."

"While me daughter suffers being an unwanted bride," Laird McTavish muttered, clearly in thought. "Still, strength begets strength. It would be a position to be envied. Me daughter has been raised to expect naught from life that she is no' willing to challenge Fate for. That is the Highland way."

"We would only expect a small amount—" Willy began, but Leif interrupted him.

"A fair amount of compensation for taking that Grant woman where she's likely to protest going."

Laird McTavish chuckled at them. It was the crusty laugh of a man who enjoyed pitting himself against the odds. "Rolfe has ridden out, ye say?"

"Aye," Leif confirmed.

Laird McTavish slowly nodded. "I'll send for ye when he's back and the time for the swapping is at hand. Ye'll take the Grant wench back to her father.

On that, I will no' tolerate ye playing me false, and ye'll do it without molesting the lass. I may be interested in using a bit of trickery to gain what will be best for the McTavish, but there will be no disgrace involved."

Leif nodded as the secretary pressed several coins into his hand. Willy's eyes brightened at the amount. It would take them months to earn as much hauling fleece, and an entire harvest to do it while farming. For sure, it was slightly dishonorable, but honor didn't keep a man's feet from feeling the chill. Good boots did that, and Willy needed coin to buy boots.

"Keep out of yer cups," McTavish ordered them. "Or ye'll be gossiping like a pair of old women. Me son Rolfe will no' break his word, so if he hears of this plan after he's struck a deal with Marcus MacPherson, he will balk. If that happens, ye'll be losing that silver as quickly as ye gained it."

"Aye, Laird."

"As ye say."

Willy and Leif nodded to him before they turned and left the chamber.

The secretary waited until Leif and Willy had left and the door was firmly closed. His laird looked at him with solid purpose in his eyes.

"Write a letter to the bishop," Laird McTavish instructed his man. "Make it…humble enough to no' offend the man's pompous ego. I have no talent for that sort of thing."

The secretary smiled as he hurried to the small table where his tools were laid out. He placed a new sheet of parchment down and dipped a quill into his inkwell. When the letter was written, he took it to his laird. The secretary read it aloud twice before his laird slapped his knee.

"There is a reason I pay ye well, man. Ye have the gift of diplomacy in yer words."

The secretary nodded once to acknowledge the compliment before heading back to his desk.

"I will seal it now," Laird McTavish said. "Find me a pair of riders who can keep their mouths shut. We'll be sending this now and beginning the process. Tell me daughter Joan to come to me. I need to tell her she's about to be wed. And no' a word to me son, on pain of losing yer tongue. Rolfe has a sense of honor that can be a hindrance in times like these when an opportunity is ripe for plucking."

❦

"This is no' helping," Bhaic said.

Marcus and Symon paid him no heed, continuing to try to choke the life out of each other. The rest of the men were placing wagers as they stood in a ring around the two combatants, shouting encouragement.

Bhaic lifted his tankard and decided to enjoy the moment, since there was no talking any sense into his brother. After all, Symon really should not have taken the risk, considering Marcus had bested him the last time they fought over Helen. It would seem that when it came to his new wife, his brother Marcus had no sense of humor.

Which was going to be something Bhaic planned to enjoy to the fullest.

Finally, Symon threw his hands up in defeat. There

was a chorus of groans as some men handed over money and others cheered as they received it.

Symon stomped over to the table where Bhaic was sitting and wiped the blood from his nose with his shirtsleeve. A girl came by with a pitcher of fresh ale that she poured into their tankards before she set the pitcher down, pulled free a cloth from her belt, and finished cleaning Symon's face.

"Later, mistress." Marcus sent her off with a tone that said he wasn't in the mood to argue. Symon watched her leave and grunted as he peered at Marcus over the rim of his mug.

Symon chuckled at the look Marcus sent him in reprimand. He set his tankard down. "By Christ's sweet mother, ye have gone and let yer heart be claimed by a woman. I never thought to see the day."

"Keep talking, and it will be the last sunrise ye enjoy," Marcus warned.

"Back to the business." Bhaic tried to gain control with a civil tone. "We've got the McTavish to deal with."

Symon took another long draw off his mug. "We're here right enough. Cooling our heels and waiting on the man. Seems he could be a bit more attentive to the matter, since he's the one gaining profit from this venture."

"He's trying to make me sweat." Marcus reached for his mug, but he drew his fingers back when he touched it. He didn't need his wits dulled, although the ale allowed him to enjoy every moment that crept by, while his mind reminded him of how possible it was for Rolfe McTavish to keep Helen.

"Marcus MacPherson," Rolfe bellowed as he came through the front door of the tavern. He came closer as men shifted away from the table. "How's the head, man?"

"Careful, McTavish," Marcus warned. "I've recently become aware of just what a bitch Fate is. She enjoys making sure she does nae miss any of us mortals."

Rolfe McTavish flashed him an arrogant grin before he lowered himself onto the stool waiting for him at the table.

The tavern was normally a boisterous place, filled with men on their way to Edinburgh and those returning to the Highlands. It was a rare spot that could be considered neutral. In spite of that fact, the occupants had fallen silent, and many of them had tossed down coin and left. The tavern might not sit on clan land, but no one missed the potential for trouble from the men sitting at the far table.

"State yer demands." Marcus made it clear he was holding his temper back.

Rolfe grinned.

"Do nae test me patience," Symon Grant warned. "Me father is on his deathbed, and I do nae care a bit for the fact that ye have made me waste time coming down here."

Rolfe sent a hard look toward Marcus. "I suppose I could have expected ye to make sure ye had a strong position when ye faced me tonight."

Marcus scoffed at him. Rolfe sobered. "Aye, to business."

❦

"That is no' Helen."

Rolfe McTavish stiffened, hearing the deadly tone of Marcus's voice.

"What game are ye playing, McTavish?" Marcus demanded.

Rolfe glared at him as they stared at each other over the heads of their horses. Their men were lined up, most of them looking rather bored. They had seen hostage exchanges before, and there wasn't likely to be any fun now that the ransom had been paid. Those men now raised their eyebrows and turned their attention toward Marcus because they heard a fight brewing.

"Helen is never so submissive." Marcus moved closer to Rolfe. "What game are ye playing, McTavish? I'll warn ye, I'm finished with being yer toy."

Several of the McTavish retainers clearly took offense at Marcus's tone, moving their hands closer to the hilts of their weapons. But Rolfe held up his hand.

"I've noticed that about her meself. That woman is a vixen and no mistake." He looked at the figure sitting meekly on top of the mare. As one of his men led the animal forward, the figure sat still, her bound hands visible through an arm slit in the cloak she wore. The hood was pulled down, hiding her face completely. Rolfe moved his horse beside her and yanked the hood off her head.

There was a squeal and a protest from the mare.

"Damn ye, Joan. What game is this?" Rolfe demanded.

Joan didn't get a chance to answer before Marcus lunged at Rolfe, knocking him clean off his stallion. The animal rose up onto its hind feet, pawing at the air. Men cursed as they shifted and tried to maintain control of their horses while Rolfe and Marcus rolled across the rocky ground.

Bhaic and Symon were the only ones who could interfere. The rest of the clansmen considered it a matter between lairds' sons and held back.

"Ye're a dead man!" Marcus shouted at Rolfe as Bhaic pulled him back.

"I've no part in this," Rolfe said, trying to defend himself.

Marcus snarled and broke free from his brother's hold. He ran straight into Joan, cursing as he realized he'd plowed right into a female. She rocked back on her heels and landed against Rolfe, who had come up behind her. He cupped her shoulders and tried to shove her aside.

"No," she insisted. "No more fighting." Joan turned her attention toward Marcus, who was growling at her. She lost a great deal of her color before she took a deep breath. "Me father did this. He ordered me to do it, and he made sure Rolfe knew nothing about it because he knew Rolfe would no' break his word to ye."

"Is nae that a pretty little speech," Marcus sneered. He turned his attention to Rolfe. The look on the man's face cut through his rage, but only enough that Marcus reined in the need to murder him. Marcus knew his share of liars, but there was disgust in Rolfe's eyes and self-loathing on his face.

"Me father," Rolfe ground out between clenched teeth, "would consider it worth the risk. To gain an alliance with the MacPhersons."

"Ye think we'd honor such a thing?" Bhaic snapped. "No' while I draw breath."

"He said ye'd ease yer thinking once ye accepted there was no being rid of me," Joan said. Marcus glared at her, wanting to detest her. Instead all he noticed was the relief in her eyes. She was a pretty enough female, but she was wary of him. His gut twisted because the one woman who didn't look at him like that was out of his reach.

"Where is Helen?" he demanded.

Joan shook her head. "I do nae know. Me father does nae explain himself to me."

"He will explain himself to me," Rolfe said in a deadly tone. Joan's eyes widened with surprise before she skirted out from between them. Rolfe locked gazes with Marcus. "I give ye me word."

❧

"Aye. Learn yer place." Leif smirked. "It is at me feet."

Helen tasted blood in her mouth. She'd hit the ground face-first because her wrists were tied behind her. The best she could manage was to turn her head to the side to protect her face as best she might. Pain went through her head; the initial connection from Leif's knuckles was now a throbbing ache.

"Ye heard Laird McTavish," Willy called out to his partner.

"The laird said we could no' molest her." Leif contemplated Helen. "I'm only teaching her to mind me."

"Ye were no' hired to be her tutor," Willy said. "Come and eat."

Helen lifted her head and rolled over. Leif watched

her strain to sit up while bound. There was no way to right her clothing, and he took a good, long look at her legs while she struggled to get her skirt to cover them.

"That rabbit does smell good," Leif said. He rubbed his groin through his kilt and grinned at her. "We're only hired to take ye home. If ye want to eat, well, ye'll have to be earning yer way since I promised no' to molest ye. Now, if ye were to throw yerself into me arms, that would no' be breaking any promise I made to Laird McTavish."

"If he told ye to conduct yerself as a man of honor, best ye think long and hard on mistreating me," Helen responded.

"Ye have been at court and with the MacPhersons, the McTavishes, and now us. No one expects ye to be virgin, so it will nae matter if I take a bit more pay for transporting ye home. It's hard enough for a man no' born to a noble line to make his way. I intend to extract all the payment I can for helping Laird McTavish gain the alliance he seeks. Ye don't eat unless ye please me."

"I prefer an empty belly."

"Ye'll change yer thinking in a few days."

Leif's expression was confident. Helen stared at the way his eyes gleamed with anticipation. Lust could be so ugly on a man. She was certain that moment lasted for an eternity, while she was tormented by the fact that hunger might be more powerful than her will at some point. Hopelessness drew its claws across her soul, leaving burning marks that were a hundred times more painful than the spot on her jaw where Leif had struck her.

Time seemed to be moving in slow motion, allowing her to realize how dire her circumstances were. In that moment, she watched the shadows shift behind Leif, like the wind blowing through the trees. A shuddering of light, and then two hands clamped down on Leif's face, one on the chin, the other on the head. There was a twist and a crunch before Leif stiffened, his eyes bulging in that last moment of life before he slumped to the ground and his breath rattled out of his chest.

She was frozen, staring at the place where Leif had stood. Helen blinked, unable to grasp what her eyes were telling her. It was too good to be true, too fine a gift from Fate, and yet Marcus knelt down beside her, remaining still for a long time while their gazes locked.

A tiny sound of relief escaped her lips. She thought she saw his mouth twitch on one side, but he moved his attention to the ropes binding her ankles.

"I have ye now, lass," Marcus whispered in her ear. For all that there was a note of possessiveness in his tone, it was the most wonderful sound she had ever heard. It cut through the pain, slicing it clean in half and leaving her with nothing to fret about. Nothing at all, which mean blackness took her as its captive, leaving her in her rescuer's arms.

Which was perfect in every possible way.

∼

"Of course I did nae tell ye," Laird McTavish said. "Yer damned sense of honor is yer Achilles' heel."

Rolfe battled against his own nature. He'd never questioned the need to respect his sire, at least not until that moment. "How could ye force Joan to such a fate? It might have been dire indeed, Father."

"By Christ, it better have not been!" His father pointed a finger at him. "If the MacPhersons had let any harm come to yer sister, it would have been paid for in blood. No one transgresses against the McTavishes. Any War Chief worth his position knows he can nae afford to have it said he has no honor."

"Do ye mean to say ye expected Marcus to conduct himself with integrity, when ye crossed him through dishonesty?" Rolfe asked incredulously.

His father chuckled like he had just bluffed his way to winning at a hand of cards and naught more. "The man would have seen the humor in it."

"I could nae disagree with ye more."

His sire grunted at him. "Ye are too young still, Rolfe. Ye think the world is a pretty place where honor is shiny and remains unblemished." He slapped the arm of his chair. "All men are beasts, me lad. Mark me word on that."

"On that point I do agree," Rolfe said. "And it would have been Joan's plight to suffer the rage ye caused."

"Yer sister has yer mother's plump breasts and fair features. After he'd wed her to avoid me declaring a feud against his clan, Marcus would have noticed those features and set about enjoying them. One woman is as good as another in this case." His father waved his hand dismissively. "Marriage is for gain and sons. Marcus would have bred her and been content or taken a mistress. That is all that concerns me."

Rolfe felt his temper straining again. His sire didn't fail to notice, either.

"Ye'll understand in time, me son. Strength is more important than anything else."

"Oh aye," Rolfe responded. "I understand yer devotion to that idea well enough." He looked down at his father's missing leg. "But I believe ye have yer pride confused with strength. For surely it's pride that has ye making a prisoner of yerself."

"It's to maintain the image of the McTavish!" his father roared, coming out of the chair.

"Ye are correct about me," Rolfe said without flinching under his father's rage. "Me honor is something I hold very dear. Ye taught me that. By example."

Laird McTavish's complexion darkened.

"It grieves me to know that the father I learned to respect has fallen into such thinking. So long as ye wish to remain here, I shall respect yer wishes to no' be considered among the living. But I will no longer assist ye in this pitiful existence ye have decided maintains the McTavish honor." Rolfe opened his hands wide. "It's yer own pride ye're nursing, and the man who raised me was never so weak. Sit here if ye must, but I will no longer witness yer decay."

Laird Malcolm McTavish stared at the door, holding his breath at the sound of it slamming behind his son like a pistol shot. He was certain it pierced his heart. He collapsed back into his chair, sitting still for long hours as he grew cold. No one came to lay a fire. His secretary never arrived to scribble away at the desk in the corner. His belly rumbled, and there was no supper brought. He was still sitting in his chair when the windows brightened with the light of dawn. He watched them with a strange sense of curiosity. First, there was only an easing of the darkness as night lost its grip. The faintest touch of pink chipped away at it more and more until he could see the beginning of the new day.

How long had it been since he'd risen at first light? Instead, he stayed shrouded in the bed curtains to hide from the light and the reality that his leg was gone.

Shrouded.

Like a breathing corpse.

He felt his chest expand and his heart thump.

He was alive.

But he'd fallen short of what his son expected of him.

He was a coward.

Malcolm looked down at the peg, staring for a long time at the piece of wood he'd allowed to make a prisoner of him.

Indeed, Rolfe was correct. About a great many things, and it was time to tell him so. Rolfe was no longer a lad. Malcolm slowly grinned as he felt his belly rumble and looked around the abandoned chamber.

No, his boy was no longer a lad. He was a man to be reckoned with. Only a fool would waste the opportunity to enjoy seeing it. Malcolm stood up, determined to stop being controlled by his pride. The first few steps were the hardest, the scrape of the peg against the floor undermining his determination.

But he was able to get to the door and pulled it open. The scent of food teased his nose as he heard the sound of his men from below, and for the first time in his life, tears burned a path down his cheeks as he realized his son had just saved his life.

There was a stench that came from being held in the dungeon. The Earl of Morton knew it and its worth.

He heard the chains clanking on Robert Gunn's ankles as the man approached the doors that led to the receiving chamber. Morton shifted, making sure he was settled firmly in the chair that was on the high ground in the room.

He smelled Robert as the doors were opened and the royal retainers pushed the man forward.

"My Lord Earl," Robert exclaimed as the door shut behind him. "What a pleasure to be invited to join ye. Needed this room stunk up, did ye? Why? Expecting the English ambassador?"

Morton chuckled. "Nay, but I'll remember to have ye brought up here the next time the man is demanding me attention. That might even shorten his overblown demands."

Robert was shackled at both ankles and wrists and had been so for the better part of two years. He reeked from it, his clothing looking dank, while his hair had grown into long mats and his beard was draped to his chest.

"What do ye want of me?" Robert Gunn didn't seem to see his position as one of weakness.

Morton hesitated for a moment, because Gunn was exactly the sort of Highlander who clung to clan before king. The type of thinking Morton had to break. Yet he needed the man because Marcus MacPherson was not going to be defeated by just any man.

"I want to know if ye are ready to be released,"

Morton replied. "And pardoned for yer part in the assassination of the late regent, the Earl of Moray."

It was a prickly subject. The Earl of Moray had been shot, and many believed the Gunn clan had helped plot it; however, evidence was thin.

Robert sent him an arrogant grin. "Ye can nae prove anything, man. If ye could, I'd be dead."

"The Earl of Moray played a large part in yer father's execution. Yer families have been locked in a blood feud for years over it."

Robert's grin faded, his eyes filling with hatred. "Stop wasting me time. I've got to get back to catching a rat for supper, and that takes a fair bit of time down where I've been laying me head."

Morton chuckled again. "Ye have balls, man. The sort I admire."

"Good," Robert replied congenially. "Get on with telling me what ye want so I can get back to the Highlands and find a woman to ease the ache in me cock."

"A woman," Morton began. "I plan to help ye with that desire."

Robert lifted an eyebrow.

"Marcus MacPherson requires a lesson."

Robert was back to grinning. "Aye, I know the tale. The guards have been wagging their tongues for a fortnight over it. But I do nae want any half-grown chit beneath me. I crave a woman who will enjoy the ride. Keep yer English child bride well away from me."

"I want ye to steal away the Grant woman who wed Marcus," Morton explained. "She's no child, and I am wedding ye to her by proxy."

"She has naught to her name," Robert replied.

"Her dowry will be yer freedom, and will restore ye to yer position of clan chief."

"I am still chief. Ye can nae take that away from me," Robert informed him. "I am no' one of yer lairds who must worry about the crown recognizing him."

Morton made a gesture with his hand. "Fine. However ye choose to see the matter. I can have ye thrown back in the dungeon, or taken above stairs where ye may bathe, eat something finer than rat, and sleep in a bed tonight while I have the contract drawn up."

"And I will do what in exchange?" Robert asked, his voice betraying his interest.

"Ye will get inside the MacPherson castle and steal away Helen Grant. I will expect ye to take yer new wife back to yer stronghold and make very sure Marcus can never reclaim her. So keep her alive for enough years to ensure the lesson is a good one."

It was a bold plan that had Robert narrowing his eyes while he contemplated it.

He grunted. "I see what ye mean to do." He nodded slowly, thinking the matter through. "Ye want to send a message to every clan in the Highlands."

"I want them all to know that they are no' beyond me reach," Morton finished for him.

"And ye knew well only another Highlander with a reason to hate ye could manage to get inside MacPherson Castle," Robert said.

"And ye, Chief Gunn, will recall that I have the means to do whatever I need to secure Scotland," Morton explained. "Yer choice is to do it in those shackles, or as a free man on yer own land with a wife at yer command anytime ye desire her flesh."

"Marcus will have had her by the time I reach MacPherson land," Robert said. "Their union can no' be annulled."

"Ye still do nae understand," Morton muttered. "I could have had that woman inspected but I did nae. Nor were her skirts looked at. I've no doubt Marcus was smart enough to bloody them, which is why I did nae check. There is no witness to the consummation. The union will be annulled. I already have the man who performed the ceremony. He will swear he heard them claim they intended to gain an annulment. If Marcus has had her in his bed, it matters not. Ye are no virgin."

Robert grinned in response, but the smirk on his lips had nothing to do with his long list of bed companions. "So ye let Marcus MacPherson out of his chains because ye knew ye could nae have his clan pissed at ye about a child bride. Well, that's something a fair number of men will take offense at. Marcus's little wedding has given ye enough time to hear the discontent being aimed yer way now that yer little plan is known. Seems ye owe the man a debt."

Morton narrowed his eyes. "The business which concerns ye is if ye will take a proxy bride of me choosing."

Robert was debating it. Morton watched the man contemplate his allegiance to his fellow Highlander against his desire to be free.

"The Gunns have no love for the MacPhersons," Morton added to sweeten the deal. "And they are allies to some of yer enemies as well."

Robert studied him. "Ye want the Highland clans to stop feuding, and yet ye use those feuds to support yer cause."

Morton only shrugged. "Each man makes his own choices. At the moment, ye may have freedom, or a few more years in those chains while ye wait for another summons from me. I promise ye, the dungeon will run low on rats while ye wait for that day to arrive."

Robert looked at the shackles. He'd have scars from them because they'd been locked around his wrists for so long. Morton was a bastard, and yet Robert couldn't see the wisdom in denying the man. It was an injustice against the woman, but females were for sealing agreements, after all. For all Robert knew, the MacPhersons might thank him for taking the unwanted bride off their hands. She had served her purpose in freeing Marcus, and now she would free Robert too.

"We have an agreement."

Morton heard the disgust in Robert's tone, but when the man looked up, there was a firm look in his eyes. "Me word on it."

The earl slowly nodded. "In that case, yer chamber has been prepared. Me secretary will be up with the marriage contracts in an hour. That will give ye time to wash the filth off ye."

Morton snapped his fingers, and one of the retainers came forward. There was a jingle of keys as he fit one into the shackles and turned it. The lock was stiff, but it gave at last and Robert's eyes brightened as the iron cuffs released his wrists. A small, satisfied smirk curled his lips. The retainer finished with the leg irons and stood up.

"Escort him above stairs," Morton instructed.

Robert stopped at the door and raised a finger. "I'll be expecting me proxy wedding night to be celebrated in proper fashion." He shot a knowing look toward the Earl of Morton. "Be sure to send me a woman who knows how to handle a cock. That way, I'll be more than satisfied with the arrangement."

Morton flicked his fingers at the retainer. The man nodded and opened the doors, taking Robert Gunn out of the receiving chamber.

There was no reason he had to grant Robert's demand for a female in his bed that night. Even if he smiled once the doors were closed because the man's audacity was admirable. Indeed, Morton saw the value of the Highlanders, but he had to bring them under crown control. His control. Of course, that now included the Gunn clan, so keeping Robert pleased with his business dealings with Morton was important. It would ensure future loyalty.

The earl slowly smiled. There was someone else who needed to know he was the master of Scotland, and she would serve as a proxy bride very well.

"Bring me Brenda Grant."

Four

MARCUS WAS HOLDING HER.

Helen woke abruptly at the thought, stiffening, and the pillow her head was resting against rumbled.

"I suppose that means ye're feeling better."

Helen blinked, but that didn't banish the darkness. She was perched sideways on a horse in front of Marcus. He'd wrapped his plaid around her head to keep the light out, but what stunned her most was the fact that he'd been holding her to keep her head from flopping about with the motion of the ride.

"Good timing, though," Marcus replied as he pulled the plaid away from her face. "We're nearly home."

Helen blinked at the bright sunlight. When her eyes stopped stinging, she was treated to a view of MacPherson Castle. Marcus stiffened behind her, and she realized she'd let out a little sigh of frustration.

Well? What did he expect her to say? It wasn't her home, and yet it was the only place she had to go to. To say her emotions were unsettled was an understatement.

"There will be a warm supper and a good bed," he offered.

"Yes." She shifted again, unsure of how to have a congenial conversation with him. Truly, she should be ashamed that she found the idea so foreign.

"Pull yer leg over the saddle, lass," he encouraged. "Now that yer awake."

Helen shifted and looked around. "I can ride on me own."

"Aye, ye've demonstrated that well enough," Marcus agreed.

But he locked his arm around her and held her against him. It really was unfair just how delightful that felt. She'd never realized two human bodies might fit together so very well or with so much comfort. He was hard, but that seemed to complement her softness.

"Put me on me own horse."

Marcus chuckled at her request. "The last conversation I had with ye, I advised ye of the merits of us becoming more accustomed to one another." He smoothed his hand along the outside of her thigh, and she struggled not to suck in her breath because the sensation was so intense.

"And I told ye, seeking an annulment was the wisest course of action."

"Yes, ye did," Marcus agreed. "And ye've had a taste of just what yer kin will do with ye if ye go back to them. So…"

He moved his hand back along her thigh to rest on her hip. Helen struggled with the urge to shift away and put her right leg on the other side of the horse. It would make her more stable, in less need of leaning back against him for support, but it would also open her thighs and she had a suspicion Marcus might enjoy that all too much.

Worse, she might enjoy it.

"So are ye suggesting that ye are now me rescuer?" she asked as she grabbed his hand, only to have him lock it around hers and slip his fingers up to stroke the delicate skin of her inner wrist. But she felt the nip of guilt and let out a sigh. "I believe ye are that indeed."

He was quiet for a long moment, the horse picking up speed as it smelled its stable.

"I suppose I am due a measure of doubt from ye, Helen," Marcus muttered. "I'll not apologize."

"I do nae want yer pity."

He chuckled at just how quickly she snapped back at him.

"And that is why," he confirmed in a tone rich with amusement, "it made ye strong—and ye were still young when I took ye."

"True enough." She'd answered him before she realized that she was agreeing with him, but even after the words were past her lips, she didn't regret them. That strength would ensure her own survival, and no one came by it without facing hardship. It was a harsh fact of life very much at the heart of living in the Highlands. The weak did not thrive.

"Thank ye." She meant it, too.

Whatever Marcus might have said was drowned out as someone started to ring a bell on the top of one of the lookout towers on the castle walls. It was quickly joined by more. He, his men, and Helen rode under the portcullis and into a courtyard that was rapidly filling with women and children. They cried out in welcome as younger boys came running from the stables to take the horses. Those lads would one day be the retainers riding out to protect the clan. Today, they were learning that the horses were key to any man's ability to defend his land.

Helen slid down and felt her boots sink into the mud. The Highlands. Where rain was something one needed to enjoy.

"Helen!"

Ailis Robertson had called her name. The crowd parted for their lady, which made Helen smile. Ailis was the daughter of the Robertson laird, which caused her forced marriage, a union that had not been warmly welcomed when she arrived at MacPherson Castle.

Now, there were smiles aimed her way as she hurried toward Helen. A few of the women reached out to touch Ailis's rounding belly. But Ailis pulled up as she sucked in a harsh breath, her eyes widening with horror.

"Who raised their hand to ye?" Ailis demanded.

It took a moment for Helen to recall what was alarming her mistress.

"Some of her kin struck a deal with Laird McTavish to trade his daughter for her," Bhaic answered his wife.

"Aye," Helen agreed. Marcus shot her a hard look.

Bhaic MacPherson pulled his wife into his embrace, but Ailis wiggled free after only a brief kiss. "I need to see to Helen."

❧

"Save yer breath."

Bhaic's eyes narrowed in response. "So sure of what I was going to say, Brother?"

Marcus finished pulling his saddlebag from his horse and let a lad lead the animal away. "Rather certain ye feel I'm owed a measure of equal grief for what ye think I did to ye when ye brought Ailis home."

Bhaic's lips split into a huge grin. "There's a solid fact. Setting yer men on us as ye did, I'll no' forget that anytime soon. Could nae get me own wife alone for a kiss, much less a tumble. And then there is the matter of ye telling me that Ailis was likely a spy. I recall that as well." Bhaic pointed at his brother. "And we can nae be forgetting about ye having us sent up to bed because we had no' consummated the union, and making sure every one of the men heard about it. Truth is, I am no' sure where to begin with ye."

Marcus flexed his fingers before making a fist. His brother snorted at him before he reached out and cupped his shoulder.

"But," Bhaic said in a jovial tone that made Marcus itch to smash him in the jaw, "I believe Father will be expecting the first shot at ye."

Marcus looked up to the main steps of the great hall where Shamus MacPherson stood.

"Do nae worry, Brother. I will nae be forgetting to take me turn," Bhaic assured him in a smug tone.

Marcus growled at him, but Bhaic only smirked back. The urge to fight was strong, but Marcus turned and went to greet his father, Bhaic right on his heels.

❧

"Do nae think that simply because ye are with child, I'll no' tell ye to stop smothering yer giggles behind me back."

Ailis turned and offered Helen an innocent look that conflicted with the merriment sparkling in her eyes.

"Thank goodness," Ailis said after she gave up the attempt to appear innocent of the charge. "It's really rather strange the way everyone is so nice to me all of a sudden."

Helen moved a lump of soap over her arms as she took the opportunity to bathe away the grime from the road. Ailis had sent all the other servants away, granting them the chance to speak freely.

"I imagine ye'll be discovering how I feel. As soon as they all learn of yer marriage to Marcus." Ailis used a large hook to pull the arm that a kettle was hanging from out of the fire. She made sure to wrap a sturdy piece of quilted wool around the handle before she picked it up and carried it over to the tub Helen sat in. Steam rose as she poured the water in near Helen's toes. It was a delight to have them warm at last, but Helen was distracted by what Ailis had said.

"No one will be changing how they treat me," Helen said. "I'll no' be staying Marcus's wife."

Ailis set the kettle on the hearth with a clunk. She contemplated Helen for a long moment.

"Say what ye're thinking," Helen said. Truthfully, she was overstepping herself, for Ailis was the mistress of MacPherson Castle. The MacPherson women had not afforded her the position automatically when she'd arrived newly wed to Bhaic. Ailis had to fight for her current status.

Ailis didn't take offense. "Marcus left looking for ye."

"He did no'." Helen rinsed the soap from her hair

and stood up. "Do nae put credit to his actions. The beast made sure to tell me that he'd gone to court because ye and Bhaic were summoned and his father sent him in yer stead because ye can no' travel."

"And the reason why he chased after yer kin?" Ailis brought Helen a length of linen with which to dry herself from where it had been warming by the fire.

"To thwart Laird McTavish's plans, of course," Helen replied as she started to pull on a chemise. "Marcus has his position to consider. No one will be respecting a War Chief who can be duped. What did ye do with Katherine?"

Ailis knew that Helen was changing the subject on purpose, but at least she didn't point it out.

"Duana is seeing to her," Ailis replied.

"Better to see to the matter personally," Helen said. "Duana hates the English more than she hates Scotswomen from other clans."

Ailis's eyes narrowed. "Ye might be right about that." She realized Helen had started to get dressed. "I'll see to it. I had Senga take supper up to yer chamber."

Ailis gave her friend a hug before she left the chamber. Helen hesitated and then snorted at herself.

There was one thing that she was certain of—that she was not going to be reduced to standing about and letting her knees knock together in fear. She'd suffered the worst MacPherson Castle had to offer before. Tonight would be no different.

❦

"The Earl of Morton is making a lot of enemies in the Highlands."

Shamus MacPherson was old. Yet at that moment, he sounded very much as he had thirty years before. There was still strength in his eyes, even if the skin around them was wrinkled by age. He looked at Marcus and smirked.

"And ye managed to bring the English prize away with ye as well?" Shamus slapped the top of his desk as he cackled. "That's the way to illustrate MacPherson strength, sure enough."

"To be fair"—Marcus spoke up—"Brenda and Helen were the ones who did the planning. The earl sets his traps well. I'd have been without recourse save for Brenda's quick wit."

"So ye said." Shamus returned to being pensive.

Marcus reached up and pulled on the corner of his cap, but his father held up a finger to keep Marcus standing in front of him.

"Ye killed a pair of Grants?"

"I did," Marcus replied without hesitation. "Ye saw me wife's face. I doubt even the Grants would like that pair back. I wonder why they were on McTavish land and looking for work."

Shamus nodded, and the moment he finished giving the grave topic due respect, he started to choke on his amusement.

"Wife, ye say?" His father asked the blunt question. "I would no' have thought that lass would allow ye any sort of relations with her."

"She did nae," Marcus admitted before turning and punching Bhaic in the shoulder. His brother half fell out of his stance before flashing him an unrepentant smirk.

"Well now, since it's bride and no' wife," Bhaic managed while trying not to choke on his laughter, "I am sure they need…witnesses."

Marcus turned and lunged at Bhaic. They ended up sprawled on the fine carpet that adorned their father's receiving chamber.

"Get off yer brother, Marcus!" Shamus bellowed.

There was a pounding on the outer door. "Laird?" the retainers questioned from behind it.

"Stay out there!" Shamus ordered.

Marcus was glaring at Bhaic, but their sire pointed at both of his sons and Marcus turned to face him respectfully.

"Ye earned that crack," Shamus informed him.

"Along with a few more," Bhaic added. "Ye can be sure I'll be taking the measure due me."

Marcus lifted his hand and sent his sibling an obscene gesture. Shamus snorted. "Well now, this will prove to be very interesting, to say the least. I'm sure even Father Matthew Peter would agree that ye are reaping what ye sowed last season."

His father couldn't finish because he was laughing so hard.

"The lot of ye can piss off," Marcus informed them. "Hire yerself a fine fool if it's laughter ye seek. I can promise ye, me union is no' going to be a source of it for ye."

Bhaic clutched his midsection and collapsed into a chair as he chuckled.

Marcus crossed his arms over his chest. "Well then, I suppose I might just let yer lovely wife know how much ye plan to exact yer revenge on me for making sure the pair of ye remained wed."

Bhaic sobered, shooting his brother a deadly look. Marcus angled his head and stared at him. "Poor lass might think ye harbor resentment, which might lead to a very cold winter for ye."

"Enough now," Shamus interrupted. "Let that lass be. She's carrying me grandchild. And enough from yer brother and me on the matter of yer wife, for the moment," he said to Marcus. "Get some sleep. Ye look as though the road was long."

Marcus took full advantage of his sire's permission to quit the chamber. But once he was outside in the passageway, he realized he didn't know where Helen slept.

"Indecision, Brother?" Bhaic asked. "No' something I'm accustomed to seeing on yer face."

"It's a good thing yer wife is breeding," Marcus muttered, stepping close enough to his brother to make sure their father didn't overhear. "Because I'm going to smash yer balls—"

"Give it yer best, man," Bhaic answered, "and Helen will remain a maiden."

Marcus was distracted by that idea. Bhaic noticed and dropped his teasing. "What is it?"

For all their picking at each other, they had a tight bond. Marcus looked both ways to make certain they were alone.

"I do nae know if Helen is a virgin."

"And that bothers ye?" Bhaic inquired.

Marcus shook his head. "Nay. I could hardly condemn her for taking comfort where she might when I dumped her here and failed to ask after her welfare." He aimed a hard look toward Bhaic. "It would seem Duana is quite the bitch when it comes to outsiders."

He suddenly felt as though his shoulders were lighter, earning a raised eyebrow from his brother.

"I wonder if Helen thinks it would matter to me," Marcus said. "Matter so much that she'd insist on an annulment to escape me reaction."

"Could be. She has no dowry, no family alliance to barter, so no' being pure might make her think ye'd reject her after the fact." Bhaic smirked again. "But I will be sorely disappointed if that female settles down after ye tell her it does no bother ye and fails to give ye the grief ye deserve."

Helen loved her hair. It was one of her few vanities, and she didn't have many opportunities to indulge it. Ailis had sent someone to her chamber to light the fire and make sure the water pitcher was filled. It was a welcome Helen treasured. It allowed her to stay in her chemise and brush out her hair while the heat from the fire gently dried it.

A rare moment of indulgence in her own vanity.

The chamber itself was not grand. No, the one she'd occupied in the McTavish tower had been larger, but she preferred hers. Located in the oldest part of the castle, the room had rougher walls, but Helen viewed them as proven. The chambers were a set of receiving and bed areas, but what she liked best was the privacy closet. There was no need for a chamber pot.

Considering she was a servant, that meant one less duty to attend to. She sat down and looked at what fare had been provided. There was cheese and bread and a portion of chicken. A fine supper, and she realized she was ravenous.

Yet once her belly was full, she felt lonely. Ailis was her only friend, besides perhaps young Senga.

But it was Marcus who came to mind as she moved over to get her comb. Helen let out a sigh as she drew it down the length of her sable hair. She had no idea whether the man fancied dark hair or light. Not that it mattered, of course, because she wouldn't allow herself to care about pleasing him.

Could she please him?

Her memory offered up what he'd said to her back in that dungeon. She was past the age of wedding, both of them were. If she hadn't been home on that fateful day or had stayed hidden, she might well have a husband now. The question was, how did a woman please a man? Such a topic was discussed often, but the conversations varied so greatly that there was little way to sift chaff from wheat.

Could she please him through obedience?

She dropped the comb, snorting at the very idea. That was what came of considering the idea of being what Marcus desired. There was no point to it, none at all. Better to set her mind to finding a way to see Laird MacPherson and begin the process of annulment.

❧

Ailis nearly ran into Marcus on her way out of the bathhouse. For some, there was private bathing, but like her, most of the inhabitants of the castle came down to the back side of the kitchens where tubs were kept and the water was always warm from the hearths. The river ran along that side of the north wing, so water could be brought up easily.

"Katherine?" he asked.

Ailis nodded. "I was just checking on her meself. I made sure Elise knows I expect Katherine to be treated well."

"I did nae know Duana was such a bitch. She should have seen to it herself," Marcus informed her in his quiet tone.

Ailis knew it well and understood that he was far from neutral when he used that tone. Marcus was a master of keeping those around him guessing at his true opinions.

"Well, I've seen to Katherine," Ailis informed him. "I'm just now off to ensure that a chamber is made ready that is appropriate to her station."

"Which is?" he asked, not willing to leave the matter to debate.

Ailis tilted her head to the side. "Yer sister. I am sure the Earl of Morton will be delighted to hear how we have taken her into the family. Even if it was no' quite in the fashion he envisioned. Still, family."

Marcus offered her a smile of appreciation. "Well played. I might even suggest to Father that his secretary write it up in a missive for the man."

With that matter lifted from his shoulders, Marcus felt every hour he'd spent with his eyes open weighing upon him. Ailis was smiling at him, and his temper was nearly frayed through. "Take yerself off to yer husband. Tomorrow will be soon enough for ye to take yer turn at extracting yer amusement from me plight."

Ailis turned and lowered herself before him. Marcus's eyes narrowed at her mockery.

"I could be ever so obedient to yer will, dearest brother by marriage."

"Or?" Marcus questioned. "Ye could do what?"

Ailis lifted her shoulders in a delicate shrug. "I could tell ye which chamber I moved Helen to, so ye do nae have to ask anyone where yer wife is or wander about lost until she decides she wants to be seen."

He made a low sound under his breath, reaching up and squeezing the bridge of his nose before sending a narrow-eyed look at his sister by marriage. "I would be in yer debt."

"I do believe that is by far the sweetest spoken manner I have ever heard from ye."

He made a low sound of frustration. "Am I to be rewarded for me efforts?"

"Before I do so, let me say, Helen is me dearest friend," Ailis warned him.

"I've noticed such."

"Good." Ailis abandoned her playfulness. "Wound her heart, and I will laugh as the staff gossips freely over ye no' knowing where yer wife is."

Marcus blinked at her before nodding. "I expect naught else from ye."

It was a compliment she recognized as Marcus's unique sort. She let out a sigh and gestured to him to follow her. MacPherson Castle had three full wings and four massive towers. Ailis made her way to one of the older towers. Marcus's expression said he didn't care for it.

"It was the best Helen would accept from me." Ailis pointed down the passageway. "However, I believe she enjoyed knowing ye sleep on the other side of the castle and there is no way to bar this door from the outside."

"That is on account of the fact that this was the convent," Marcus stated. "And the door bars from the inside."

"Yes," Ailis agreed. "That chamber is where the abbess slept. Beware of ghosts. The ones in this wing might be very pious."

Marcus grinned. "Yet, we are wed, so there should be no objection."

Ailis smothered a snicker behind her hand. "Unless Helen is dead, I highly doubt that, sir."

Marcus narrowed his eyes at her before she turned and disappeared into the shadows.

He slowly smiled until his teeth were showing.

Let the challenge begin.

❧

"Ailis did right by ye."

Helen jumped, catching the comb just before it went tumbling to the floor. Again. Marcus sent her a grin that was the opposite of repentant as he came through the door of her chamber and closed it firmly behind him. Had she conjured him from her thoughts? The strangest sensation rippled across her skin, as though she was more aware of him than any other person she'd ever met.

"What are ye doing?"

It was really quite a foolish question. He was stripped down to his shirt and kilt, water still glistening in his hair, proving that he'd washed the dirt from the road away before coming to her. He hadn't bothered to strap on his second belt or sword, simply carrying them into the chamber and laying them beside the bed.

"I am going to get some sleep, lass."

He wasn't really complaining, his tone still crusty and full of strength, but she realized it was the closest thing she'd ever heard from him that might indicate fatigue. Having him there with her was strange and unsettling, but she couldn't help but look closer in an attempt to deduce what his game was.

He was tired.

She saw the dark circles beneath his eyes as he sat on the bed and kicked his boots off because they too were not laced fully.

"I've had precious little rest since I went down to see the good Earl of Morton." He stretched his arms, rotating them and his neck before he opened his eyes and considered her. "And I'll no' sleep very soundly if I do nae know where ye are, so indulge me for the service I have given ye in getting ye away from those cousins of yers."

She felt a touch of guilt for the way she was nearly flattened against the wall. "I did appreciate ye coming for me."

He nodded and rotated his arm again. Helen suddenly realized why.

"Yer arm is stiff from holding me head." The chamber was so small that she was already at the bedside by the time she thought to question her impulse to help him. It was too late by that point. Their gazes locked, and she felt her insides quiver. She cupped his shoulder and pushed him back. He went, only because he wanted to. Beneath her fingertips, she could feel just how strong he was under that shirt.

She liked the way he felt.

It was a shocking thought that left a hot trail across her mind. One that was sprouting with new, wicked ideas. She battled them, trying to focus on what needed doing. He let out a soft, male sound of enjoyment as she started to rub his shoulder and arm. He rolled over, giving her better access to his back as she sat down on the bed next to him. The ropes groaned as they took the weight of both of them, but held.

She was intent on her work and didn't realize Marcus had fallen asleep until she heard his breathing deepen. A sense of accomplishment filled her, lifting the corners of her lips. He wasn't a man who let his guard down easily, yet he'd fallen asleep next to her. What did that mean? She shied away from deciding just what and started to stand.

Pain suddenly went through her scalp. At some point, Marcus had grasped a handful of her hair and pulled it up to his nose. A tingle went through her as she looked at the way he was clutching her hair. So simple and yet somehow intimate in a way she'd never expected. This was so lacking in sin and flesh. Yet it struck her as being purer than any declaration of flowery compliments might have been.

However, she was stuck. She tried to pull the strands from his fingers, but he had wound the length around them and closed his hand. Helen debated waking him, but that seemed a very poor way to show her gratitude. The long hours on the road were taking their toll on her too. Her eyelids felt too heavy to hold open. So she crawled over him and lay down beside him.

Marcus was warm, and his hold on her hair didn't allow her to move away from him. She only had another moment to contemplate the wisdom of sleeping with him before sleep claimed her.

❧

Marcus opened his eyes and considered Helen. It wasn't his way to be dishonest, but the sight of her next to him might make him consider changing his ways.

The only light in the room was from the fire. It cast a red and orange flicker over her. He'd never seen so much of her, and his cock hardened. The chemise she wore was new but of soft linen that lay across her curves like liquid. He could see the little beads of her nipples and had to force himself to reach for the bedding and pull it up and over them both.

Damn, but he liked the way she smelled. More than one woman had chased him through the years—although it was fairer to say they had been pursuing his position—and those females often applied lavender oil or honey or some other essence to their skin. He leaned down and inhaled the scent of Helen's hair.

His cock began to throb.

There was some hint of amber from the soap she'd bathed with, but nothing else. No, that was an unfair thing to think. There was plenty more. She smelled like sunshine and strength. He wanted to nuzzle against her. Combine her scent with the taste of her, and he wanted to stroke her until she let him cup her sweet breasts. His mind was full of the progression of what he craved, the appetite she seemed to build in him, the one he was gaining a new understanding of as he lay there and cradled her close while letting her sleep. It was a strangely erotic experience, a new one for him. He savored it because there was one thing he knew for certain: Helen wasn't going to make it easy to catch her.

But then again, he had to admit to enjoying that facet of her personality too.

❦

It felt good to be touched.

Helen let out a little sound of contentment and rotated her head so whoever was stroking her might reach more of her skin.

Delightful.

Little ripples of enjoyment moved across her skin, waking her gently while she enjoyed the warmth of the bed. Normally her toes were chilled and getting up was the only way to warm herself because the fire would have gone cold during the night.

Today, she smiled as her bed was deliciously warm and inviting to linger in. She slid her fingers along the warmth beneath her and froze when she heard a husky chuckle.

Marcus grinned at her when she opened her eyes and looked into his face, her eyes as wide as full moons.

"What are ye doing?" she demanded.

"Well now, lass." He tried to contain his mirth. "Ye're the one lying on top of me."

She was. Helen looked down in horror to see that her fingers were splayed on his chest. With a little cry, she rolled away from him and right off the edge of the bed. Marcus laughed. For the second time that day, she was stunned. She'd seen the man amused before, but this was pure and freely expressed. He wasn't hiding behind his control, and she got the distinct feeling it was a privilege to see him in such a private moment.

"I could get accustomed to waking up to ye in me bed, Helen, and that is a fact."

She'd edged her way around the foot of the bed as he sat up and put his feet on the floor. His expression tightened, his lips thinning as he looked at her. "Aye, ye're a handsome woman, and I've a mind to order ye some of that fine cotton to make yer chemises out of. So I can see through it when ye venture near the candlelight in the evenings."

Helen wrapped her arms around herself, trying to keep him from seeing through her linen chemise. "That would be pure waste."

"Aye," he agreed as he sent her a grin that made her blush. "I'd much rather ye wore naught at all when we're in private." He crooked his finger at her. "Come back here, lass. Let me pet ye some more."

She shook her head.

"Ye were enjoying it."

He was still sitting on the end of the bed, but she heard the determination in his tone. She realized he was gripping the sheeting in his effort to remain poised there, to make it her choice. That idea burst on her like spring after a hard, long winter. It was ripe with opportunities that she'd only dreamed about.

"What game are ye playing?" she asked. "Are ye trying to have me before yer father has me sent on me way? Make a mistress of me so me ruin will be complete?"

That had to be it, and she would be wise to remember the facts of her circumstances.

"Ye're wrong about that."

There was something in his tone that made her take him more seriously. She turned to make eye contact with him.

"I never kept a mistress because I am no' the sort of man who ruins a woman's name simply so he can have her in his bed whenever he wants her," Marcus informed her gravely. "I know what happens to discarded bedmates."

"At least the females," she added.

"Aye," he agreed. "And me father was too busy laughing to say anything else. He considers ye a fine match for me. So." He patted the bed beside him.

"Ye'll no' be taking the last thing I have of me own."

"I would have rolled ye onto yer back and kissed ye until ye kissed me back if taking was what I had on me mind, Helen."

He was speaking the truth. She heard the frustration in his voice, but he sat there, looking both ridiculous and appealing. He was suddenly more tempting than any man she'd ever seen. All of her senses felt awakened by him and heightened now that she'd taken the time to notice how good it felt to be in contact with him.

Kissed by him…

"Aye, that is so, and I'll likely be damned for me

weak will," she admitted before she found her skirt and lifted it over her head.

When she looked up from lacing the waistband closed, she found Marcus standing in front of her. His expression had gone serious and she felt something inside her tighten, as though he was going to say something vitally important.

"I'll no' renounce ye if ye are no' a maiden, Helen."

She felt her cheeks catch fire.

"I could hardly blame ye for taking what comfort ye could when I dropped ye here and never looked in on yer circumstances."

"So ye think I turned slut?" She reached up and slapped him. As small as the chamber was, the sound was loud. "I'll have ye know, Marcus MacPherson, that I am stronger than anything ye might ever do to me, and I will no' be shaming meself or squandering the one gift I have left to give to the man I choose."

His cheek was dark where her hand had struck him. The chamber was silent for a long moment as he looked into her eyes, seeking proof to support her words. She'd acted brazenly, but she stood tall and faced him, ready to take whatever retribution he decided was hers.

What he did stunned her to the core. Marcus MacPherson, War Chief of the clan, opened his arms and lowered himself before her. She caught sight of a wink sent her way as he straightened before scooping up his sword and heading toward the door.

"In that case, mistress"—he paused with his hand on the door latch—"I suggest ye get below and have a good breakfast. We've a courtship to begin today, and I can assure ye, best to make sure ye have all the strength ye can muster." Determination glittered in his eyes. "I promise ye shall need it."

⁂

"Wife or bride?"

Marcus stiffened, hearing his own words coming out of his brother's mouth. Bhaic was leaning against the passageway wall, clearly waiting for him.

"I suppose it was too much to hope that ye'd let me be." Marcus passed him and went toward the newer section of the castle where his chamber was.

"Well now," Bhaic said, "seems that leaving the castle open to having its defenses known would be a terrible oversight. If Helen is still a bride, well, just as ye said when I brought Ailis here, there is an issue that needs attention."

"I know what my reasoning was when ye brought Ailis here," Marcus replied, cutting his brother off. "Helen does nae have a father who can ride out against us."

Bhaic offered him an unrepentant shrug.

"Actually, I was waiting about to see if she killed ye when she found ye in her bedchamber."

"It was yer wife who showed me the way last evening."

Bhaic was surprised by that. "So does that mean ye plan to keep her?"

Marcus drew in a deep breath and sent a hard look toward Bhaic. "Ye think me that great a fool? That I'm blind to what ye have with Ailis, and do nae notice Helen draws me attention as no other female ever has? For whatever good that is, considering she loathes me."

"Some would say justifiably."

Marcus growled. "I was ensuring peace."

"I know that," Bhaic answered.

"So does she." Marcus stopped as they approached the more inhabited portions of the castle.

"So where is the difficulty?" Bhaic asked seriously.

Marcus shook his head. "The same thing ye once told me concerning yer bride. How did ye put it? 'I'll no' take me rights when she is worn down by a day that has been too long and I have no' courted her.' Well, Helen has had a long year due to me trusting that Duana would see to her needs. I've no right to expect her to trust me. That's something I'll have to earn with effort."

Bhaic had been listening intently, but his lips split into a smirk as Marcus finished. "So, are ye saying ye plan to court the lass?" His tone was thick with disbelief.

"What is so amusing about that?" Marcus demanded. "Am I some sort of beast who can no' show a woman she is worthy of winning over?"

"Beast?" Bhaic was trying to talk through his snickers. "Maybe no' quite that bad, but ye are…well… rough around the edges."

Marcus offered his brother a grin, the same one he often sent his sibling right before he sent his fist into his jaw.

"Am I being less than helpful?" Bhaic asked.

"Aye," Marcus snapped, but stopped and thought for a moment. "Where did ye take yer bride that night ye two snuck away?"

"The astrologer's house," Bhaic answered.

"Ah. To see the stars. The lasses like that sort of thing."

"Well, I do nae suggest it in yer case. The only way up to view the sights is a ladder," Bhaic said. "Helen will kick ye right off it or pull ye down when ye offer her a hand. Either way, ye'll end up with yer fool neck broken."

Marcus grunted. "Ye and Ailis were lifelong enemies, and she did no' kick ye."

"Aye," Bhaic agreed. "But she never hit me with a pitcher either."

His brother meant it as a cutting jest, but Marcus slowly grinned. He reached out and patted Bhaic on the shoulder in mock sympathy. "Well now, do nae be too jealous, Brother."

Bhaic sent him a look that would wither a lesser man. Marcus enjoyed it before he took off down the passageway again. He'd court Helen. It couldn't be that difficult.

❧

"Helen."

Laird Shamus MacPherson had called her name. He was seated in the middle of the huge table that sat on the high ground in the great hall. His captains were in places of honor beside him. Ailis was there as well, one seat away from the man, because the one beside her was reserved for Shamus's son.

Helen rose from the bench where she'd sat down to enjoy her midday meal and lowered herself.

"Since yer husband is off in the training yard, allow me to welcome ye to the high table."

Several of Shamus's captains didn't care for what their laird said. Their eyes narrowed at the sight of an outsider being giving such an honor.

"Thank ye kindly." Helen spoke evenly, fighting for a measure of meekness she knew she fell short of achieving. "I am—"

"Skittish."

Marcus came up behind her, his voice booming over the heads of those enjoying their meal at the lower tables. Which was a great many people. The MacPhersons were one of the largest clans in the Highlands; their retainers alone numbered more than three hundred. There was a rumble of male amusement from those watching.

"Ye'll need to be attending to that condition, me boy," Shamus remarked, to the growing delight of his men. "Or ye'll get thrown when ye try to ride her."

Helen felt her cheeks heating as the hall erupted into laughter. She lowered herself and turned to leave, only to end up facing Marcus. He reached out and grasped her hand, lifting it to his lips and kissing the back of it like a gallant knight It carried him a few chuckles before she snatched her hand away.

"Enough," she muttered under her breath.

"Am I no' impressing ye?"

Helen rolled her eyes, earning a chuckle from him.

"I suppose that allows me only boldness to achieve me goals."

He didn't allow her time to decipher the meaning of his words before leaning over and kissing the side of her neck.

"That's it, me lad!" Shamus pounded the table in

approval. "Get a whiff of her scent. Make sure she has a reason to want to let ye into her bed!"

The MacPherson men were laughing hysterically. Helen took the opportunity to dash around Marcus and out of the hall.

"Christ, woman." Marcus caught her by the elbow. "Do Grants nae jest?"

Helen turned on him, her skirts flaring out and showing off her ankles because she moved so fast.

"What the devil is yer quarrel with me now, Helen?"

"Me?" Helen demanded. "Ye dare to say I am the one acting ridiculously?"

"Aye," he confirmed. "Running as if yer skirt is on fire."

Helen seethed. She pointed at him, her finger only a few inches from his chest. "I warned ye before. I will nae be subject to a public display where ye take liberties with me person. I am no' a slut."

"Ye're me wife," Marcus said firmly. "I was showing ye affection, courting ye."

"Ye put yer hands on me right there in the hall like a woman ye hired for the night in a tavern," Helen declared. "As ye told me, I'm assumed a slut because of my lack of relatives here."

"Ye are the first woman I've ever courted," he replied, defending himself. "And ye are the one who reminded me that I offered ye to me men. Madam, I am making certain that matter is corrected. No' a single one of them will make the mistake of trying their hand at ye."

To his way of thinking, it was a sound reason. Or at the least, not an unkind gesture on his part.

"Ye have no right to do such a thing," she argued. "Because ye know I want an annulment, and ye owe it to me on account of the fact that I saved ye from committing an atrocity."

They were nose to nose, their breath rasping between their teeth, and while they were intent on each other, Helen suddenly felt as if her mother had just caught her sneaking bread before the meal was blessed by her father. That guilty little tingle on the nape of her neck. She turned her head and Marcus did too, so both of them ended up staring straight into the eyes of Father Matthew Peter.

The priest was red-faced and had clearly stormed across the courtyard to pull them apart. Helen felt her belly do a flip. All of the youths practicing in the yard had stopped and were staring at them, while the steps behind them were crowded with women and girls who had come out of the hall to enjoy the spectacle they were providing.

Father Matthew Peter opened his mouth and shut it several times. He never managed to speak. Instead he stuck his arm out, pointing toward the church. Helen turned and started toward the church, and then had to bite her lip as she realized the good father was staring at Marcus with his arm still extended toward the church. There was a collective hush in the yard as those watching waited to see what Marcus would do. Women were covering their mouths with their hands to remain silent while Marcus and the monk stared at each other.

And then Marcus MacPherson, War Chief of the clan, nodded once before falling into step beside Helen to walk in shame on their way to be reprimanded.

❧

"Twelve lashes," Morton said with a hint of admiration in his tone. "I expected ye to fold much sooner."

Brenda flinched and chided herself for showing any reaction, but damned if she couldn't still hear the snap of the leather before it bit into her back. Morton moved further into the chamber, grinning at her. He stopped and looked at the bed. The sheets were stained with blood that had come from the welts on her back. She still felt a great deal of satisfaction in seeing it, because she'd proven herself strong enough to endure.

At least in some part she had been, but there was only so much pain anybody could endure before the will to survive overrode everything else. She could have taken more lashes, but she had been forced to face the truth of her own limited strength. So she'd agreed to do Morton's bidding, and Gunn had made good use of her weakness.

It was a lesson she focused on, letting it feed her hatred of men.

"Perhaps ye understand now who yer master is?" Morton asked softly.

Brenda remained still, looking straight at him, her chin level. Her silence earned her a soft *tsk*. "In that case," he muttered, "ye can be sure there will be further demonstrations of me power over ye."

Morton had walked toward her, stopping when he was close enough to tap her on her cheek with a fingertip. "Ye are a damned handsome woman. With a body that matches yer face. Ye shall fuck when I tell ye. No one will care if yer back is scarred or the soles of yer feet burned."

He left her to his men. The only mercy afforded her was that he ordered them to keep their hands off her. She was a treat only to be enjoyed by those he decided to gift her to. His retainers grumbled as they took her to the chambers that served as her cell.

It was more of a haven than the earl ever would have guessed. With the door closed, she was free to indulge in the tears she'd kept locked inside during the night.

But she wiped them away, angry with herself for giving Gunn or Morton any part of herself. It was a lesson she'd learned with her husband and would do well to recall. Men were not worthy.

Oh, perhaps men such as Bhaic and Marcus were, but at court, there were only ambitious, self-centered males, and it would seem she was to keep company with them. It shouldn't have surprised her. Her entire life had been one of service to the ambitions of the males who surrounded her. Her current circumstances were nothing new.

So she would not cry.

Ever again.

And as for scars…Brenda pulled her chemise off and turned to look at her back in a mirror. She would wear each one with pride. Morton would learn something from her as well.

She was a Highlander too.

⊱⊰

"Helen?" Ailis poked her head into the small cell.

"Aye, I am here."

Ailis opened the door wide, or at least as wide as

it could be opened. The small chamber was used as a sewing room. Three steps down from the narrow doorway was a single cot and a wardrobe that could be locked to safeguard the lengths of linen kept inside it. Fabric was very expensive and sometimes impossible to find. There were also fine shears, carefully sharpened lest a burr catch any of the costly fabric while it was being cut. Needles and pins were also stored there, along with thread and buttons. A ring of keys lay on the table where Helen had placed it after opening the wardrobe.

"I have been lectured on the duties of a wife and the need my immortal soul has to perform them," Helen explained as she pulled a needle up from the piece of linen she was working with. "And that making me *husband*"—she sighed on the word—"a shirt, as a devoted wife should, is the penance I owe for me behavior this afternoon."

Helen jabbed the needle back into the cloth with a soft snarl.

Ailis smothered a chuckle. "Ye were…quite angry."

Helen lifted her head while pulling the thread tight. "I was bloody well ready to clock that bastard on the side of the head again. Ye witnessed what he did, right enough."

"Aye, I did," Ailis confirmed. "A poor attempt at courting. However, given that we are talking about Marcus, I believe he did rather well."

Helen offered her a snort in response. "That man acts more like a stallion, doing his best to run off any competition."

Ailis turned red, and Helen rolled her eyes as her

mistress burst out laughing. She kept at it until tears ran down her cheeks.

"Oh, Helen, I am sorry, and yet I am not truly repentant. Perhaps I need to make ye a chemise."

"According to the good Father, this task"—Helen stabbed the needle down again—"will help me settle in."

"Marcus would be disappointed if ye did," Ailis remarked. She'd come closer and leaned over to peer intently at what Helen was stitching. "Helen, are those—?"

Helen looked up with a wicked smile on her lips. She pulled the needle up, allowing Ailis to see the color of the thread she was using. It was pink. Helen looked back down, using the needle carefully as she worked the pink thread into the outline of a posy.

"Ye are putting flowers on Marcus's collar." Ailis began choking on her mirth again.

Helen offered her a pleased little smirk as she pulled the needle up into the air once more. "Father Peter will not fault me for shorting him on the amount of attention I give to the task he's set me, and Marcus will no' be refusing to wear the shirt Father Peter insisted I make for him."

"Nay," Ailis agreed, tears glittering in her eyes. "Ye are certainly…toiling…devotedly… Marcus will, of course, have to wear what ye made…as penance." She collapsed into another fit of giggles, ending up on the small cot in the cell.

"Oh, do hush," Helen scolded her. "At least until I finish. I want to make sure the beast has to wear it. That's little enough payback for him kissing me before one and all."

Ailis was turning purple as she clamped her lips shut and smothered her laughter behind her hand. When she at last drew breath, there were tears sparkling in her eyes. "Oh, Helen, forgive me, but I do think ye are that man's match after all."

"Naught to forgive. I agree."

Ailis sat up, albeit slowly because her belly was rounded. "Ye do?"

Helen smiled and looked back at the posy she was stitching. "Marcus is going to discover that I will be having my way in this and getting my annulment."

For the first time, that idea didn't give her the burst of satisfaction it had before. Helen contemplated why. An annulment was what she craved, so why was she not happily basking in the glow of contentment? It made little sense, which was true about many of her feelings concerning Marcus. That was solid, irrefutable reasoning for why she had to go through with her plan to end their union before she did something irreversible.

Such as consummating it.

❧

"Helen."

Shamus called out to her the moment she entered the great hall. Truthfully, Helen was impressed with the man's eyesight. His hair was gray and his skin more wrinkled than an apple in May, but he spotted her trying to fill a bowl with stew at the far side of the hall.

"Ye'll join me."

It was an order she could not disobey. He was the master of the castle, even if age had made it so that his sons shouldered most of the duties he'd once performed.

One of the serving women reached out and took the bowl right out of her hands. Helen lowered herself before making her way down the aisle. Conversation hushed, the men watching her approach the high ground and lower herself again before she climbed the six steps to the dais that raised the laird's table above the others in the hall. Finley was there, pulling a chair out for her and pushing it back in once she'd sat down.

Shamus nodded approvingly. "I look forward to having grandchildren to bounce on me knee now that both me sons have taken wives."

There was a cheer from his men. Women began serving again as conversation picked up. Marcus and Bhaic arrived at last, tugging on the corners of their bonnets before they sat down. Marcus angled his head and considered her for a long moment before he ripped a loaf of bread apart and offered a section to her.

Helen reached for it and felt her hand shaking. She dropped the bread onto her plate as every bit of composure deserted her. Everyone was staring at her. The scrutiny made her feel as if her jaw was too stiff to open when she tried to put a piece of the bread into her mouth. Every motion of chewing sounded too loud and obnoxious, so she swallowed too soon and ended up drinking to wash the lump of half-chewed bread down her throat. It left her feeling as if she had stretched the inside of her neck.

And the staring continued.

The conversation was stilling again. Those who had watched them march off to the church hoped to be entertained further. Helen picked up her eating knife, but it clattered out of her fingers onto her plate. Unlike the lower tables, the laird's was set with silver plates. Hers made a horrific sound as the knife hit it. Marcus finally drew in a deep breath and cupped her elbow.

"We managed to share a bed last night without ye shaking, woman. Can ye no' settle down and enjoy supper without making it appear to one and all that ye fully expect me to ravish ye right here upon the table because I have no restraint?"

"What are ye accusing me of now?" Helen demanded as quietly as she could manage. She'd missed half of what Marcus had said because she was so focused on those watching her. "I have never sat at a high table in me life, much less been served by others. I'll tell ye truthfully, I hardly notice ye are beside me."

Her voice was rising with every word. Shamus turned and caught the last thing she uttered. He flashed a huge grin at them. "I see ye've no' yet proven yerself to the lass, Marcus. She's still skittish."

The table went quiet, his captains ending their conversations to listen intently to what their chief was saying. Shamus contemplated Helen as he chewed and swallowed. He washed the food down before pointing his eating knife at her. "A female like that needs a man who can satisfy her passions."

Her cheeks heated, but more with temper than anything else. She was out of patience with everyone's interest in her maidenhead. "All I long for is a man who is no' completely convinced that his cock will solve all of the troubles in the world."

There was silence at the table. Two of the captains

had stopped in mid-chew as her comment was being repeated below them, and the hall became still.

Shamus wasn't shocked into silence as she'd first suspected. No, he waited a full three seconds before letting out a whoop of amusement and tossing his head back with a roar. His eyes glittered when he looked back at her and slapped the tabletop.

"Ye mistake me, lass," he said through a huge smile. "'Tis yer husband who has nae proven himself by putting his face between yer thighs and showing ye he can move ye to ecstasy so ye'll know he's worthy of yer maidenhead."

It took only a second for his captains to absorb what he'd said. In the next, hysteria ensued. Cups were overturned, and one man actually fell out of his chair because he was doubled over laughing so hard.

"Marcus, ye lazy dog!" Shamus bellowed. "Only a fool would no' make time for a treat such as yer wife."

There was a harsh grating sound as Marcus pushed his chair back. A second later, he was dragging hers away from the table.

"Marcus—" Helen only got out his name before he reached out, grabbed her wrist, and pulled her right over his shoulder.

The hall grew louder, if such a thing were possible, while Marcus carried her out dangling over his shoulder.

"And ye claimed me behavior was going to have one and all thinking ye a brute," she admonished him when they were inside a chamber.

Marcus closed the door. He turned and looked at her. "It seemed more of a kindness to get ye out of the hall. I will fully admit I was no' willing to stay there and suffer more of me father's ever-so-sage advice. Me father does nae answer to Matthew Peter quite the same way ye and I do. Trust me, me father was just getting started."

Somehow, in that moment, Marcus looked every bit as finished with being the source of everyone's amusement as she was. Their gazes met, understanding passing between them. He offered her a genuine grin before she sent back a shy smile. Marcus reached up and rubbed his forehead.

Helen started giggling. Oh, her timing couldn't have been worse, but she couldn't seem to help herself.

Marcus raised an eyebrow. "Laughing at me expense?"

She shook her head. "I just realized we're both on the same side of this issue, and, well…I am no' used to being on even ground with ye."

Understanding flashed through his eyes a moment before his expression softened. The man truly was handsome when he wasn't intent on making sure she was intimidated by him. She felt a desire to see him relax more often.

"Aye, we are at that, lass," he agreed. "No one is going to let either of us off lightly."

She nodded, but ended up stopping when their gazes met and fused. It felt as if the world had shifted off center, her insides twisting as they had when she was a child and her father tossed her up into the air. Only this time, the sensation settled into her flesh, heating parts of her she'd never thought much about.

"I truly was nervous about sitting there," she said softly.

The chamber was silent for a long moment.

"I recall the first time I sat at the high table."

His words surprised her. He had never shared something personal with her.

"Me mother refused to wed me father," Marcus continued. "Shamus had me educated and trained, but I broke bread at the lower tables until I was eighteen because her status was mine, since she would no' take vows with me sire. He called out to me the first night after me mother's passing. I never knew that hall was so very long. The walk felt as though it went on forever."

"Aye, it did feel that way tonight," she agreed.

"And I understand what ye mean by no' being accustomed to someone serving ye. It's bloody unsettling at first."

"I thought me spine was going to break because I was sitting so straight," she admitted. "I suppose when I was small, I daydreamed of being a lady of station." She let out a little sigh. "The reality is rather more of a responsibility than I realized. How do ye eat with everyone staring at ye?"

"With care," Marcus agreed. "I believe Father Matthew Peter was making sure ye and I know we need to be setting a proper example." A naughty smile curved his lips. "I miss the days when I could indulge in a good tussle just for the fun of it. I think that's why me father is enjoying himself so greatly at our expense. He's waited nearly an entire lifetime to be above reproach. No one tells him what to do anymore."

They both laughed at the idea.

She realized Marcus had brought her to his chambers. They were larger than hers, of course, but furnished with only the essentials. No carpets upon the stone floor or tapestries hung on the walls. There were only sturdy chairs and a table in the outer room. Through an arched doorway, she glimpsed the huge bed. Her nipples actually began to contract, making her shift her attention away from it.

She was clearly turning into a wanton.

He reached down and pulled a flask from the top of his boot. A quick twist and he had the top open. "Share a drink with me, lass, for the rest of the clan is no' going to give us any peace until they've had their measure of fun at our expense. Hence, we need a nip or two or eight."

She took the flask and tipped it up to her lips. Marcus was watching her when she lowered it. "What? Ye do nae think a Grant can drink?"

He toasted her with the flask before taking a long swig of it. "I am most pleasantly surprised. But then again, ye do that rather often to me."

His words warmed her. Sure, she might have blamed the whisky, but the truth was, it was nice to know she kept him guessing. She reached for the flask again. "Ye only encouraged them with how ye carried me off."

Marcus waited until she'd finished drinking before answering. "I was hoping to expedite matters. Once they think we've made things official, they'll leave us be."

"It won't be soon if yer brother has anything to say about it." She let out a little sigh. "Ye tested his patience sorely when he brought Ailis here."

Marcus only smirked at her and took the flask back. Helen returned his smile. "Ye really are a swine at times, Marcus MacPherson."

"And ye, madam," he countered through a chuckle, "are pure vixen. I've the bites to prove it."

"Every one of them was richly deserved," she informed him with a grin.

Enjoyment flickered in his eyes. It made her groan, but out of camaraderie rather than frustration. Marcus didn't miss her reaction.

"Admit it," he said over the top of the flask. "Ye enjoy pitting yerself against me. Ye would have no stomach for a man who quoted the holy book in his effort to put ye in yer place." He raised a finger in the air and waved it about. "'Woman was made to serve man...'"

She nodded, laughing softly at the idea.

There was a bump outside the chamber door and some scratching. "I'm getting to it." Someone's words came through in a muffled jumble. "It's quiet. Maybe they're finished."

"They've no' been up here long enough," someone answered.

"So open the door and have a peek."

Marcus sent it an annoyed look. "Seems ye may be right about Bhaic wanting to extract a full measure of vengeance."

"Well, we can nae let them go on thinking I've surrendered so quickly." Helen stood up, her legs feeling a little wobbly and overly warm. She selected a bowl that was sitting on the table and sent it hurling at the door just as it was pushed in. "Swine!" she bellowed as Finley started to peek inside.

Marcus threw his head back and roared. The chair he was in tipped back, and he gave a push so he went tumbling heels over chin and landed on his feet in front of the door. "Vixen!" He kicked back, his foot connecting with the door and sending it slamming shut. There was a muffled expletive from outside in the hallway before Marcus started turning over the rest of the furniture while growling like a hungry wolf. Helen squealed in amusement as tears glittered in her eyes.

It was all finished in a few moments, leaving them breathless and laughing at the mess they'd made. Her head was spinning, her thoughts flying apart from the combination of activity and whisky. She was breathless and so was he as they stood facing each other. She stared at him in fascination as he laid his hands on either side of her face. The contact raced down her spine, all the way to her toes, where it set off a tingling. If he'd pulled her to him, she might have balked, but this kindness was so sweet that she stood there, anticipation building like the tempo of a springtime dance as he leaned forward and slowly sealed her lips beneath his.

The kiss was scalding hot, searing a path through her as her breath caught. They were suspended in the moment, like a bubble where the fae danced forever in merriment. She reached for him, flattening her hands on his chest and shivering as she slipped her hands across the ridges of muscle beneath his clothing.

He lifted his head from hers, looking down into her eyes as though he wanted to see what effect he had on her.

"Yer eyes glitter with passion when I kiss ye, Helen."

She could have told him he was mistaken, but she

realized such a taunt would be cowardly. An attempt to goad him into action and remove all responsibility from her hands for what happened when she gave in to her cravings.

He deserved better than that from her. So she nodded before she shifted away from him. Uncertainty was sweeping through her, as hard as winter winds. It left her caught between the two forces—that flickering lick of passion's flames and the chill of not knowing what she wanted, only that it felt so right to be in his arms.

He watched her for a moment before he let out a long sigh. "Aye. Let's lay our heads down and sleep, lass. Tomorrow will be soon enough to puzzle through what we plan to do with each other."

Helen cast a look toward the bed.

His bed.

"We've shared a bed before," Marcus reminded her in that low, gravelly tone that he used when he was hiding his feelings. She'd heard him use it on his men plenty of times, and it made her suspicious.

"Because ye had hold of me hair and were snoring," She took another step away from him. She couldn't seem to stand still. Marcus stopped, planting his feet shoulder-width apart as he crossed his arms over his chest.

"Father Matthew Peter made me swear to wait upon yer whim."

Helen choked. "He would no' do such a thing. The church says I am yer property."

Marcus lifted a finger into the air. "It was a personal penance given to me. That I might better understand the merits of patience and no' harboring the sin of wrath."

She shouldn't laugh.

Yet she did. Marcus closed his eyes, but his lips parted in a grin. He took another swallow before offering it to her. Helen eyed it for a bit, contemplating just how much like bait it was.

Oh, for heaven's sake! Stiffen yer spine!

She moved forward and took the flask, their fingers brushing as she gripped it. "Yer word, then."

"I gave it."

He drained the last of the whisky before walking into the bedchamber and laying the flask down on a small table. Helen watched him for a long time. She wasn't so much nervous as curious. He was in a private moment now, something she knew without a doubt few ever witnessed. She felt privileged, something she had not experienced in a very long time.

There was a bench in the bedchamber. She sat on it to take off her boots. Marcus sat on another one, doing the same. They were a pair, that was for certain. Never had she thought that men suffered the same trials as women when it came to marriage. It had always seemed that men held all the power, and perhaps that was true for many. Marcus was the son of the laird though, and as such, he had expectations from the clan to fulfill. Even when their vows were swept aside by a lawyer's quill, he would still have to perform as expected. Perhaps Fate was not simply unkind to her. No, Marcus would have a pound of flesh demanded of him as well.

Somehow, that made him easier to approach.

Beneath his gruff exterior, he was a man who was being told to suffer the will of others over his own. Helen lay beside him, listening to him breathe, and lamented the fact that she would have to leave his side. Part of her truly wanted more private time with him. Lying there beside him, she felt more at ease than she could ever recall. Sleep came easily as she settled into the bed, enjoying the warmth Marcus added to it.

Indeed, she was turning wanton for the one man she should know better than to fancy, but at that moment, she didn't care a bit.

❧

She'd gone to sleep with a soft throbbing at the front of her sex. A mild annoyance that never truly ebbed during the night. Helen shifted and sighed, not quite ready to awaken. There was a nip in the air that promised snow, and the bed was delightfully warm.

And that throbbing? Well, it was becoming something different now. There was pleasure involved, a deep enjoyment that made her let out a little sound of pure bliss. Her dreams had never included such a sensation, only the building need that went from that little throbbing spot down into her core. It became a yearning that frustrated her because she didn't know how to ease it.

Today, though, there was more than easement; there was pleasure. It soothed away the ache, growing as intense as the need. She wanted more of it and felt herself straining upward, seeking... Well, she didn't know just what, only that she couldn't think beyond the need for it.

It all snapped, unleashing a rush of pleasure so intense that she cried out and arched, her entire body caught in the grip of it for one mind-numbing moment. She opened her eyes and heard herself gasping. Her heart was racing, and sensation was still rippling across her skin when she looked down her body and gasped.

"Ye lied to me." She wanted be outraged, but her voice was husky with satisfaction.

Marcus offered her a cocky grin from where his head was hovering just a few inches above her spread sex. His lips were wet, and she realized in horror exactly why.

"I did nae have me hands on ye at all, lass," he responded arrogantly. "And I owe me sire a wee bit of an apology for me thinking last evening, because his advice is sound."

She rolled over and over and right off the edge of the huge bed, but her knees were shaky, so she stumbled, grasping one of the posts that held the bed curtains. Marcus watched her, his grin widening as he took in his effect on her. He was wearing nothing but his shirt, and his member was sticking out in the front of it.

He'd lulled her into a false sense of ease. She realized he was every bit as menacing as ever and had simply waited for his moment to pounce on her.

"Do nae look at me like that, Helen." Marcus sat up on the side of the bed and watched her move away. "Ye told me yer maidenhead was the only thing ye have left that is yer own, so I pleasured ye without taking it. Is it so hard to think of me as a man who does nae want to act the brute to ye?" He patted the surface of the bed. "I want ye to choose me."

Did she dare?

Dare was certainly the correct word. He was looking at her, every inch the hardened man she'd faced time and again, and yet there was much more to him now. He was attempting to push inside her, to that place where no one had ever been, to her deepest feelings. However, he was offering her a glimpse at his own in return.

Such a tangle of possibilities.

She looked at the pile of clothing that she'd left on the bench, caught between the need to maintain her pride and the desire to simply let it go in favor of... Well, she wasn't sure what exactly she'd find in his bed. She ended up looking back toward him, seeking the answer in his eyes.

"Naught to say?" he asked. "There is a first."

"Oh, for Christ's sake," she exclaimed with her hip roll half laced. "There was a time when I knew how to speak kindly. Why do ye needle me until I can nae hold me tongue?"

He flashed her an arrogant grin. "Because I like ye the way ye are, no' disguising yer nature to appease everyone about ye. Do ye have any idea how long it has been since a lass was honest with me? Since one came to me seeking me, and no' me position? Ye are not the only one who feels isolated. As War Chief, I must be hard on the young lads, lest they fail to build up enough strength to survive. Smiling at them would be a disservice."

Sometime during the night, he'd taken the time to pleat his kilt on a table that ran along the side of the bedchamber. His wide belt was already under it. It took only a moment for him to lean back, grasp the sides of the belt, and pull it all around himself. Most men used the floor, but clearly Marcus wanted to be ready, should there be a need to dress in a hurry during the night.

"It fell to me to either take ye or know without a doubt that I'd be sending me own men up against yer brothers because they refused to admit the cattle were ours." He was buckling a second belt in place to make sure his kilt was secure. "Ye think I enjoyed it?"

"Yes, ye did," she answered him. "Somewhat, anyhow. Admit it. Yer nature is suited to yer position."

He offered her a cocky grin. "If ye'll match me by admitting ye did nae think to notice I do nae always care for what me duty demands of me. That's the thing about duty. Ye do it because it needs doing and others depend on ye seeing things through."

"Fairly spoken," she said softly while pulling her skirts over her head. The waistband caught on her hip roll, and she began to lace the waistband closed. "Ye are no' a brute." His smile was widening with victory. "But *swine* fits well, for ye knew well ye were twisting words last evening to get me into yer bed."

He chuckled and opened his arms wide. "Taming a vixen requires cunning."

Helen felt her temper stir at the use of the word *taming*.

Something else also flickered inside her too, and she'd be a liar if she claimed she hadn't enjoyed being the recipient of his attention. She picked up her bodice and shrugged into it to avoid letting him see the indecision in her eyes. He'd notice, all right—the man had an uncanny ability to see right into her soul. Or so it seemed.

He sat and laced his boots while Helen continued to dress. His silence didn't make her think he'd forgotten her; no, she felt his gaze on her as the only sounds in the chamber were the ones made by cloth moving.

"Ye'll have a few days to think on things," he said when he'd finished.

Helen lifted her attention from her boots to him.

"I'll need to move some of the cattle now that it's going to snow."

"I see."

He adopted the pose she was used to seeing him in: feet braced shoulder-width apart with his arms crossed over his wide chest. Without his doublet on, she could see the muscles of his upper arms flex.

Damned if that didn't warm her insides.

"Will ye promise me ye'll be here when I get back?"

He was reluctant to ask her. She heard it in his tone. Indecision was flickering in his eyes, and she realized he was debating the merits of setting guards on her. "Ye'd accept me word?"

He stepped toward her, his expression relaxing. "I do want to. The truth is, I want nothing more than to make very certain ye are here when I return, but I also crave yer approval, and I can nae have it if I imprison ye. So, I'm asking ye."

It was an admission he was not completely comfortable with.

"I will be here. But I suggest ye think long and hard about yer impulse to see this union solidified. Ye stole me to ensure the MacPhersons remain strong. Our marriage will put yer clan at a disadvantage because all of yer neighbors will say ye are soft at heart for no' making a better match."

"They might." He moved closer and slipped his arm around her waist when she stood her ground. "At the moment, I'm anything but soft, lass, and I want ye here when I return so I can show ye how much better I can please ye."

His meaning was impossible to miss. The hard length of his erection was pressed against her belly, hot and tempting as he leaned down and kissed her. There was a promise in his kiss, as well as a warning that he wasn't going to be deterred. She should have pulled away, but there was a challenge there too that she couldn't seem to resist answering. Maybe she needed to feel she was woman enough to not shiver in his embrace. Whatever the reason, she slid her hand along the ridges of his chest and up to his neck, where she held him in place as surely as he was cradling her nape.

She felt his passion growing, seemed to recognize it deep inside herself. The throbbing returned at the front of her sex. Only this time, she was very aware of how empty her passage felt. It was a stark, blunt realization that swept aside the last of her innocence about why women were happy to follow men like Marcus into the shadows. She now understood the brightness in their eyes when they returned, and realized that she craved it deeply.

Ye can have it…

In fact, she could take that satisfaction any moment

she cared to. She pulled back from him, her mind trying frantically to make a choice. A lifetime of warnings and lectures on piety were battling against the surge of need and hunger burning inside her. It left her feeling as though the very ground was crumbling beneath her feet.

"Stop fretting, Helen." Marcus stroked her cheek with the backs of his fingers. "We're wed. It's no' a sin."

"It's surrender," she whispered without meaning to.

His jaw tightened. "Well now, it seems ye have as much pride as I do. Ye might just have to be tempering yer thoughts on me."

There was a rap on the door. Marcus leaned down and pressed a hard kiss against her mouth before striding across the chamber to where his sword was. He slung the harness over one shoulder and settled the hilt into position.

"Ye gave yer word, Helen. Honor it."

&

Shamus could override a promise given to Marcus.

It took Helen several days to realize that fact. Of course, her days had been filled with the frantic last rush to bring in any remaining crops and store them for the coming winter. There wasn't a pot not in use as squash and other gourds were stewed down. As the castle had grown, new kitchens had been added to provide for the increased needs of its retainers. Even the older kitchens were fired up for the last push of the season.

By the end of the week, they were all aching from the workload and there was still more to do. Helen fell into her bed late in the evening, too exhausted to do anything but sleep. For certain, she wanted to go to Shamus and do what was best for Marcus, but there simply wasn't any time.

That thought sobered her, but it pleased her as well. Somehow, she'd become concerned over what would happen to Marcus. She liked knowing that, because it finally broke away the anger that seemed to have been stuck to her for so long. Her marriage would have to be considered a blessing for freeing her from that. Even if she still needed to end it.

Near the end of the week, Helen heard Shamus shuffling in the passageway on his way to the hall. She dusted off her hands and untied her apron. The Laird of the MacPhersons noticed her immediately. He slowed his step as she came out of the older portion of the castle where she'd been working. She lowered herself as he lifted his hand and gestured for the two captains who had been trailing him to move back.

"What do ye seek, lass?" Shamus asked. "Even if I am fairly certain I already know what it is."

There was a note in his voice that wasn't promising. In fact, she recognized it as the same one Marcus so often used when he was putting his duty first.

"I am still a maiden." She resisted the urge to be too delicate in her word choices. For all that age had had its way with Shamus MacPherson, he was Marcus's sire and she'd best recall that fact.

Shamus slowly grinned. "Aye, as I told me son, he has yet to impress ye. Do nae worry, lass. He'll return soon, and the snow will keep him here. The pair of ye shall have a nice, cold winter to enjoy."

"Surely ye must have offers for him," Helen said as her cheeks heated from the image his words had painted.

"Aye," Shamus confirmed. "Many."

She'd known it, but hearing the words felt as though something had just cut across the surface of her heart. Helen drew in a deep breath. "Help me gain an annulment so Marcus can be the son the MacPhersons expect him to be."

Shamus had been watching her with a serious expression. As her words sank in, his lips rose into a satisfied smile.

Helen felt as if he'd reached right into her chest and ripped her heart out.

"Me son said ye gave him yer word that ye'd be here when he returned."

Helen nodded. "As his sire and laird—"

"Aye, I can do what is best for him, and ye could be content ye did nae break a promise."

Helen nodded again, grateful for the semidarkness in the passageway. It helped hide the glitter of unshed tears in her eyes. It was all for the best, but it hurt so dreadfully

"Let me tell ye, mistress, why I never matched either of me sons." Shamus took a moment to look around before continuing. "I loved his mother. Marcus's, that is." His eyes lit with the memory. "Oh, she was a fine woman and no mistake. A true daughter of the Highlands with a spirit as wild as the lands we live on. That same spirit is in yer eyes, lass."

Helen started to shake her head. Shamus held up a finger to keep her silent.

"I am a liar."

His confession shocked her, and he smiled as he watched the impact of his words.

"Aye. It's true," Shamus confirmed. "For all me days, I've told one and all that she would nae wed me because of a difference in faith. No, Clare refused to let me make her me wife when the clan expected me to bring home a bride who came with a dowry and an alliance. She loved me enough to set her own happiness aside so I would nae suffer shame."

For a moment he went silent, lost in the memory.

"So I did it, after five long years of waiting for her to soften her thinking on the matter. At last, I decided to let her shield me, and I pleased me father by telling him I'd wed the match he selected for me." His voice was edged with bitterness. "Bhaic's mother was everything she should have been. Sweet and obedient, and she gave me a son and a daughter. She had waited to give her heart away, placing her faith in her parents' choice of husband for her." Shamus aimed a hard look at Helen.

"I watched her heart break because I could no' stop meself from loving another, and she witnessed the truth of it when I looked at Clare. Me own daughter hates me for what I did to her mother, but I'm grateful Bhaic never saw it. It takes men longer to understand the delicate nature of women. Me daughter, on the other hand, watched her mother wither and die because I could nae love her, and she would no' take a lover out of respect for me."

The tears escaped Helen's eyes and Shamus nodded.

"Aye. It's a hard story to tell and hear. The truth is, I would have gladly gone to the noose Morton had strung up for me instead of watching me son be forced to wed. Why do ye think I let young Ailis go back to her father on that first day? I am no' so great a fool as to think that angering the Earl of Morton is a good decision for me to make."

"My union with Marcus enraged him."

"Well now." Shamus's voice had taken on a hard edge. "That is another matter altogether. Ye were right to notice Katherine is too young for bedding. On that account, the earl will have to suffer me disobedience, and I've written him to let him know what I think of the matter. Marcus agreed to the wedding but no' the bedding, as any decent man would do. The earl will soften his will on it, or I will let the truth of the matter be known, and he'll lose more than one supporter."

Helen drew in a breath to steady herself.

"Save yer breath, lass," Shamus warned her. "I will no' agree to an annulment. The fact that ye care what is thought of me son has confirmed how right ye are for him. Too many believe Marcus is a hard, callous man. He has a heart, ye have noticed. If not, ye would no' be asking me to help ye leave him for his own good. Marcus gives enough to his clan."

Shamus reached out and touched her cheek, where the tears had left her skin wet. He smiled at the sensation, a strange, sweet smile that vanished almost as quickly as it appeared. He nodded as he withdrew his hand.

"Ye'll be here when he returns, and the pair of ye can get back to circling each other."

"Yet surely—"

Shamus made a slashing motion with his hand. "Another word, mistress, and I will put me own men on ye to ensure it is so."

"I do nae break me word."

Shamus chuckled. "Aye, there it is, that devil-take-heed spirit. I've half a mind to set a few of the lads to dodging yer hem, just for the lesson it will prove to be when they underestimate ye. That's the sort of thing ye can tell a man, but until he comes up against it, he'll not believe ye. Takes the experience to set it into the mind." He tapped his temple with his fingertip.

Helen felt her temper heating. Shamus laughed at her and slapped his thigh before he turned and gestured to his waiting captains. They were quick to stride forward, both of them sending her looks designed to get her to relinquish their laird's attention.

Helen lowered herself as Shamus continued on his way.

The conversation left Helen feeling strangely relieved. She should have been nursing her temper over being yet again forced to bend to a MacPherson's will.

But she wasn't.

No, there was a complete lack of resentment inside her. So much so that the fatigue weighing on her shoulders felt lifted. And that left her prey to the anticipation she'd been trying to ignore. Now, it flooded her, drowning her insistence.

Should she leave her situation as Fate seemed to want it? The question chewed into her thoughts into the next day as she toiled along with the rest of the household.

Was being Marcus's wife such a terrible fate? Perhaps not for her. Many would think she'd acted the fool by not ensuring Marcus was bound to her when she had the opportunity to seal their vows. Well after sunset, she was still pondering her feelings when she decided to seek her bed. Ailis had taken to her chamber hours before, in spite of her insistence that she stay and see to her house. But her ankles had been nearly as swollen as her middle, so she'd lost the battle and retired. Helen had promised to finish, and now, well into the late hours of the night, she stretched her neck and smiled at a job finally done.

At least in the smaller kitchen it was. In the main kitchens, there most likely was more to be done. That could wait until sunrise, though. Helen made her way through the passageways, intent on finding her chamber.

"Sleeping, are ye?"

Helen felt a bolt of cold memory go down her spine. She knew that tone of voice from Duana. She jumped when she heard a swish and then a blunt connection.

That was a sound branded into her memory. Helen grabbed her skirts and ran. Something had certainly changed in her, and she didn't take the time to think the impulse through. She went around the corner and through one of the back entrances to the kitchen in time to see Duana raising her rod for another blow.

Katherine was cringing on a stool, her eyes bright but her cheeks dry because she knew tears would gain her nothing but more punishment.

"Do nae ye dare strike her!" Helen ordered.

Duana rounded on her as though she'd dared some sort of inexcusable blasphemy. Of course, to the Head of House, it was very much the same.

"Ye'll mind yer place, Grant," Duana hissed before

she turned back toward Katherine and raised the rod. "I'll teach this one what happens to lazy English whelps in me kitchen. Ye have nothing without me goodwill…naught."

Plenty of women were watching, as well as the younger lads who served in the kitchens. Helen stepped forward and grabbed the rod. "I told ye nay."

Duana rounded on her and slapped her hard. She landed the blow because Helen was busy pulling the rod out of the mistress's reach. Pain went zipping through Helen's jaw and teeth, hard enough to make her ears ring. She had to quell the impulse to strike the woman back.

"And ye will mind me, Duana."

There was a collective gasp from their audience. As well as a shuffle, but Helen kept her attention on Duana.

"And just who do ye think ye are to be telling me what I can and can nae do in these kitchens?" the Head of House demanded.

"I am Marcus's wife."

"Ye're his slut!" Duana insisted. "Maybe ye're warming his cock now, but he'll cast ye out when the spring comes because ye have naught to offer him but a warm bed for the winter. No one will blame him for setting ye aside when yer family fails to provide any dowry. There was no contract, so the vows will be easily broken. Everyone knows it."

Duana opened her hands wide, and the rest of the inhabitants of the kitchens all looked at Helen with condemning gazes. Perhaps some of the younger ones pitied her, but that would change. They'd soon see her as an example of why they must obey their parents when it came to matters of marriage. It was a business that needed contracts—sealed and witnessed to be binding.

Helen broke the rod over her knee anyway. "Well, I am here now, and ye will no' be striking this child. Katherine, leave the kitchens now."

The girl went, but not before she took off the apron she wore and slapped it down on the stool in defiance. Duana grunted.

"Ye'll be mine again before ye know it, English bastard girl. I promise ye that." There was a hard edge to Duana's voice that sent a ripple of memory across Helen's skin. But Katherine was looking to her, the child's eyes wide in her face. Helen banished the specter, refusing to be prey to its grip.

"Do nae listen to her." Helen tried to soothe Katherine once they were away from the kitchens. "She's a woman who has spent too many years hating."

Katherine may have been young, but she looked at Helen with a world of knowledge in her eyes. "If ye had no contract, do ye think to gain your husband's love? The queen's mother had her father's love, but he took her head when that love drove him insane."

"So I've heard." Helen took a small lantern hanging on an iron hook in the wall to light their way. The fate of Anne Boleyn was well known and often told to remind young girls of the danger of wedding for love. Men might fall prey to that madness, but it was insanity. In the end, they were still men, and it was a man's world.

Helen looked around. "Where are ye going, Katherine?"

"To me chamber," she answered. "I was sleeping on me stool."

"Ailis gave ye a chamber in the new tower."

They were in the bowels of the castle now, where wide arches supported the structure above them. Most of the chambers here were storage rooms and sewing cells because there was no way to vent smoke from hearths.

"Duana told me I was to sleep here."

Helen looked at the narrow door Katherine indicated. Inside was a tiny nun's cell dating back to when a convent was attached to what would become MacPherson Castle. Inside, the chamber was so small that Helen could stretch her hands out on either side and touch both walls. A narrow cot was against one wall, with a thin pallet and single blanket.

Katherine started to strike a flint into the bowl of tinder sitting on the little two-foot-wide table that held a candle. But she sighed. "I forgot to fill it this morning in me rush to answer Duana's summons. No matter. I am so tired, I do nae need light."

She started to sit down on the cot.

"Ye are no' sleeping here," Helen informed her. "The mistress will be very displeased when she discovers ye here."

"Truly"—Katherine covered a huge yawn—"I only need a bed, and the mistress needs her strength, with the babe due to arrive soon."

"Aye, she needs her sleep," Helen agreed. "Come along. Ye'll have me old chamber until the mistress sorts matters out."

Katherine had started to settle onto the cot. She blinked and stood.

Helen led Katherine down a passageway to where the abbess's chamber was. She pushed open the door. "And ye can bar the door if anyone bothers ye."

Katherine looked around the set of chambers and smiled.

"Go on, the bed is quite nice and the blankets thick."

The girl shed her garments, and Helen realized they were her old clothing. Duana had considered rags good enough for an English girl. Once she was wearing only the tattered chemise, Katherine went to the bed and climbed in. A few moments later, her soft breathing told Helen she was fast asleep.

And Helen knew exactly why too. Her temper kept her from regretting too much about what she'd done. Let it filter through the castle that she'd used her position to face down the Head of House. She didn't really care what any of them thought. Lord knew none of them had ever befriended her.

Yet her steps slowed when she stood facing the doors to Marcus's chambers. She squared her shoulders and entered. Inside, she was assaulted by just how much she missed him. It was something in the scent of the chamber, a lingering essence of the man who used it as a haven from the rest of the clan. As she stripped down and crawled into the bed, she noticed how cold it was without him and lamented not taking the invitation he'd offered when he was there.

And when he returns?

Well, to be sure, she needed to ponder that question, but she was simply too tired to do so now. She slipped into sleep. Marcus's scent teased her senses and took her to a dream-filled world where he was there beside her and nothing else mattered.

Helen stayed out of the kitchens the next day. The hours crept by as she waited for the Head of House to exact her retaliation. It would come—Helen was sure of that—but time kept ticking away and snow started to fall around noon. There was a hustle again now; supper had to be a rushed affair so the benches might be rearranged for the court Shamus MacPherson held each month.

It was a time for disputes to be settled and business agreed upon. Anyone might step forward to have their case heard. Shamus had long ago begun allowing his sons to sit on the high ground with him during such courts. Ailis had duly taken a position as well, so that any issue considered to be a woman's matter might be judged by a female.

The court was held on the full moon. Marcus rode back into the yard just before sunset. Helen felt his arrival as much as she witnessed it. He came up the steps into the hall as she was working to clear away the remains of supper. He paused, making eye contact with her. She caught a hint of a smile curving his lips and felt a shiver go down her spine. She knew the look on his face: it was pure promise.

"Marcus!" Shamus called from the high ground. "Ye've just enough time to clean up before court."

Marcus turned his attention to his father, reaching up to tug on the corner of his bonnet before disappearing down the passageway toward the bathhouse.

"Well then."

Helen turned to find Duana standing near her. The Head of House had clearly decided the moment of her revenge was at hand. "Are ye going to stand here while yer husband goes to bathe?" Duana was enjoying putting Helen's declaration to the test. "After ye claimed to be his wife and all? Of course, none of us has seen a soiled sheet flying from the window."

There was a round of snickers from the other women. "I did nae see one."

"Nor I."

"Heard there was no consummation from me cousin on McTavish land."

Duana narrowed her eyes and snapped her fingers. "And where have ye been?" she called out to Katherine. "Isn't it just like the English to think they've the right to sleep the day away while still filling their bellies?"

"Katherine was under my direction today." Helen stepped between Duana and the English girl.

The Head of House didn't back down. "I see. So ye are still Marcus's wife?"

Helen nodded firmly. Duana extended her arm toward the bathhouse. "Then ye'd best get to scrubbing his back."

"I shall." The words were out of Helen's mouth before she had really thought them through. Duana smiled, knowing full well she was daring Helen to prove herself or be known as a liar. Helen straightened her spine because the one who would truly suffer would be Katherine. The Head of House would claim the English girl back with a snap of her fingers if Helen refused to take up her task. For the first time, she found a sense of satisfaction in knowing everyone was watching her.

❧

"I wondered if Duana would send ye down to tend me." Marcus reclined in a tub, his back to the door. He poured a mug full of water over his head.

"I am yer wife."

"Are ye?" He grasped the sides of the tub and stood. Her breath caught in her chest as the firelight shimmered off the water running down his bare form. Every inch of him was hard and cut, and he made sure she saw all of it, lifting his leg and climbing out of the tub before he very deliberately turned to face her.

Helen gasped at the look on his face.

"Aye, I'm right furious with ye and no mistake."

This was a side of him she knew how to deal with. "I see yer father has sent ye word."

"He did," Marcus confirmed.

Helen went past him, intent on getting a length of linen from where it rested on a warming rack. Marcus reached out and grasped her arm, pulling her around and pushing her back against the wall.

"Stop trying to intimidate me." She flattened her hands on his chest and then regretted it because he felt so much better than her recollections.

"Ye gave me yer word, Helen," he said, refusing to move.

"And I did no' break it," she insisted.

"What do ye call going to me father?" he demanded, framing her face with his hands when she looked away.

"As if I'd expect ye to understand." She curled her

fingers into talons and felt her nails sink into his flesh. "Get off me."

"Understand?" he rasped, so close his breath teased her lips. "'Tis a simple matter. Ye gave yer word to be here when I returned, and ye tried to place me father between us." He pressed all the way against her, so that she felt every inch of his body. "Here is something for ye to understand, Helen. There will be no one between ye and me."

He angled his head and pressed his mouth against hers. Was it a kiss? She wasn't really sure. His lips connected with hers, pressing them apart so he could thrust his tongue into her mouth. It was a claiming, a declaration of intent, and she fought against it.

But it was Marcus who decided to release her. He slapped his hands on either side of the wall next to her head and pushed away from her with a snarl. "Ye are driving me to insanity, woman."

"Ye?" She went after him and cupped his shoulder. He spun around, shocked to have her chasing after him. "Ye said ye were no' going to take what I do nae offer, and here ye are pushing me against a wall because we've disagreed."

"It's bloody more than a disagreement." He grabbed his shirt and put it on. For a moment, the fabric interrupted their conversation. With a snap and tug, he pulled the creamy linen over his head, which drew her attention to the collar.

"What are ye doing wearing that shirt?"

It took him a moment to understand her change in topic. He worked the buttons on one cuff and then the other as he contemplated her.

"Ye made it for me." He closed his eyes and drew in a deep breath, clearly fighting for patience.

The pink posies she'd diligently embroidered on the collar showed up even in the meager light of the bathhouse.

"Well, I certainly never thought ye'd wear it in public."

That comment earned her a half grin. "Did ye nae, Helen?" He reached up and touched one of the pink embellishments. "Ye were daring me to put it on. Spitting in the eye of what ye were told was yer place. Well, lass, I will rise to yer challenges every time. I promise ye."

Damned if his declaration didn't make her tingle again. He had a way of making what everyone else thought was the sin of stubbornness into something admirable, of making her into someone to be admired.

The posies suddenly made her feel guilty. "But during...yer father's court?"

He started to button it up the chest. "Aye."

That one firm word sent her sagging against the wall. He came toward her, this time his pace firm and solid but not threatening. He flattened his hands on either side of her head as their gazes met.

"I adore that facet of yer spirit," he said softly. "Yer need to face me down and test me."

This time, when he kissed her, it was sweet and seeking. An invitation to join him in a moment of intimacy. She didn't resist. No, she slid her hand into the open collar of the shirt and enjoyed the feeling of his skin beneath her fingertips as she opened her mouth and teased his lower lip with the tip of her tongue.

His chest rumbled, the sound deep and male. It struck some chord within her, making her pull him toward her as need became a living force inside her.

But he pulled back. "Nay. We've no' the time just now."

His cock was hard against her belly, and she suddenly felt so very unbalanced. He liked when she kissed him back, and that idea led to another one that scorched her cheeks but made her confidence swell. She shifted and slid her hand beneath his shirt, then up his thigh until she had his organ grasped in her hand.

"Sweet Christ," he gasped as he leaned on his hands.

His face drew tight, his jaw clenching. She recalled feeling just the same while he'd driven her to ecstasy. Satisfaction flooded her as she stroked his length and heard him draw in a ragged breath. This was what she craved: proof that she wasn't just his for the taking.

He was hers, too.

And she was going to make sure he knew it. She slid down the wall until his member was at face level.

"Helen, ye should nae do that..." His voice was rough and strained, delighting her completely.

She cast a quick look up to see his hands still braced on the wall, his fingers curled into talons as she worked her hands up and down his length, even cupping the sacs that hung beneath his member.

"What did ye tell me ye were doing?" she asked. "Oh yes, proving yerself to me. Well now, Marcus MacPherson, ye just told me how much ye enjoy the facet of me personality that makes me spit in the eye of what me place is said to be."

He drew in a hissing breath through gritted teeth.

Helen lowered her attention to his staff, opening her lips and closing them around the head of it. She felt him jerk, satisfaction flooding her at the proof she could reduce him to that same level of surrender.

He cursed.

It was low and deep, and pleased her greatly. It also encouraged her. Helen opened her mouth wide, taking more of his length inside before applying her tongue to the underside of the head. She heard his fingernails scraping the stone wall and used her hands on the portion of his staff that wouldn't fit in her mouth.

"Lass..." he forced out. "Ye've got to stop..."

Helen doubled her efforts. Moving her hands faster, taking him deeper and closing her lips tightly around him. His cock was harder now, and he was thrusting it toward her with little jerking motions of his hips, sounds of male delight escaping his lips.

She'd been the same way.

It wasn't vengeance—it was proving that she really was able to stand up to him in all things. Perhaps she was on her knees, but she was proving her point. She felt him tense, and then his seed was spurting into her mouth. She took it all, sucking him through the moment. He shuddered, a harsh groan filling the stone-walled chamber. She sat back, rubbing his thighs with her hands as she felt the tremors running down them.

So strong, and yet vulnerable to her touch.

"Come here, woman."

He reached down and hooked her upper arms, pulling her to her feet. A moment later, he was rucking up the fabric of her skirt with one hand while he threaded his left hand into her hair and angled her head up so their eyes met.

"Someone…could walk in on us." She meant it as a warning, but her voice was husky with desire.

He found her thigh and grasped it, making her breath catch. In his eyes, she watched the ebbing satisfaction give way to determination.

"Ye should know very well I'll not let that sort of challenge go unanswered," he promised her wickedly.

Her insides twisted with anticipation while her clitoris throbbed insistently. He slid his hand along her thigh, sending ripples of pleasure across the surface of her skin. She felt gooseflesh rise up in response to his intimate touch. All she wanted to do was open her thighs so he could touch her throbbing sex and give her the same ecstasy that had haunted her dreams.

Someone pounded on the door. "Yer father is calling for ye!"

"Fuck." Marcus opened his eyes and locked gazes with her. A promise glittered in them, one in which her body was very interested. His hand had gone still, his grip tightening just a bit as he fought the urge to release her.

He did—with a snarl and another round of profanity. Helen ended up giggling as her skirt fell back down to cover her legs. Marcus turned to eye her.

"Father Matthew Peter is going to have something to say about yer language."

Marcus moved back toward her and tapped the open collar of his shirt. "I wonder what he'll think of the fine shirt ye made me while contemplating yer penitence?"

Helen didn't fold under his veiled threat. "Likely

insist that I need more lessons in humility. Knowing the good Father, I would expect to spend hours and hours toiling upon the labors he sets me to." Helen let out a sigh. "I'd no' get to bed until very, very late, if at all."

Marcus had been grinning, enjoying teasing her, but his lips set into a hard line as she finished.

"As I'm thinking on it"—he was unbuttoning the cuffs—"I've decided to keep this shirt for our chamber. It's simply too dear to me heart to share."

❧

"Who are ye?"

Robert Gunn raised his head and looked at the retainer who had stepped into his path. The man was no coward, which pleased him. There was a moment of indecision as the man considered him before he nodded and grinned.

"Chief." He reached up to tug on the corner of his cap.

There were other Gunn clansmen sitting at the tables in the hall. It was a small one, because as chief, Robert only commanded one of the branches of the Gunn clan. But the single tower was sweeter-looking than all of Stirling Castle. It was his home.

"Ye all look fat and bored," he declared. "Who wants to join me on a venture to bring us gain?"

The men contemplated him before they began to grin. Hands went into the air, confirming his hold on their loyalty. Robert accepted a mug of ale as his clansmen began to toast his return. He enjoyed the cool slide of the beverage across his tongue and grinned as a buxom lass leaned over to place a bowl of stew in front of him, allowing him a good, long look down her cleavage.

Home.

He didn't bother to think about what needed doing at sunrise. Everything in life had a price. There was little point in taking on the burden of guilt over making hard choices. A man did what he had to do. Life was a matter of winners and losers, and he was going to claim victory. Now that he had his men, he could make good on his word to the Earl of Morton.

Five

THE MONTHLY COURT WAS DRAWING TO A CLOSE. Marcus felt as though it had drawn on for an eternity, but there were fewer cases than normal. The last of the MacPherson clansmen had their say before his father passed judgment. Marcus had never struggled so hard to maintain his focus, nor had his damned cock ever been so hard within an hour of losing his load.

He ground his teeth in frustration, trying to rein in his thoughts and keep his attention on the men in front of them seeking justice.

At least there were signs of the court drawing to a close. At the far end of the hall, people were starting to lose their serious expressions in anticipation of mead being served and the music beginning. But Katherine stepped forward, lowering herself before Shamus.

The English girl drew everyone's attention. However, she proved her worth by standing straight and still under the scrutiny. Marcus realized she was still wearing the rags of Helen's clothing that she'd escaped in.

"Do ye have a matter to bring to me attention, Mistress Katherine?" Shamus asked.

"If I am allowed," she answered strongly and clearly.

There were curious looks sent her way, as well as a few nods of appreciation for her boldness, at least from the men. Marcus considered the way the women shifted back into the shadows.

"As me son Marcus's *sister*"—Shamus stressed the last word—"ye do have the right to be heard if ye feel someone has transgressed against ye."

There was a rise of hushed comments from the back of the hall.

"Not against me," Katherine explained. "Yet I witnessed such an act."

The hall grew quiet as people moved in closer to hear the case. Shamus made a motion with his hand. "Let's hear it, lass."

"Duana struck Mistress Helen across the face. Many saw it, and you could see the mark it left if Mistress Helen was not wearing a partlet."

Marcus felt his temper straining to break free. He was out of his chair and beside Helen before she realized what Katherine had said in front of all. He moved the collar of her partlet aside, revealing the dark bruise.

"Duana," he rasped out. "Present yerself."

The crowd parted as the Head of House came forward. She lowered herself before her laird.

"Helen," Shamus called over his shoulder since she was seated on the high ground beside Ailis.

Helen stood and joined Katherine. She lowered herself as well, and Duana lifted her chin confidently.

"Now," Shamus began, "what manner of quarrel moved ye to strike me daughter-by-marriage?"

Duana opened her hands wide. "There has been

talk of forced vows, but no proof of a wedding celebration," she said clearly and loudly to the approval of many. "I agree full well that Helen did what any decent soul would under the circumstances, but that does nae grant her the right to interfere in the way I run the kitchens. Not when the McTavishes are telling one and all that they heard the union was unconsummated, and there has been no sheet flown nor has her kin been here to agree to contracts. She broke my rod, and I put her back in her place."

There was a rumble of agreement from those watching. Shamus allowed it to die down before switching his attention to Helen. "Broke her rod, did ye?"

"Indeed."

Shamus looked at Katherine. "Why do ye think Helen broke Mistress Duana's rod?"

"Ye ask an English bastard girl?" Duana demanded. "I have served in this house for thirty years."

"Something we are grateful for." Shamus lifted a finger to keep her from saying anything further. "Yet when it comes to this matter of me son's vows, it is a complicated one, as are all the dealings with court and the king's regent. What should be simple is nae, which is why I am ever glad I was born in the Highlands."

Duana nodded, her lips pressed into an expression of distaste.

"Answer the question, Mistress Katherine," Shamus repeated.

"Me," she replied simply.

There was a round of comments from those watching. Marcus felt his temper straining, but his father held up his hand. The hall was suddenly so quiet, they heard the thump of the hound's tail as he wagged it next to Shamus's feet.

"As I said, I am ever grateful to have been born in the Highlands," Shamus said. "Decency is something we do nae just talk about. Helen will be respected for the service she did me son Marcus, yer War Chief."

There was a grudging round of nods from those listening.

"The Earl of Morton is the regent of Scotland, and we are Scots," Shamus continued. "It was his wish that Katherine Carew become a member of me family. As a loyal Scot, I will accept his will. She is Marcus's sister and, thereby, me daughter."

Shamus spoke clearly and slowly. Men reached up and tugged on the corners of their caps in response as the women lowered themselves. Duana lowered herself very quickly before she turned and retreated.

"Now, some music!" Shamus proclaimed. "This court is finished. Marcus, good night to ye and yer bride. Off to bed with ye both now."

≈

Everyone was staring at her. Helen felt as if daggers were being thrown at her back.

Someone began to play at the rear of the hall. Whoever it was, they were joined in short order as people started to talk. It was a hushed, frantic sort of conversation at first, clearly about what had just transpired.

"Helen." Marcus waited only a moment for his father's word to be heeded before he stood and called out to her. It stilled the budding conversations as those behind them took in his actions.

"Shall we retire?"

Marcus was still on the high ground and he'd used a voice every MacPherson knew. It was controlled and tight and carried to the back of the hall. He stood there with his hand out, palm facing up. It was Helen's place to be meek, the position of the wife to follow her husband. He risked a great deal standing there and making an invitation to her.

The truth burst on her as she realized it was a gift, and she had earned it. He was making sure his men knew he trusted her. She placed her hand in his and heard the whispers behind them. She didn't turn to look because she was too captivated by the way Marcus's eyes were lit.

❧

Katherine Carew watched Marcus and Helen leave. There was music now and laughter as conversation flowed. Duana had withdrawn, and many of her maids with her. That left Katherine keeping company with the men.

Not that she minded. She was accustomed to not being accepted. Her mother had been a mistress, scorned by the legitimate wife of the house. Katherine wasn't naive enough to question why that was.

Coin.

Her father was a rich man, and his wife liked keeping that coin in their coffers. So she'd made sure Katherine knew she was owed nothing, not even protection, which was how she'd landed in Scotland.

Still, it was a great adventure.

So much better than reading tales in musty old

books. She caught several of the maids glaring at her and sent them a look straight back. Let them scorn her; she was used to such. For certain, she would get a great deal more sleep now that she did not have to work in the kitchens. She looked around and found several boys her age grappling with each other. They looked up when she came closer.

"What do ye want?" one questioned.

"To learn how to do that," Katherine answered. "That part when you broke his hold on you—how do you do it?"

The boy looked confused. "Ye're a lass."

"I'm very clever, though," Katherine said. "Unless… hmmm… Perhaps you are not a good enough teacher."

"I can teach anyone how to do it, even a lass," the boy informed her with budding pride.

Katherine lowered herself and smiled at him. "I am ready to be instructed."

Truly, she was. It looked so much more fun than dancing or making her stitches perfect on linen strips so she might someday impress a would-be suitor with her skills. Learning how to keep from being abducted—now there was a skill she wished she'd learned before being taken from England.

Then again, Scotland seemed a much better place. No one in England would call her *sister* or teach her how to wrestle. Yes, she was growing to like Scotland very much indeed.

In fact, there was no reason ever to go back to England.

"I will have words with Duana." Marcus spoke the moment the chamber door was closed.

"There truly is no need."

He put his sword down and sent Helen a harsh look.

"I dismissed her opinion of me long ago," she explained before Marcus was able to argue. "The only reason I challenged her was because—"

"It was the bloody right thing to do," Marcus finished for her.

"And so I did it. It is finished." She moved over to where her comb was and started to pull the braid out of her hair. Marcus was watching her again, and she looked toward him.

"Yer comb is here," he noted.

"Yes. Duana had put Katherine in one of the novice cells, so I gave her my chamber and came here."

She felt uncertain as she explained because she hadn't thought about it much. He started to smile but stopped.

"I'm still angry ye went to me father," Marcus informed her tersely. "Ye gave me yer word, Helen, and ye went to the only person with whom I could no' argue."

Helen held her chin steady. She'd known full well what she was doing and wouldn't shirk from the reprimand. Marcus muttered in Gaelic, frustration edging his words.

"And ye are no' sorry, is that it?" he asked.

"A fact ye should thank me for." Helen finally broke her silence. "Do ye know what Duana said to me? Told me I was nothing, and ye'd put me aside without a thought once spring comes."

"I've never said anything of the sort," Marcus growled. "For Christ's sake, woman, I rode all the way to court after ye."

Her eyes widened and his narrowed as he realized what he'd said.

"Aye," Marcus said in a tired voice. "I did go after ye."

The idea warmed her heart.

Marcus suddenly tilted his head to one side, his gaze sharpening. "Yet ye stood up to Duana, even broke her rod. Why now, Helen?"

Helen shifted, but she realized she was taking the coward's way out and he'd only discover the facts of the matter anyway. "Ye should know when to leave well enough alone."

He slowly grinned, and there was nothing pleasant about it. The expression was pure intent. "What did ye say to Duana?"

"I told her I was yer wife."

Marcus considered her for a long moment. "I see. That would be when she told ye I would abandon ye come spring, and then ye went to me father."

"Every person in the kitchens agreed with her," Helen defended herself. "And it is no' a matter of me caring so much for what they think of me. Yer clan expects ye to marry a bride who brings the MacPhersons something."

He was smiling now, and it was one of victory. But what drew her attention to him even more was the way his eyes were sparkling. He was pleased, and she liked the look of it a great deal.

"Ye're trying to protect me," he said. "Keep me from doing something that will no' sit well with the clan."

Helen lifted one shoulder in a half shrug as she removed the partlet she'd worn to keep her neck warm during the court. "Is that so wrong?"

He shrugged out of his sword belt and placed it on the table. "It is very right, even if I do nae care for how ye've gone about it."

"As if I have many ways at me disposal."

Marcus chuckled as he began to unbutton his doublet. "I enjoy knowing ye want to shelter me, lass."

He let the doublet slide down his arms and tossed it over a chair. Her heart was accelerating now. Excitement teased her in all the spots that seemed to come alive when he was close enough to touch. Her lips tingled, begging for his kiss, while her breasts felt smashed inside her bodice, freedom the only solution.

"I'd do the same for a litter of puppies in the stable," she offered as a means of shielding her weak response to him.

"In that case…" His kilt hit the floor and he walked over to the bed, rolling onto it and stretching out on its surface. He'd stopped on his stomach, his head near the foot well. "If I roll over and offer ye me belly, will ye scratch it?"

Her cheeks caught fire, but so did the rest of her. That little nub at the top of her sex was throbbing incessantly now, demanding she take action. Of course, that only brought to mind just how much she enjoyed it when Marcus dealt with her hungers.

"So, ready to be at me mercy again?" Her voice had turned husky, but that seemed to suit the moment. She was going to share more than the bed with him. There was no doubt in her mind of it, but she was not nervous.

No, *excited* was more the appropriate word. She turned and set her comb down. The front of her bodice was held together with lacings. She pulled the knot up from where it was tucked into her cleavage and untied it.

"Allow me, lass…" Marcus was suddenly there. He cupped her shoulders and stroked down to where the swells of her breasts rose above the neckline of her bodice. "I've dreamed of cupping these." He lingered for a moment on her breasts before dipping his finger into the lacing on her bodice. He pulled each crossing free, the front of her dress sagging until it was entirely open.

It felt wonderful to have her breasts free. Somehow, being near him made her feel trapped in her clothing, desperate for freedom. Her sleeves were laced to her bodice, and the whole thing slid down her arms easily.

She tugged at the ties on her waistband while Marcus made good on his desire and cupped her breasts. Her fingers fumbled on the knots as she lost track of what she was doing in favor of leaning back against him so he could better fondle her.

Why had she never noticed how sensitive her breasts were? In his hands, the skin was more sensitive than she'd ever imagined possible, her nipples drawing into tight little points that he leaned over to taste after turning her around.

"Mmm…" Helen wasn't sure she could form words at the moment and didn't particularly care. Not when there was so much bliss to enjoy. Marcus licked one little point and then gave its twin the same attention.

"Sweet." He pulled his head up and ripped at the

laces on her waistband. He reached right in and opened her hip roll too, so the whole jumble just slid down her legs. She stepped out of the puddle of her skirts and he scooped her off her feet.

"Not yet," Helen said when he tried to follow her down onto the bed. She heard him groan as she rolled away from him and came up on her knees in the middle of the bed. "There was a time when I dreamed of me wedding night…"

He'd paused on the edge of the bed, a magnificent creature covered in creamy skin carved with hard muscles. The only soft spot on him was the restraint he employed to remain where he was.

"And what exactly did ye dream of, Helen?"

She offered him a brazen look. "I was nude." The bed shook as he came up onto it. Her breath caught as he knelt in front of her, his body close enough for her to feel the heat from his skin teasing hers.

"Is that a fact?" he inquired softly.

"As bare as a fae creature on May Day," she confirmed. "I never confessed that, though."

"A rather wise idea." He reached out and opened the tie that held the neckline of her chemise closed. "But where did ye hear about wedding nights?"

There was a touch of jealousy in his tone, and she liked it full well. "May Day festival, of course." She reached out and trailed her fingers along the open patch of skin his unbuttoned shirt offered her. Once again she shivered, the contact between their skin stunning her.

He watched her as she struggled to collect her composure. "Where do ye suppose I heard about Frenching?"

His eyes narrowed as her words hit him. He hadn't

expected her to say anything so brazen, and she liked seeing the impact.

"Enjoy shocking me, do ye?"

She offered him a shrug that sent the edges of her chemise over the curves of her shoulders. She clasped her arms around herself to keep the fabric in place. "Shouldn't I?" She meant it to be a brazen comment, but instead her voice was high and thin, betraying how nervous she truly was.

"I suppose ye think ye've been dancing to my tune so long that it's my time to be yer fool."

She laughed. A single sound of amusement that helped her cling to the last morsels of her composure. "As if ye could ever be anyone's fool."

"That does no' mean I am a beast." He reached up and grasped his shirt, pulling it over his shoulders in a hard motion that made the fabric snap. He tossed it aside but waited for her response.

"No," she whispered. "Ye are no' a beast. At least no' at the moment."

Which was a gift. She recognized it and felt it warming her heart. He certainly didn't have to cater to her delicate feelings. Yet he was, watching her as the fire began to die down, lowering the light in the chamber. The darkness suited her well, and she opened her arms so the chemise slithered down her body and pooled around her hips.

"Ye are stunning, lass." His voice was thick with desire. She recognized it from the times she'd heard the whispered liaisons of couples hiding in the darkened corners of the kitchens while the rest of the clan enjoyed the evening revels.

It was different, though, far more personal and intimate. She realized he was still waiting, so she lifted her hand and offered it to him. Ridiculous? Perhaps, since her breasts were bare and only a single layer of linen guarded her sex.

Satisfaction lit his eyes, his expression showing his growing anticipation. He took her hand and raised it up to his mouth for a soft kiss. She shivered, the contact fanning the flames that seemed to be licking at her insides.

A moment later, she was clasped against him. He'd slid a hard arm around her waist and pulled her to him. She gasped, and he captured that little breathless sound with his lips as he kissed her. There was strength in his kiss, the sort that made her belly twist. Not that she understood why she craved him or had any inclination to ponder it.

No, thinking was becoming impossible. Impulses were rising up from somewhere inside her, like vapors through the floorboards. Soon, there was nothing to see but what had risen up to encompass them.

She reached for him, smoothing her hands along his chest and purring with delight at the way he felt. So hard, and she seemed to be soft in comparison. Her breasts pressed in against his chest as he teased her lower lip with the tip of his tongue, running it along skin that suddenly felt delicate and alive with sensation. He thrust his tongue deep into her mouth, making her passage ache for the same.

Blunt and brazen but so very true.

She wanted to be beneath him, and Marcus didn't disappoint her. The bed ropes groaned as he rolled her onto the surface of the bed. He cupped her breasts, cradling them in his large hands.

"Damn me, but I've wanted to do this for a very long time."

He was looking at her breasts in his hands, his eyes bright with male satisfaction. There was a note of possessiveness in his voice that should have made her angry. Instead, she enjoyed it.

In some deep part of herself, she had hidden all her cravings for things she had been schooled to think of as forbidden and sinful. Like cradling him between her open thighs.

So very forbidden, unless he was her husband, and even then, enjoying it was frowned upon.

Well, she did enjoy it. Right then, he felt perfect, and she closed her legs around him, holding him.

But it wasn't perfect, not just yet. Marcus raised his attention to her face, locking gazes with her as his cock lay across the open folds of her sex. She was wet and needy, her passage aching. He knew it; she could see the understanding in his eyes. Only it was more. It was a moment in which they shared the same cravings for each other.

He reached down, shifting off to the side so he could rub her throbbing little bud once more. The thing was almost unbearably sensitive.

"Get on with it," she ordered in a husky voice she barely recognized.

Marcus didn't bend to her will. He teased her little pearl, keeping her in place when she tried to wiggle out from under him.

"No' just yet. I'll hurt ye."

"It can nae be all that bad," she rasped out. "I'm no' weak."

His fingers stilled as his jaw tightened. She watched the need dance in his eyes as his nostrils flared. "No, ye are not."

It was a compliment, and given in his rough voice, it struck her as more honest than many a flowery phrase. "So, get…on…with it."

His lips curled into a wolfish grin. "Vixen." He rolled back onto her fully.

His weight pleased her, sending a flash of enjoyment through her. His wider frame kept her spread, the folds of her sex opening wide.

"My vixen." The head of his cock nestled into the open center of her body.

She realized exactly why she was wet. It was so his member could slide into her. The slickness that seemed to seep from her whenever he touched her was a welcome from her core.

"Oh Christ," he grunted as he seemed to sink in farther than he intended.

She didn't give him the chance to withdraw, but lifted her hips so he continued forward, impaling her on his staff.

Pain ripped through her. It was like a bolt of lightning, unannounced, that blinded her for a moment while the thunder came behind it.

"Ye should have stayed still," he admonished her.

Helen opened her eyes, not really sure when she'd closed them. The look on his face was savage, held back only by sheer will. "I am a vixen. Do nae ever expect me to lie still beneath ye."

He chuckled, the sound more warning than anything else. "Ye are that, lass, and ye are mine."

He'd pulled out of her and pressed back in as he spoke, his voice becoming strained when he was once more sheathed to the hilt. She let her eyes slip shut once more so she could focus on the intensity of having him inside her.

It was a whole new level of pleasure that she was eager to experience. Her heart was accelerating, her breathing increasing to keep pace. His was as well, and she reached for him, digging her fingers into his shoulders as she lifted her hips to welcome every downward plunge of his cock.

The pleasure was growing, increasing with their motions. She felt as though something was going to burst inside her, and just possibly, her heart might do so as well.

It didn't matter. The only thing that held any meaning was moving with him. Feeling him drive deep into her, filling her, and satisfying the need that was ripping up her insides. There was nothing but him and her cravings, which he fulfilled. When it all broke, she arched up, digging her fingernails into his skin and crying out. Pleasure burned through her in a single white-hot flare that taught her the true meaning of the word *rapture*.

She heard him reach that same zenith, felt him drive into her with hard determination that finished off her own moment of ecstasy. A deep connection seemed to complete everything as he spilled his seed inside her, holding her beneath him as she clasped him to her with her thighs.

Intimate.

She hadn't really understood that word before. She did now, and she happily let the moment wash over her, pushing her into unconsciousness. If she never woke up, she'd die content.

&

"It's going to start snowing. Hard."

Robert Gunn heard his man and nodded. His response didn't please his man any. "That's what we're waiting for," he explained. "The MacPhersons will no' invite us inside their castle if it is no' a matter of life and death, and none of us appear to be unsuited to our surroundings."

There was a chuckle from his men. Robert hunkered down and pulled out a flask of whisky. He sipped at it while his men huddled out of the wind. For himself, he rather enjoyed the bite of the frost. It was a damned fine thing to feel the wind on his neck, even if it was laced with ice.

&

For all her doubts about returning to the world of the living, Helen opened her eyes and found herself staring at the canopy above the bed. It was a luxury, there to keep the bedding clean and help the occupants stay warm with the aid of the curtains that hung at the large corner posts.

Marcus lifted his hand, the glow from the fire shining off his flask as he offered it to her. Helen giggled.

He came into view, propping himself up on one elbow so he could look down into her face, one of his eyebrows raised in question. Helen rolled up to sitting and took the flask. She drew off a long sip of the whisky, feeling it burn a path across her tongue and down her throat, before she opened her eyes and smiled at him while snickering some more.

"Who would have known that all I had to do was offer ye me flask to get ye to stop spitting at me." He took it back and scooted up to lean against the pillows stacked next to the headboard. He started to lift the flask to his lips, but paused. "No, that's no' it. Tell me what amuses ye, woman."

He was as keen as always. She reached for the flask, but he held it up and raised that eyebrow once more.

"I was just thinking," she offered as she felt the chill of the night air for the first time. Her chemise was hanging over the foot rail where it had been tossed. She plucked it up and put it on.

"Just thinking…what, Helen?"

He looked disappointed as the linen fabric covered her.

"That tomorrow, when yer gilly finds yer flask needs refilling, the man will be sure that we emptied it before going to…bed."

Marcus slowly smiled and chuckled as he extended his arm so she could reach the flask. "I can nae be having that."

Helen lowered the flask and offered him a flutter of her eyelashes. "Of course no'." She burst into giggles again.

Marcus took the flask away as she rolled back and laughed at the canopy. The bed rocked, and the ropes supporting the mattress groaned. She discovered why a moment later when Marcus landed on top of her.

She sucked in her breath as he pinned her down, holding enough of his body weight on his elbows to keep her from being crushed.

"I do nae think ye are being very respectful... Wife," he growled playfully. "I am going to have to take ye in hand."

Helen reached down and grasped his member. His face tightened, his lips curling back from his teeth as he arched back to give her more access. "If ye have any illusions as to what manner of wife I will be to ye, Marcus, I advise ye to think long and hard on the matter. For when that door is closed, I'll no' be meek."

He rolled onto his back as she followed him, stroking his hardening cock.

"Yer ideas have me captivated." He let out a moan.

She liked hearing how she affected him. It unleashed a boldness in her that seemed to have no bounds and absolutely no shame. Helen leaned forward and licked the spot on the underside of his cock head that seemed to be as sensitive as her nub. His hands curled into talons, clawing at the sheet while she trailed her tongue through the slit on the top of his member. There was a drop of salty fluid there, and he moaned again, long and deep.

"There are many men who think a wife should lie on her back while he labors over her."

Marcus opened his eyes and sent her a wicked look. A moment later, the bed rocked as he flipped and turned and pinned her beneath him. He had a knee pressed between her thighs, opening them so he could reach down and tease her with his fingertips.

"Ye might enjoy it," he rasped as he rubbed her.

When she shifted, he caught her wrists and raised them above her head, pressing them to the bed and holding them there as he nuzzled against her neck. It was a dramatic shift that ripped away any illusion she might have of him being docile. He was choosing to be kind to her and court her sweetly.

"Marcus MacPherson," she muttered softly, "ye are by far the most unlikely man I ever thought would take the time to woo."

He lifted his head but held her wrists down. The only light came from the fire that had reduced itself to a bed of glowing red coals. The ruby light bathed his features, allowing her to glimpse the unguarded expression on his face. She had the feeling that very few souls alive had seen this side of him.

"Ye think I like the idea of being used any more than ye do?"

"No," she answered.

He contemplated her for a long moment before he shifted his hands and flattened them against the bed to lever himself up and off her. She felt his withdrawal keenly, reality rushing back in to remind her she did not know him at all.

And trust? The only certainty she had was in his nature to devote himself to his duty. She sat up so her chemise fluttered down to cover her. The silence was nearly deafening, and she realized he was withdrawing from her, bound by her own insistence that her body was her only remaining possession.

So she went to him, not really understanding what she was doing, only that she was so tired of being alone and couldn't bear to inflict the same on another person. He'd ended up leaning on the stack of pillows, and she crawled right up onto his lap. He clasped her to him, smoothing his hands along her sides and down to cup her hips. It seemed so natural to open her thighs and let his member slide up into her body. There was a twinge of discomfort as he stretched her once more, but it was worth it to be united with him again.

"Jesus...Helen..." He was muttering against her neck, kissing her skin and sending ripples of delight down her body. She rose and fell as he guided her with his hands, teaching her the motion.

The pleasure and need built slowly this time, coming from deeper inside her. The pace was hers to control; her cravings were hers to satisfy. Confidence filled her as she arched back. For some reason, she enjoyed with an insane intensity the grip he had on her hips. It was demanding, and yet she flourished with the knowledge that he was intent on having her.

Right, wrong, none of that mattered. There was only room in her mind for the growing need to feed their appetites. The bed ropes protested, the canopy swaying as she increased her pace and he lifted up off the bed to meet every one of her downward plunges. He was penetrating deeper, all the way to her core. She felt herself nearing that moment of explosion, and when it happened, she would have sworn her passage gripped him, trying to milk his member.

He gasped at her, thrusting up into her body as his seed began to spew inside her. It was hot and triggered a second wave of delight that literally stole her breath. She didn't much care, collapsing onto the body of her lover, somewhat aware of him turning her so they ended up sprawled on the surface of the bed, their rasping breaths filling the chamber.

∽

"Good morning!"

Bhaic MacPherson pushed the door open as Marcus snarled and landed on his feet next to the bed. Helen grabbed the bed clothing while Bhaic smirked at his brother.

"Still sleeping, Marcus?" Bhaic asked. "Whatever could keep ye in bed?"

"Ye're a dead man," Marcus declared before he set off after his sibling. They cleared the outer chamber and disappeared while Helen was still blinking away the last of slumber's hold.

"Here now." Ailis was suddenly there with a chemise in hand. "Best get something on," her friend said. "Half the clan is set to descend here and extract their share of amusement."

Helen sat up and then stopped as pain went through her passage.

"Aye." Ailis came closer and dropped the chemise over Helen's head. "Takes ye by surprise, does it no'?"

Helen found the sleeves and pushed her hands into them. Senga was there as well, holding out Helen's hip roll. Helen had barely reached for it when there was another loud entrance into the room.

"Morning, mistress!"

"Fine day to ye!"

Helen found herself flat against the wall of the bedchamber with Ailis shielding her while Finley and Skene ripped the bedding aside to get at the sheet.

They hooted in victory and pulled it off the bed before nearly running across the chamber.

"What are ye doing?" Helen demanded.

Finley stopped near the door. "Well now, mistress, it's fixing to snow, so we're going to hang this in the hall."

Helen felt the blood drain from her face. Finley chuckled at her response before he disappeared down the passageway.

"I am suddenly no' very hungry."

❧

"Ye're looking for me."

Helen jumped, but Marcus anticipated her motions. He'd come up behind her and captured her startled body against his as he made a soft sound next to her ear.

"Admit it," he insisted as he placed a kiss on the side of her neck.

"Just because I am looking out of a window does no' mean—"

He opened his lips and gently bit the skin on the side of her neck. She shivered, her knees going weak. Her body seemed to have no interest in putting up a good front. No, her flesh was far more inclined to melt into his embrace.

"Ye are looking out to the training yard." He smoothed his hands along her arms without giving her enough space to disengage from the embrace. "For me."

She had been, and he'd noticed the details that condemned her, as he so often did. Part of her was excited by the way he noticed things about her. "Perhaps I was making sure I could avoid ye."

Her voice lacked any sharp edges. Instead, it came across as a teasing challenge that earned her a soft chuckle from Marcus. He'd buried his face in her hair, inhaling deeply.

"I like the way ye smell, Helen." He shifted closer, allowing her to feel just how true his words were.

"I do nae use any oils." She wasn't sure why she said anything, just that she was suddenly shy and uncertain.

"Ye do nae need any." He nuzzled against her neck again, but one of his hands ventured lower. "Especially here."

He'd covered her mons. The fabric of her skirts suddenly felt too thin.

"What are ye about?" she asked. "Ye never leave the training yard this time of day."

He chuckled again. "And ye know that?" He made a low sound of approval. "We're better suited to each other than either of us knows."

"Ye're the one who lined yer men up in front of me after your father told ye to take me home." She wasn't sure why she spoke, hadn't really realized how much it bothered her. Marcus stiffened behind her. A moment later, he turned her around but stood squarely in her path.

"Ye want to hear me admit I thought ye'd no' have me?"

Helen was distracted by the swelling around one of his eyes. She reached up to touch him, the topic of their conversation completely lost in her concern.

"Bhaic looks worse." He captured her hand and pressed a kiss against the open palm. "Do nae ignore me, Helen. I must ride out, and I would no' have something left unresolved between us."

"Ride out?" She turned her head and looked out the window again. "There is a storm brewing. A heavy one." The sky was turning black with the promise of snow.

"Ye would care?"

She looked back at him with her lower lip rolled in as she worried it. But there was something flickering in his eyes that made her nod. Some need she'd never considered him the sort to feel, and yet it was there. Just like the night before, when she'd glimpsed the man inside him that craved approval just as she did.

"Ye should wait."

He smiled at her request. "I can nae. Me father can see just fine. He'd no' have asked me to venture out if the matter were no' an important one."

She nodded but didn't really agree. Of course, she didn't know his reasoning. She realized that she would have to become accustomed to him not sharing details with her. When it came to his position, she was still very much an outsider.

There was a step in the passageway behind them. Marcus turned his head slightly to catch the sound before shifting to the side and taking her with him. They ended up behind a weapons rack, hidden from anyone who might venture too close.

"And I can nae face me duty without a last taste of ye."

It was an admission he whispered as he pressed her against the wall. He covered her mouth with his, kissing her firmly as she twisted from the overwhelming need gripping her. How and where it had come from, she really didn't know. Somehow, having him near simply gave rise to a riot of sensations that assaulted her reasoning skills until they fell away and let her cravings reign supreme.

She reached for him in a frantic way, the knowledge that he was leaving making her desperate to touch him. He seemed in agreement, kissing her hard as he yanked her skirts up and lifted her knee so he could touch the center of her body. She locked her leg around his waist, making him pull his head up and consider her with an eyebrow raised.

"I was always in the kitchens when everyone else was at the hall," she explained. "What do ye think I saw?"

He offered her a cocky grin before she pulled his kilt up and felt his member against her thigh. He teased her slit for a moment, plunging his finger into her cleft to stroke her bud. She jerked, sharp need feeling as if it were splitting her open. But he didn't feed it just yet. He teased her, not stopping until his fingers were slick with the flow from her body.

"Now ye're ready…" he whispered with satisfaction. He'd threaded his other hand into her hair and tightened it so that she was his captive. They locked gazes, his eyes shining with intent. "Never before ye're hungry for me, Helen. I swear that to ye."

It was a blunt, savage declaration that made her feel more cherished than she ever had. He pulled her close, the head of his cock slipping between the folds of her sex before he eased himself inside her. His jaw was tight with the effort of holding back the urge to impale her. She felt him straining to maintain a slow pace, and decided it didn't suit her at all.

"I didn't want one of yer men"—she dug her fingernails into the skin on his neck—"because they would never have demanded I accept them."

She drew her nails across his skin, watched the way his lips curled back to expose his gritted teeth. His hands tightened on her hips as his eyes glowed with anticipation.

"I did nae have the right to." He plunged up inside her. Time froze as they both absorbed being locked together. It was the purest form of intimacy she'd ever experienced. Her body was stretching around his, gripping his member as she trembled in reaction to being taken. "And now, I will never let ye go."

It was a declaration. One that both delighted and frightened her. The combination was intoxicating, making a mockery of everything she thought she wanted. At that moment, there was only him and the way she craved being his. Marcus didn't disappoint her. He took her, driving the breath from her body as she strained to make it easier for him to drive himself all the way to her core. There was only the way their bodies met and parted and the growing need to move faster, harder, deeper.

He pushed her head against his shoulder to muffle her cries, clenching his jaw to contain his own. When she reached the zenith, she cried out into the linen of his shirt, feeling as if her bones might break as he clasped her against him in those final moments while he found his release.

He leaned on the wall that she was pressed to, both

of them panting. He cupped her jaw, raising her face so that he could look into her eyes. "Mine."

It was the demand she didn't want to admit she craved. She curled her fingers into his shirt, unsure if she wanted to push him away or yank him closer. She let out a snort of frustration.

"Ye make me feel insane, Marcus MacPherson."

Her comment earned her a grin that was every bit as smug and arrogant as she expected from him, and yet it was very personal too. He pulled away from her, allowing her skirts to fall and cover her legs.

She felt the parting keenly, reaching out for him in spite of the fact that she knew he would go, no matter what she said. Helen stopped with her hand inches from his shoulder. "Sorry."

He caught her hand and raised it to his lips. "I have to go and fetch me sister."

"Yer sister?"

Marcus nodded, looking less than pleased with his impending duty. It was a look she recognized well from the day he'd stolen her.

"With Morton intent on making alliances through marriage, me father fears Jocelyn is at risk. I'm to bring her back from where she has been fostered with Laird McLeod so she might be protected."

Helen covered her lips with her hand, Shamus's confession rising from her memory. Marcus shared a look with her.

"Ye know me sister has no love for our sire?" he asked quietly.

Helen nodded. "From yer father's own lips."

Marcus crossed his arms over his chest. He was

staring her down, or at least doing his best to make her give up what she knew. Helen drew herself up. "Ye'll have to ask yer father what he said, no' expect me to carry his secrets. I am no' a gossip, Marcus, and I've no plans to become one. Father Matthew Peter has quite enough to say to me as it is."

Marcus slowly grinned before he backed up and went around the weapons rack. He turned in the passageway and shot her a look full of wicked intent. "He'll likely have something more to say today, since he's waiting in the yard with me men to bless us before we depart."

Her cheeks turned crimson as Marcus winked at her before his expression went serious. "Make yerself some chemises, lass. No one will dare tell ye the fabric is no' yers for the using. And if they do, indulge me and let me know, so I can thrash them."

"Well, that will not happen," she informed him, her hands on her hips. "I do nae need ye to take care of me, Marcus."

He ran his tongue over his lower lip. "Yes, ye do, and yes, I will."

She ended up flushed and breathless as she recalled vividly how it had felt to have him prove himself to her. He pressed his lips into a silent kiss before he turned and left, the longer folds of his kilt swaying behind him.

❧

"Ye should be ashamed," Ailis whispered.

Bhaic flashed her a completely unrepentant grin. He reached under the table and gripped her thigh.

"Marcus looks worse than I do."

"Fighting with yer brother is a sin," Ailis continued.

"Marcus chasing me below floors as bare as a new-born was sinful." Bhaic smirked. "However, now that he's wed, the swine will likely escape Father Matthew Peter's wrath because he wasn't tempting the other lasses in the hall."

"Ye began it."

Bhaic held up a finger. "I disagree, Wife."

Ailis ended up conceding the point. She fluttered her eyelashes, enjoying the moment, even if she had lost the argument. It afforded her a chance to look across the hall.

"Who is that?"

"Chief Gunn," Bhaic supplied. "One of Laird Gunn's men. Another man feeling the bite of Morton's demands. Seems he was no' given leave from court in time to beat the snow home. Mind ye, I believe he only asked for shelter for the good of his horses. The man is from the northern Highlands. I am no' sure this is enough snow to stop him."

Ailis looked at the man in question. He wore a full sheepskin down his back, the wool facing her. Part of it was sewn into a hood that might be raised when the weather turned foul. His men all had similar attire. They were suited to their environment: rough, hardened, and clearing away every morsel of food placed in front of them, because they knew it might be the last they had for some time.

Her baby kicked, drawing her attention to her rounded belly. Bhaic noted her shifting her gaze downward and reached over so she might place his hand over the spot where the babe was moving. His face lit with enjoyment as he felt the motions of his child.

"I adore ye, Ailis Robertson." He uttered the name he'd been raised to curse.

Ailis reached up and stroked his jawline. "And I love ye, Bhaic MacPherson."

❦

"There's something a man does nae see very often."

Robert glanced behind him at Ailis and Bhaic and turned back around with a sniff. "I'd lose me appetite if it wasn't pleasing me so much to eat as much MacPherson food as I can." He reached over and grabbed a round of bread that he shoved into his shirt. "His grandfather would piss on him if he could see him dancing to his enemy's tune."

"Heard it was the Earl of Morton that made them wed."

Robert shrugged. "And so they did, and her belly is swelling. There's no need for him to sit there simpering like a French fop. Better to set the Robertson bitch aside since she's serving her purpose. Ye can be sure I will no' have a wife sitting on the high ground beside me."

His men chuckled. "Aye, a woman's place is beneath a man," one of them said.

Robert nodded. "A real man makes sure they know it."

And a true man made his own fortune. Robert emptied his mug and shoved another round of bread into his shirt before closing his doublet. His men took his lead, making ready for the hard road ahead of them.

"Don't leave at the same time," he cautioned them before he stood and made his way toward the back of the hall where the maids were. Robert smiled at them, seeking out one who would give him the information he needed.

❧

"Ye likely think yerself clever."

Helen looked up as Duana came into the sewing cell. The Head of House was pleased with herself and had clearly snuck away during supper so no one would witness whatever she wanted to say.

"I see ye have wasted no time in taking what ye can," Duana remarked as she looked at the linen Helen was sewing.

"A measure I earned full well in yer kitchen." Helen stood up to face her. "Every quartering day, ye made me stand there with an empty palm while ye paid out the wages, knowing full well I worked more hours than any other."

Duana made a little scoffing sound beneath her breath. "Ye were fed. Since yer father does nae serve this clan, that was yer due."

It wasn't an uncommon belief. That was the reason clansmen were so loyal to their laird. The service they gave ensured that their families were fed and had a place. Her family was the Grants and she hadn't had a husband who was a MacPherson, so every mouthful of bread was something she'd had to earn.

"What do ye want, Duana?" Helen suddenly felt very tired. "Are ye truly no' finished with yer hatred? Ye've had over a year to vent yer spleen on me. No matter how justified ye think yerself, bitterness leads to a poor life."

"So now ye think to preach to me as well?" Duana demanded. "Ye still have many years to live before ye have the experience I have."

Helen quelled the urge to quarrel with the woman. "That is true."

Duana wasn't expecting agreement. She paused, pursing her lips disapprovingly as she decided on her next course of action.

"It is done, Duana." Helen spoke as controlled as she could. "I am wed to Marcus. We shall have to find a way to live in harmony. Or at least in quiet."

The Head of House shook her head. "Are ye sure it's done?"

Helen looked at the woman in confusion. Duana looked behind her before she spoke again. "If ye want to leave, I can arrange an escort for ye."

Helen stared at her in shock, which pleased the Head of House. "It's all arranged. There is a pair of lads down at the stable who will take ye away."

How she would have adored hearing those words once. Was it truly only a few months past?

"Is nae that what ye craved? Escape?" the Head of House continued.

"It was," Helen agreed. "What a bitch ye are to offer me such a thing now. Ye kept me as yer slave and only now offer me freedom because ye will no' see me set above ye."

All effort to be congenial was abandoned as Helen faced off with the woman who had tormented her mercilessly.

"Mind yer tongue," Duana warned her.

"I will no'," Helen hissed back.

Duana's eyes bulged, her lips moving silently like a fresh-caught fish, and then suddenly she dropped to the floor, leaving Helen facing a huge man.

He stood there, pleased with his actions, a bloody sword in his grasp. "I assure ye Helen, ye'll learn to hold yer tongue with me, or I will cut it out of yer mouth."

Six

SKENE DIDN'T CARE FOR BEING LEFT BEHIND. HE HAD no wife, and his mother had died several winters past. He liked to ride out with Marcus because he knew the day was coming when he would have other responsibilities and would have to remain at the castle while the younger lads went out to seek adventure.

He sat in the hall, long after the supper had been cleared away and the conversation had died to hushed whispers. Men had unbelted their kilts and lain down for the night. He heard a quick step on the stone floor and looked up. Young Senga Robertson was hurrying along, her eyes on him. He started to smile until he realized her eyes were wide with horror and there was fresh blood on her hands.

"Come quickly…" She reached out for him, unaware her hands were covered in blood. "Oh please, come very quickly."

Her frantic tone gained plenty of attention. Men who had been doing their best to woo the household maids came out of the shadows as those sleeping awoke and raised their heads. They all instantly recognized the scent of blood.

Skene knew the men were getting to their feet, but he followed Senga as she pulled him down the passageway and back into the darkened areas of the castle.

"Here now, lass." He pulled her to a stop as he drew his sword. More men caught up to them, and he let Senga lead him to a small cell.

"She is dying," Senga said as Skene took in Duana.

He put his sword down and dropped to his knees next to the Head of House. She struggled to draw in breath, her clothing soaked with her life's blood.

"Ye there." Skene spoke to a younger lad who stood with his sword still drawn. "Wake the castle and the Tanis. Lower the gate, and get the mistress down here to see what can be done. Quickly, man."

There was immediate action. In a few moments, Skene heard the bells on the walls ringing. The level of light increased as torches kept at the ready for emergencies were lit.

"There is…naught…to do." Duana's voice was just a strained whisper. Skene reached for her hand, at a complete loss as to how to comfort a dying woman.

Ailis Robertson came into the room in only a dressing robe, her husband on her heels. "Here now, mistress."

Ailis knelt down and looked at the wound, but Duana had been run straight through her body. Her firmly laced bodice had kept her alive because it kept the wound from spilling her blood too quickly. She opened her eyes and looked at Ailis.

"Ye…likely think…it…just…of Fate."

"I think nothing of the sort." Ailis took Duana's hand as Skene gratefully relinquished it.

"Who did this?" Bhaic was there on one knee, his expression grim. Duana had lowered her eyelids. He tightened his jaw and reached out to press on the wound. "Duana, I must know."

The Head of House jumped as pain went through her. But she opened her eyes and looked at Bhaic. "Robert Gunn," she answered softly. "He…claimed he was…wed…by proxy to…Helen…and took…"

Duana was out of breath. She struggled to draw in more, but there was a rattle in her chest. She looked at Bhaic and then smiled as she appeared to be looking beyond him. "Oh, Willie…" she whispered with a smile on her lips. "It's been so long…since I saw ye… me sweet husband."

Suddenly sitting up, Duana reached out to someone only she could see, with a smile that spoke of love. It was so bright, her eyes glittered with it, and in the next moment, her body slumped back into Bhaic's arms, her chest still as her eyes shut and death took her. He laid her down gently while those watching made the sign of the cross.

"Skene." Bhaic spoke quietly. "I charge ye with me wife."

Ailis looked up. Bhaic offered her a hand, helping her gain her feet before he nodded. "I must go. Ye'll stay in our chambers until I am certain Helen was the only target of Morton's attack." He looked past her at Skene. "Take no chances."

"Aye," Skene responded.

Bhaic gave his wife a quick kiss before he was out

the door and heading toward the hall. He cursed when he arrived at the doors, because the storm was fully on them. Snow came down in plump, wet clumps. Tracks would be filled in quickly as the wind swept snow into drifts, and the horses wouldn't be happy about venturing out.

But there was no choice. Because there was no way he was going to tell his brother he'd let his wife be taken.

Even though that was exactly what had happened.

❧

Robert Gunn didn't share his food with her.

At first, Helen would gladly have refused. Three days later, it was becoming harder to take comfort in her pride because her belly ached and the cold threatened to snap her in half. She tried to eat the snow, but it soon left a ring of blisters on the inside of her mouth.

Robert came and sat near her at last. He considered her as he chewed on a piece of bread. Her belly rumbled low and long in response. She looked away only to hear him grunt at her efforts to maintain her pride.

"I do nae want a wife," he declared firmly.

"Excellent." Helen looked back at him and lifted her bound hands up.

"The Earl of Morton wed us by proxy."

Helen glared at him in response.

Robert snorted, a hint of a smile raising the corners of his lips. "No argument? I expected one from ye."

"When it comes to the Earl of Morton and his ideas concerning marriage, there is no sense in pointing out what is logical. The man seems to have no care for anything but his agendas."

"Aye," Robert agreed, noting her surprise. "The man forced me to accept his arrangement, sure enough. I've no desire to strike a blow at me fellow Highlanders."

"The MacPhersons will no' take doing murder inside their castle while they gave ye shelter as anything else."

Robert Gunn knew what he'd done and was content with his actions. It was horrifying to look into the eyes of a man who felt no remorse. He viewed his choices as ones he'd made for the best reasons. That meant she was at his mercy.

Completely at his mercy.

❧

Marcus raised his fist, telling his men to pull up.

He turned his head, listening intently as he tried to identify what had gained his attention.

"Marcus!" Kam raised his hand and waved in the air from just over the rise behind them.

"That lad is killing his horse," Finley growled.

Kam struggled up to them, his horse snorting as it was allowed to stop for a rest. "Trouble at the castle," Kam got out between the snorts coming from his horse.

Marcus felt a chill go down his spine. "What sort of trouble?"

❧

The weather broke at last, granting them a clear blue sky and bright sun that made the new snow sparkle. It was magical, unless one's toes were frozen.

Helen tried to curl hers in an effort to get some warmth into them.

They'd only stopped because the horses were exhausted and the Gunns had decided the remedy was to steal fresh mounts.

Robert tied her to a tree with a wink. "Do nae worry, lass. As soon as we arrive home, I'll have more time for ye."

"Why are ye playing the puppet to Morton?"

Robert stopped and considered her as he slid his dagger into a scabbard hanging from his belt. "I gave me word to the man. So I'll see it through."

"He is a long way from here, and the MacPhersons are much closer," she warned him.

She caught a flicker of distaste in his eyes. "And yet, we've all felt his reach. Have we no', mistress? Only a fool would anger him." Robert sent her a hard look. "Ye did so, and now ye see the man has plenty of resources to strike back at ye."

"I would have thought a fellow Highlander would no' have anything to do with Morton's vengeance."

Robert leaned down and lowered his voice. "Marcus was in chains for a day. I was rotting in that dungeon for two years. Wedding ye was a price I was willing to pay to be free."

"I am another man's wife."

"With no dowry and the wrath of the regent aimed at him for keeping ye?" Robert shook his head. "With ye gone, his father will make Marcus see reason. As a bastard, he'll be wise to accept. Just as I was when I took Morton's offer. Ye"—Robert's tone took on a stern warning—"will do the same, for I'll no' be suffering yer discontent. Ye will no' be fed unless ye please me."

He turned and left her, disappearing over the rise. Her chest tightened as she fought against the rope binding her to the tree. She felt the skin on her wrists tearing, but that didn't deter her. She was fighting for her life, one of her own choosing.

Marcus.

He was her choice. As she worked her wrists back and forth across the rough bark of the tree, she fought back the lash of reality. The MacPhersons would be in better standing with Morton if she were gone. Marcus would also be viewed in a kinder light by his fellow clansmen.

Stop it! she chided herself. Marcus had declared himself to her. All her fretting was an insult to his integrity.

And still, she fought against the tide of her doubts just as surely as she battled to free herself from the rope around her wrists. It felt as if she were trying to change all of the world and make life suit her whims. Of course that was ridiculous. Well, as ridiculous as realizing she needed Marcus as much as her next breath.

She loved him.

For a moment, she leaned back against the tree, exhausted by the admission and nearly smothering beneath the weight of her guilt for having resisted acknowledging it until now.

Now, when it was too late to tell him.

No.

It was more than a word; it was a rejection of all her circumstances. Marcus would never surrender, and neither would she. Helen yanked on her bindings, and one of the coils of rope suddenly gave. It slipped right off her wrist. She gasped and pulled on her arms until one hand popped completely free. She sat stunned for a moment as she looked at the bloody mess her hands had become. Her fingers were so cold that she couldn't feel them, and she realized that the rope had slipped free because her body was contracting as it tried to conserve warmth.

The new blanket of snow surrounded her. She stared at it for only a moment before she started across it because there was no help for it. Robert might return at any moment. The worn-out horses were clustered under a tree, trying to huddle together and ease their suffering. The Gunn had provided no food for the poor creatures, abandoning them now that they had no more strength to be used.

Helen spoke softly to one, reaching out to run a kind hand along its neck. "Carry me away, and I will find ye a stable."

She didn't know if she was trying to convince herself or the horse of that fact, only that she had to concentrate on doing what she could instead of the very real fact that Robert would easily ride her down if he succeeded in stealing a fresh horse.

The animal was reluctant to leave the shelter it had found but it did, beginning to trot down the road they'd come. Helen forced a smile onto her lips, refusing to let doubt into her thoughts. She had to succeed, and what frightened her more than anything was the certain knowledge that Robert Gunn felt just as strongly about making good on his word to keep her.

She would be an unwanted thing for the rest of her days.

※

The horse's strength truly was spent.

Helen felt the poor beast limping as it slowed. She rubbed its neck but accepted that she couldn't ride it any longer. There was nothing in sight, and it grieved her to know she could not make good on her promise to find it a stable. All she might do was see it to a thicket, where the animal tossed its head at her in farewell.

"Aye, good luck to ye too," Helen muttered as she surveyed the landscape.

The trail they'd left was plain, making her feel as though her efforts were hopeless. While she stood contemplating her options, she heard the sound of water.

The water wouldn't show her tracks.

Of course, she might freeze if she got her feet wet.

It was a chance she had to take. So was turning and moving back upstream. She'd find where the river split and take a different route south. It was slow going as she climbed over boulders and trudged through ankle-deep water. She tucked her skirts up high to keep them from the water as she tried to ignore the way her belly hurt.

She had never been so hungry.

But there was nothing to do but go on. She only wished she didn't know just how alike she and the horse were. At some point, she would have to accept she had no more strength, and then she'd have to wait for her death.

❧

Helen understood how the horse felt now.

There was something about a thicket of tree branches that was inviting, sheltering, and really very comforting. She lay down on a patch of fallen leaves that was bare of snow and enjoyed the way it felt warm against her back.

Yes. So nice.

She drew in a deep breath, and then another slower one. She'd been trembling for so long, it felt rather normal. Yet as she stared up into the tangle of dry leaves and bare branches, she felt the tremors leaving her body.

That was much better. In fact, she didn't feel so very cold any longer. Just tired. So weary. Sleep offered her release and balm for her aches, so she went to it willingly, happily wrapped in its embrace.

❧

Helen was gone by the time Marcus tracked her to the thicket.

He reached down and felt the ground but there was no warmth left, only the faint indentation from her body. Bhaic was farther down the slope, inspecting the tracks that led away from the spot.

Marcus joined his brother, both of them working their way to the top of a rise. They stayed low to the ground, hugging the earth as they peered over it.

"She never knew how close she was to shelter," Marcus said bitterly. Below them was the castle of the Earl of Sutherland.

"One can never be sure if the Sutherlands can be trusted," Bhaic answered.

"Just what we need," Marcus replied. "Another earl who thinks himself king."

"Aye," Bhaic said. "But if Helen is still alive, she's down there. Someone picked her up."

Marcus nodded. "I'm going after her."

"Agreed," Bhaic said.

"Ye are no' joining me, Brother."

"The hell I'm not," Bhaic argued.

Marcus caught his brother by the bicep. "We can nae allow the Sutherlands to have both of us. Ye must leave me here."

"So ye can ride up to that castle alone?"

Marcus slowly grinned. "I was no' thinking of riding up."

Bhaic felt his lips twitch at his brother's daring. "Marcus, the Sutherlands make a good show of supporting the king. Cormac might well put ye back in chains and write to Morton."

"Aye," Marcus agreed. "He might at that."

Bhaic shoved his brother when all Marcus did was continue to look down on the castle.

"Perhaps it might be better to gain Symon's support in getting Helen back."

Marcus turned a hard look on his brother. "Ye'd never have left Ailis. So do nae ask me to do anything of the sort with Helen. She is mine."

Bhaic slowly nodded. He clasped his brother's hand. "I'll be waiting for ye." His voice never faltered, but every man among them knew the situation didn't favor them. Not one bit.

Marcus didn't hesitate. He pulled his kilt off, leaving his legs covered in a set of plain trews that protected him during the colder months. He reached up and pulled the fine brooch off his bonnet before trading swords with one of his men for one that had a plainer hilt.

Indeed, it was deceptive and the Sutherlands wouldn't take it kindly if they discovered him. Men could be hung for disguising who they were in the Highlands.

Marcus didn't give it another thought. At that moment, there was only the need to get Helen back.

So that was what he was going to do.

God help the man who stepped into his path.

❦

Helen gasped, her eyes opening wide because it felt as if someone was peeling the skin off her feet.

"I know, it stings," someone said softly. "Yet it will keep ye from losing yer toes to the frost."

Helen looked at the girl sitting beside her. She was pretty, with golden hair and large, blue eyes. "I am Annella. Ye are at Sutherland Castle."

Helen was slumped in a huge chair with a padded seat and back. At her feet, two maids were gently working her stockings free from her toes. The firelight made the ice crystals sparkle. Annella offered her a glass. "This will dull the pain."

Helen sniffed the liquid and discovered it was nothing more than whisky. She downed it and gasped as it burned a path to her empty stomach.

"Who are ye?" Annella asked. "Yer arisaid is plain."

So it was. Helen had adopted a brown length of cloth down her back instead of one with clan colors when Marcus dropped her in the MacPherson yard. "I am Helen Grant."

"And who is yer father?" Annella asked sweetly.

Too sweetly, Helen decided. She looked past the girl toward the shadows of the room and heard a grunt. Annella offered her a smile before she stood and walked away.

"I have nothing to hide," Helen said.

The man who emerged from the shadows was just as massive as Marcus. He had the same golden hair and blue eyes as Annella, but there was nothing sweet about him. He was a hardened clansman, and the gold brooch on his bonnet winked at her.

"Cormac Sutherland?" Helen asked.

His lips twitched. "So ye know who I am."

"No' really," she answered as the maids finished and left her feet soaking in a basin of warm water. Helen was avoiding looking down. If she was going to lose any of her toes, she would have to mourn them later, once she'd determined her circumstances. "I know what gold looks like and who is the eldest son of the Earl of Sutherland."

Cormac nodded once. "Yet I do nae know who ye are, mistress."

"Helen Grant. Me father has a small home that me brothers farm."

"I see," Cormac answered. "No one of any importance, is that what ye would have me believe?"

Helen made a motion over her clothing. "Do I look as though I come from a family with means?"

He shook his head but looked at her boots. "Those are fine work." He swept his eyes over her once again and aimed a hard look at her. "So tell me why yer wrists are bleeding from being bound. If ye are no one of any importance."

Helen looked at her wrists. Honestly, she'd forgotten about them, but now that she was warming up, the wounds were throbbing. In fact, the pain felt as though it was traveling up her body in a thick wave that knocked her back into unconsciousness when it hit her head.

⁓

"Ye might have let her eat something first," Annella said to her brother.

"I need to know if we are bringing someone dangerous into the castle," Cormac replied. He considered their guest with frustration.

"Oh aye," his sister replied. "She appears so very fearsome."

"I detest that tone of yers," Cormac informed her. "What did our aunt teach ye, anyway? How to vex men?"

"I believe she called it minding me place." His sister shot him a look full of loathing. "That I might always be pleasing to my lord-and-master husband. According to our dear aunt, that is a woman's place."

"And ye are still angry with Father for sending ye south," Cormac said. He made a soft sound under his breath before he scooped Helen up and carried her to the bed. The maids hurried in front of him to pull down the bedding. "I need to know more of why she was found out there."

"Clearly someone stole her," Annella answered her

brother. "Is nae that what ye forever warn me might happen if I stray from the care of yer men?"

"If that is so, then ye know I have no' just been trying to frustrate ye with me warnings."

Annella stuck her tongue out at him in response.

"I hope ye never have reason to know that me warnings are justified, Annella. There are men in this world who differ little from beasts."

"A few women as well," Annella responded. "I met them at court." She shuddered.

His sister smiled at him, hugging him before she went on her way, two of his men trailing her. Cormac took a moment outside the chamber door to instruct the guards to ensure that their guest remained inside the chamber until he'd had a chance to learn her story. It had better be a good one, supported by facts he could see for himself, because the times were uncertain, and he would not allow a would-be assassin into his father's castle.

She wouldn't be the first woman used for such a purpose, which meant he wouldn't be the first man to have to stomach his distaste for hanging a woman.

But he'd do what had to be done to ensure the safety of the Sutherlands.

❧

Robert stopped and looked at the tracks where they disappeared into the water. He gave a little grunt before he straightened and rejoined his men.

"How does a hot meal sound, lads?"

His captain offered him a doubtful look. "At Sutherland, ye mean?"

"Aye," Robert confirmed. "Since we no longer have a captive to hide, we can blend in with the merchants going up to the castle. I hear the Sutherlands still keep a lower table for travelers."

It was an old tradition that dated back to the Crusades. The last table in the hall would be open to anyone seeking food. Of course, it was not wise to enter the castle of your enemy, but there were advantages to being only a chief of a branch of the Gunn clan. No one would think of taking Robert hostage because the laird could easily replace him instead of paying a ransom.

"Let's fill our bellies before making our way north."

"And yer wife?" his captain inquired.

Robert shrugged and looked up the river. "She surprised me, no doubt about it, but she'll no' last much longer. No' with how empty her belly is. Likely better this way. I did nae want a wife, and the wolves will take care of her body."

It was harsh, just like life. He admired Helen for taking a hand in her own fate. Fate was a bitch, and all a man might really ask was to die well.

Helen had achieved that goal. It made him just a bit sorry that he wouldn't be getting a son from her. Strength had to be bred into offspring. She would have produced a fine litter for him, but at least she'd given him a clear idea of what to seek in a bride.

❧

Marcus was in her dreams.

But in reality, she was stuck inside another castle. Helen awoke at first light and tested her feet. There was still pain, but she was relieved to see that all her toes were pink. She wrinkled her nose when she looked at her stockings. They had dried during the night but were stained with mud and muck and smelled to high heaven.

There was a rap on the door as she was contemplating them and the necessity of dressing.

"I've brought ye something much nicer to wear," Annella said as she pushed the door wide, without a care for the fact that Helen was wearing only a chemise and there were three retainers looking in on her.

Two maids followed their mistress, their arms heavy with clothing. Annella might have been young, but clearly she was experienced in commanding the staff. She pointed at the table, and the maids laid down their burdens. The retainers sent Helen a look that made it clear they'd snap her neck if they heard even a tiny sound of alarm from inside the chamber.

"Me father wishes to see ye."

The door hadn't fully closed, and now two young men came through, shouldering a tub. They set it down, and a line of other boys began to dump water into it.

"We'll have ye fit for him in no time at all," Annella declared as the last of the boys left after pouring steaming hot water into the tub.

One of the maids had come right over to Helen and begun to gather up her chemise in order to pull it over her head. The door was barely closed when Helen was stripped bare. She happily climbed into the tub for the shelter it offered, but the maids followed her, scrubbing every inch of her body while their mistress looked on.

"Out now," Annella said. "It's too cold to linger."

Helen tried not to shirk, but Annella noticed. "Does no' yer father's house have servants who bathe ye?"

"Nay," Helen answered as the maids dried her body before one of them offered her a clean chemise.

"Hmmm," Annella offered by way of response. "Me mother instructed me on no' flinching while I was being bathed because there would be gossip that I had something to hide, such as a witch mark."

Helen sat down and pulled on stockings that a maid tied securely above her knee with a garter. "Well, me father's house is modest. There are nae servants to tend to the tasks I can do meself."

She stood and had a hip bolster fastened around her. Next came an underskirt of thick wool flannel. She enjoyed the weight of it against her legs while it cut out the chill, and then one of the maids brought over a pleated skirt.

It had been a long time since she'd worn a bodice and skirt that matched. So long, that she realized clothing wasn't very important. No, being with the people you loved, that was what mattered.

She'd never told Marcus she wanted to be his wife. It was a failing she prayed she would receive an opportunity to correct.

Of course, Fate had never been given to granting her desires.

෴

Cormac Sutherland had learned a great deal from his father.

The earl considered Helen as she was brought into

his private study. Cormac stood off to one side, clearly there to protect his father should the need arise.

Such was the way life was. A wise person always took precautions against attack. Helen felt a nip of guilt for how hard her thoughts had been toward Marcus. He was only doing what harsh reality had taught men to do in order to defend their own families.

"Me son claims ye say yer father is a man of no great name," the earl began.

"That is true," Helen answered. She'd lowered herself to the man and stood waiting for him to decide what her fate was. "Although he has more than many. A small plot of land to call his own and a good house."

"And ye have brothers?" the earl asked.

Helen nodded.

"No man should ask for more than enough and healthy children he is blessed with seeing grow to adulthood. Three sons, aye, that's a fine thing for a man to have."

His eyes glazed over for a moment, making it clear he knew about loss from personal experience.

"Let me see yer wrists."

She'd had her hands clasped behind her back. It took a moment for her to extend them.

"Closer, me eyesight is no' what it once was."

Cormac moved with her, making sure he was close enough to intercede should she lunge at his father.

"A man of no great name, and yet"—the earl looked up from the torn mess of her wrists—"someone took ye by force."

Helen stepped back.

"Deciding whether or no' to trust me with the tale?" the earl deduced.

"I'd surely be a fool to think ye do nae hold a great deal of power over me." Marcus would have had something to say about her sharp tongue, and she let out a little scoffing sound.

"I know that sound," the earl declared. "There's a man who's told ye that ye have spirit."

"More than is healthy for me, in his opinion," Helen confirmed.

"Who?" Cormac wasn't willing to let the conversation dissolve into one of pleasantries.

"Marcus MacPherson."

The earl's eyes narrowed. "Shamus's bastard? He'd say something like that. Marcus is a fine War Chief, and no mistake, I'd ride beside him. What are ye to him?"

Helen debated her answer; it might serve as her deliverance or her undoing. The Sutherlands ruled as kings in the north. There was no telling what they'd do with her once they established that she had worth.

"And who stole ye from him?" Cormac demanded.

"Robert Gunn." Helen took the opportunity to shift attention from herself, looking at Cormac in time to see the man's eyes widen.

"Bloody hell. The man is inside the hall this very moment." He cursed before he went toward the door. At the last second, he turned and looked at her. "With me, mistress, and do nae make me drag ye. I will no' be leaving ye here with me father."

"I'm coming with ye," the earl announced. "I would see what Robert has to say for himself."

Fear went through Helen, and she recoiled. It

wasn't a choice; it was pure reaction. "Robert is inside yer castle?"

Cormac had the door open. "I just said so."

"He murdered the MacPherson's Head of House."

She gained a glimpse of Cormac's rage before the man ran down the passageway. Retainers noticed him and joined the charge. One of them caught her by the bicep and dragged her along. The hall of the Sutherlands was as grand as that of the MacPhersons. Helen only had a moment to note the noble coat of arms displayed above the high ground before Cormac was shouting at men sitting at the end of the hall.

"Chief Robert Gunn," Cormac bellowed in a voice laced with authority. "Ye will stand and explain yerself."

Everyone in the hall came to a stop. Children were pushed behind adults as Sutherland retainers flooded in from the passageways in response to Cormac's tone. More than one sword was pulled, and the few beggars who had been breaking bread at the low table scurried away, leaving Robert and his men to face the Sutherland.

Robert stood and caught sight of her. His lips actually twitched. He faced Cormac.

"I see ye found me wife," Robert began.

"Yer what?" Cormac turned to look at Helen. But he caught sight of someone behind her and his eyes widened.

"She's my wife," Marcus announced. "And I'm going to enjoy choking the life out of ye for taking her, Robert Gunn."

The Sutherlands were alarmed to discover Marcus in their midst. There was a scuffle as they moved toward Marcus, and he threw a couple of them off him like puppies. Helen gasped, trying to run toward him, but the men beside her grabbed her around the waist, lifting her right off her feet as she struggled against their strength. Marcus let out a roar but directed his words toward Cormac.

"Tell yer men to get their hands off me wife." Only Marcus would be brash enough to issue an order while standing in the hall of another clan.

Damned if she didn't love him all the more for it, while at the same time, fear snaked down her spine because of the very real danger he was in.

"Hold!"

It was the earl who spoke, and his people responded to his command instantly, turning to look toward him.

"I will be the one to decide this matter." The earl spoke evenly and firmly. "Since ye have both brought it into me hall."

The earl didn't climb up to his high ground. He sat down on a bench nearby and gestured for his men who were holding Helen to release her. She stumbled because they did so very quickly. Their unbreakable grips just opened, and she had to catch herself. The earl pointed to a spot near him. She drew herself up straight and went to it.

"Now, lass," the earl began. "Who are ye married to?"

She felt Marcus watching her. Oh, there were so many others there, but the only one who mattered was Marcus and the fool he'd made of himself by risking his neck to come after her.

Which warmed her heart and her temper equally.

"Marcus MacPherson," she answered clearly.

The earl swept her from head to toe before he looked past her to Marcus. His men released him but stayed close.

"The Earl of Morton"—Robert stepped forward, a parchment in his hand—"wed me to her by proxy."

"We were already wed, man," Marcus argued. "And the vows celebrated."

"No' when ye left court, they weren't," Robert argued. "That makes her yer slut, no' yer wife."

Marcus let out a warning sound. "When a man and woman speak their vows before a priest, that's a wedding, lad."

"But ye did nae fuck her there." Robert didn't hesitate to be blunt. "The earl dissolved the union and wed me to her before ye had her in yer bed. She is my wife and an adulteress."

Cormac took the parchment from Robert and read it through. He looked up at his father. "It's sealed, all right." He handed it to his father, who took a long moment to read the document.

"If ye're a true subject of the king," Robert announced, "ye will give her to me."

"So, ye think to call upon me sense of justice." The earl spoke clearly, even if his tone was edged with age.

"Aye." Robert pointed at the parchment. "That is the will of the Earl of Morton. Regent of Scotland. I am a loyal subject."

"Ye are nothing of the sort," the earl snapped back, betraying just how quick his wit still was. "Ye were part of the assassination of the Earl of Moray and a supporter of Bothwell and Mary Stuart. Now that ye know yer cause is lost, ye are licking Morton's balls like the cur ye are."

There was a round of crusty amusement from the Sutherland retainers.

The earl wasn't finished, though. "However, I do nae care what this piece of paper says. Ye came to me home after doing murder and stealing another man's wife. If ye think I am going to grant ye shelter from the justice of the man ye wronged because of some piece of parchment, ye are nae as intelligent as some of me hounds."

"I took her by order of the Earl of Morton," Robert insisted.

"Did he instruct ye to do murder?" Marcus asked. "Ye ran a woman through, under me father's roof."

There was a ripple of anger among the Sutherlands.

"At least I am no' the one who snuck into this castle after taking off me plaid so no one knows who I am." Robert made sure his voice was heard throughout the hall. "Ye are spying on the Sutherlands."

"No, ye bastard," Marcus snarled softly. "I'm making sure ye do nae escape, no matter who ye try to hide behind. Ye'll no' scare me into letting ye live. Ye ran Duana through in a sewing cell."

"Ye should hang him." Robert turned to address the earl. "Before ye find yer castle overrun by the MacPhersons and all yer throats cut."

The earl was still, his face tight as he contemplated both men. Helen felt her blood running cold because his will would be done. More than a hundred men were looking on, just waiting to do their laird's bidding. She felt as though her breath was lodged in her throat as the earl raised his hand for silence.

"Marcus MacPherson," the earl said, "I do nae care very much for ye sneaking into me home."

There was a ripple of angry agreement from those pressing forward. Marcus adopted his favorite pose—feet braced shoulder-width apart, arms crossed over his chest—and stared straight at the earl without flinching.

"But I admire ye for having the balls to do it."

There was a scoffing sound from Cormac.

"It's a Highlander's way sometimes to do what needs doing, no matter the risk," the earl continued. He made a motion with his hands. "Back up, lads. No Sutherland will be interfering in this fight."

Marcus smiled. It was a slow, menacing expression. Helen gripped her skirt, staying in place only by sheer force of will. She needed to interfere but knew it was a lost cause. She'd be asking him to discard who he was, and that wasn't something Marcus would ever do.

And Duana deserved justice. No matter how bitter the woman had been, Robert had murdered her simply because she was in his way. Marcus couldn't let the injustice go, and that was the part of him that she realized she'd always known was there.

Marcus spared her one glance and Robert took full advantage of it, launching himself at Marcus. There was a grumble from the watching Sutherlands, but Marcus proved himself worthy by lifting his foot and planting it in Robert's midsection while he rolled back under the force of the attack. They hit the floor, and Marcus kicked Robert up and off him before flipping over with a motion that showed how strong he was.

"Ye like to hit yer enemies when they aren't looking, do nae ye, Gunn?" Marcus moved in a slow circle, taking the time to unbutton his doublet and shrug out of it.

"I like victory." Robert pulled a dagger from his boot. "I'm going to fuck yer woman tonight, while ye're rotting in a grave."

He raised the knife up high, proving he knew how to use it. Both men were hard and trained. It was going to be a matter of who made a mistake first.

Helen's fingers ached from how tightly she was clenching them into fists. Cormac had made his way behind her and caught a handful of her skirt at some point, but she never moved, never made a sound, hardly even drew breath as the fight went on.

It seemed to last forever. Robert drew first blood, slicing a path across Marcus's forearm as Marcus blocked the blow. Marcus turned and smashed Robert in the groin with his foot, to the delight of those watching. Robert stumbled back, and Marcus pressed his advantage.

The two men ended up on the floor, grunting as they tried to kill one another.

That was of course their common goal. But the similarities ended there. Robert fought to claim a victory that wasn't rightfully his, so he was choosing to win through might. Marcus refused to allow him to claim it. From the outside, there was little difference between them, but inside, there was a great divide. Honor separated them, and Helen prayed it would be enough.

But Robert's men weren't willing to lose. One of them threw a dagger that sank into Marcus's shoulder. He growled, turning instinctually toward the new attack. Robert lunged forward, his dagger raised high to sink its blade into Marcus's exposed throat.

Helen surged forward, breaking Cormac's grip. She watched that dagger moving toward Marcus, the tip looking deadly sharp.

Marcus whipped around, dropping his own weapon as he clasped his hands around Robert's wrist. Robert jerked as Marcus twisted and turned the knife on him. Robert recoiled, and the two men fell back onto the floor.

Cormac grabbed Helen from behind, pulling her to a stop, while the fight ended as quickly as it had begun. Helen searched both men for signs of life, her eyes widening with horror as a puddle of bright-red blood began to seep across the stone floor.

Helen felt her heart stop. Everyone in the hall seemed frozen, waiting to see which man would rise. Marcus's shoulder was turning red, the thrown dagger having fallen out to leave the wound open.

He moved. Helen blinked, thinking she had willed him to do so, but he flattened his hands on the floor and pushed himself up and off Robert, who lay staring at the ceiling, his eyes lifeless.

Marcus fixed the Earl of Sutherland with a hard look. "Would ye be so kind as to summon yer priest? I have need of the man."

Helen broke loose and went to him, inspecting the wound, but she discovered that although it was bleeding heavily, it was not dangerous. Marcus pulled her in front of him.

"It seems we need to be married again."

❧

Finley and the other MacPherson retainers were reluctant to come inside the Sutherland stronghold. Marcus rode out with Helen to meet them, not bothering to explain the fresh blood on his shirt. They rode long and hard for the next few days, stopping only when they had left Sutherland land behind.

The tavern where they stopped was better than the last one Marcus had taken her to, but he still had Finley take her above stairs while Marcus tended to the horses. As soon as the door shut, Helen found her composure crumbling. All of the fear she'd refused to show escaped. Tears stung her eyes as she paced around the room, caught between relief that Marcus was alive and anger for the chance he'd taken with his life. Her control seemed exhausted, leaving her furious.

He came into the room without knocking, opening and closing the door with a look that made it plain he felt it his right to share the room with her.

Which it was, but that only made her temper flare when she spied the dried blood on his shirt. That just drove deep how close he'd come to dying.

"What were ye thinking?" she asked. "Going into the Sutherland castle like that? Ye might have been hanged."

He walked over and put his sword and doublet on the table. "I was thinking I was rescuing ye."

"Ye were," she agreed, but her tone was sharp. "But ye should no' have risked yer life."

He considered her from behind an unreadable expression, but it broke as his lips twitched and he grinned at her. "Ye were worried about me."

"Of course I was. Ye acted the damn fool."

"I acted as yer husband," he said in a low tone edged with hard certainty. It was hypnotic in a way, especially when she coupled the sound with the way he was looking at her. As though she were something precious to him.

"Come here, lass." He crooked a finger at her. "I want to hold ye."

She lifted her chin. "Ye would have been furious with me if I'd done something so dangerous."

His expression darkened. "Ye can be sure I would. Do nae ye ever test me on that, Helen. I'd have to take ye to task for yer own good."

"Yet ye expect me to come to ye now, when ye have acted with so little regard for yer safety?"

His lips slowly curled up, and he flashed his teeth at her. "I do."

She propped her hands on her hips. "I warned ye I would nae be obedient behind closed doors."

She watched the challenge flash through his blue eyes a moment before he intercepted her and pulled her close. She wiggled, squirming against his hold.

"Have done," he demanded, clearly becoming exasperated. "It was me duty to see justice done."

"I know that." She sent him a hard look.

He let out a little huff and released her. The moment he unlocked his arms, she realized the problem was inside herself, and there was no running from that.

He'd crossed his arms over his chest. "If ye know me nature, why are ye so angry with me?"

"Why?" she asked. She caught the glitter in his eyes even as he controlled his expression. "Oh!" She went back toward him and slapped his chest. Her blow landed with a soft sound; she'd hit him with her open palm because she couldn't truly hurt him. Indeed, the conflict was within herself, and that was a solid fact.

"Ye know me. Me duty is a part of me."

"Yes." She stepped back, feeling as exposed as if she were stripped to her skin. "That's why I could never truly hate ye. Lord knows, I asked meself why I did no', and now…"

He lifted her chin. "And now?"

The memory of how much she'd lamented not telling him how she felt tormented her. "I love ye."

There. She watched her words impact him, saw the way his eyes flickered with emotion before brightening with satisfaction.

"Come." He pulled her close again.

He nuzzled against her hair, drawing in a deep breath. The memory of him doing so before he left stirred, rising to smother her discontentment. He was hard and warm against her.

"Does that mean ye will have me, lass?" He tilted his head to the side so his lips were next to her ear. "I fear I will lose what little control I have left if ye say no."

She could no more deny him than hold back the coming winter. "Good." She slid her hands up his chest. "It seems only fair that ye understand how ye make me feel. As though me mind is no' me own."

He cupped her cheeks in his large hands, sending a ripple of awareness across her skin. Her flesh was awakening, becoming eager for his. "For all that it makes me sound like a savage, Helen, I will tell ye the only way I can think of ye is as mine."

That was perfect. She smiled as his words sank in, and for a moment, their gazes locked together, making them feel as though their very souls were connected. And then he was kissing her, driving away every thought, sweeping them aside like items carefully placed on a tabletop, scattering them onto the floor in a tangle of unrecognizable things that meant nothing. She kissed him back, rising onto her toes so she could press her mouth firmly against his. He cupped the back of her head, keeping her in place while he teased her tongue with his own.

But that wasn't enough. Both of them craved more than teasing and were impatient to be joined together. He turned her around, seeking out the lacings that held the bodice closed.

"I thought to give ye proper clothing…" Marcus exclaimed as he fought with the ties. "But now I'm rethinking the matter."

The fabric made a threatening sound that made her squeal. "Do nae ye dare," she warned him. "I've no' had a proper dress in years."

He yanked the laces free and the bodice slid down; at the same time she released the waistband of the skirt and reached inside to pop the little tie that held the hip roll in place. Her skirts slipped down her legs and puddled around her ankles, leaving her in a corset and chemise. Marcus cupped her shoulder and turned her, passion brightening his eyes, and he froze.

"I swear, I am going to make sure ye have a dozen of those contraptions," he declared as he took in the sight of her with her breasts pushed up by the corset.

Helen stepped out of her skirts, putting distance

between them. The look on his face made her bold, filling her with a confidence she'd never experienced. She teased the swell of one of her breasts where it sat plump and supported by the corset with just the edge of her chemise peeking out. "Oh, like it, do ye?"

He unbuckled his belt and let his kilt drop to the floor. His member was already stiff, pushing out the front of his shirt. "I do."

"As do I," she responded breathlessly.

She moved toward him, undoing one cuff and then the other. He reached over his head and tugged the shirt up and off before facing her in nothing but skin. Helen paused, her attention caught by the bandaging around his wound.

"It's naught," he informed her, scooping her up and carrying her to the bed.

They sank onto it in a tangle of limbs, seeking solace in each other's embrace. Their skin warmed as their hearts accelerated and passion built. Helen couldn't seem to touch him enough, couldn't draw in enough of his scent, couldn't move close enough.

Marcus kissed her again and again. Refusing to sink into her flesh as she craved, instead he cupped her cheeks and took a long time to explore her mouth with his. She made little sounds and listened to the way he growled gently next to her ear. Her need was raging. So was his, and yet he stroked her tenderly, slowly, making her feel cherished.

She returned the favor, showing him with every touch how deeply she needed to be near him.

"Mine," she muttered against his neck, pressing a kiss to the place where she could feel the beat of his heart.

He caught her head and angled her face up so their eyes met. "Mine," he said through gritted teeth.

He pushed her back at last, and she purred as he settled between her thighs. Her body was made to cradle his, to take the deep thrust of his hard flesh. Satisfaction was their reward, coming to sweep them both into bliss unmatched by anything else.

❦

Every castle had its spies.

Sutherland was no exception.

The Earl of Morton read the letter twice before he cursed. Winter was raging around them and the letter had been written two months past, so the matter was well and truly done now.

Well then, Marcus could keep his wife, the earl thought. Of course, there was nothing he could do about it, but Morton had never been one to admit defeat.

Action had to be taken against the MacPhersons.

Some might advise him to allow the lesson to stand as it was. Their castle had been invaded, something no Highlander would sleep easy knowing. It was a good blow against those in the north who believed themselves so far removed from his reach.

Still, he was not content.

But that only made him chuckle.

A wise man was never willing to think he'd done all that he might to further his family. That was the difference between a noble and a commoner. Common men accepted their place, while men such as himself strived to climb higher, against the odds in many cases, and even in defiance of what was considered moral.

Still, he climbed.

The need set him apart, above other men. That was the reason he ruled Scotland: He'd earned it. Someday, he'd answer to God, but until then, he would make other men answer to him.

The Highlanders would learn to respect his will.

Seven

"WILL WINTER NEVER END?" AILIS STOPPED AT A window and scowled at the sky. "It has never lasted so long."

Helen didn't answer Ailis, but she had Helen's full attention.

"Oh stop it," Ailis exclaimed as she turned around. She meant to do it quickly, but her belly was huge and it made her clumsy. She missed a step and ended up catching herself against the wall as Finley and Lyel both jumped forward to catch her.

"I warned ye." Ailis pointed at the pair of retainers. They stopped and hooked their hands on their wide belts, making it plain they were not going to depart, no matter how much she snarled at them.

"Helen," Ailis implored her friend.

"Oh, all right." Helen stood up. "Ye need no' sound as though ye are going to weep." Helen sent Ailis a wink her mistress didn't miss.

"Oh…but…it's just that I am…*so very tired of winter*…" Ailis began to whimper.

"We'll be nearby if ye need us," Finley mumbled

before he dashed through the chamber door with Lyel on his heels.

"At last." Ailis rubbed her belly. "I swear, I am nearly mad from the way everyone watches me." She collapsed into a chair. "As if this child is going to spring forth in a few moments and one of them might miss its arrival." She snorted. "It would not be called labor if it were so simple."

Helen laughed softly. Ailis looked at her. "Enough about me. Tell me what it is ye will not talk about."

Helen pulled a needle through the skirt she was making. "Ye have asked me that question every day since I returned, and the answer has no' changed."

"I know." Ailis spread her arms wide. "Ye persist in keeping yer thoughts to yerself. I would nae have to keep asking ye if ye explained why ye will nae tell me what is on yer mind." Ailis pointed at her. "And ye know very well I am talking about yer husband."

"There is naught to say."

Ailis smiled at her, but it was the sort of expression that promised Helen an interrogation.

"I'm hungry," Helen announced as she stood and left her half-sewn skirt in the chair behind her. "I'll go fetch us something from the kitchens. Best stay here, or the boys will be on yer heels in a moment. Ye know Bhaic told them he'd tan their hides if they let ye go down the stairs without help."

"Me husband can sleep in the stable for all I care."

Helen smiled as she left the chamber. Finley and Lyel were leaning against the wall near the top of the stairs. They tugged on the corners of their bonnets as she passed.

What was she thinking? Truly, she wished she knew.

In many ways, her life was so perfect. But that was what alarmed her. Perfection wasn't something that reality offered. At least, she had never found such to be the case. Happiness might come and touch her for magical moments that warmed her to the center of her heart, but it never lasted.

She felt on edge, as though she were waiting for something to crash through the window she was looking out and allow the bitter cold to blow against her. The snow was so beautiful when one was buffered against its chill.

He hadn't said he loved her.

It shouldn't bother her so much, or if it did, she should collect her courage and confront him. But if she did so, he might destroy the contentment they enjoyed by telling her he did not share her feelings.

Coward.

She was surely that, and yet not without reason. Her life was good now, far better than she might have expected from any match her father could have made for her. With Duana gone, the rest of the staff was showing her respect, while Marcus made certain she was well satisfied every night in their bed.

Coward? Perhaps *wise* was more the word.

It would be foolish to demand more, and most men did not think love was for their gender. They might indulge it, even smile when it was bestowed upon them, but they did not return it.

Indeed, it would be wise to see how full her life was and not long for more.

Yet she did.

The kitchens were warm and filled with the scent of roasting meat. Bhaic had ordered more livestock slaughtered so his wife could have fresh meat, even during the months when most made do with oats and ale. It was a luxury, and Helen drew in a deep breath before instantly regretting it.

Her belly heaved, and she clamped her mouth shut as the urge to retch nearly strangled her. She raced to the privacy closet, getting there just in time before losing what was left of her dinner. Yet that did not relieve the nausea. It seemed to have her locked in its grip as she tried to collect her composure.

"I wondered when that would happen," Senga said when Helen emerged. She snapped her fingers at a younger maid who stood with a bowl and a cloth in hand. The young Robertson who Bhaic had rescued with Ailis was now taking command as personal attendant to Ailis and Helen. "The laird will be overjoyed."

The scent of the roasting meat was still enough to make Helen heave. She didn't pay much attention to Senga, instead hurrying out of the kitchen, and gulping in fresh air. It helped, so she went all the way onto the steps to gain air that wasn't stale from being inside the castle walls. There was still a chill in the air, but her stomach settled and she sighed with relief.

"Ye haven't bled in months."

Senga had followed her. Helen turned to look at the young woman. "How would ye know?"

Senga offered her a satisfied look. "As I told the mistress, I will prove meself. Ye have no' asked for any cloth, and it has been four months since yer return from Sutherland."

Four months?

There was a scuff on the stairs as Finley came down them fast enough to break his neck. His eyes were wide, and he reached for Helen while he was still running.

"The mistress... Quick now, woman... She's having that babe."

"Should ye nae be above stairs with the women?"

Katherine looked at Robbie and shook her head.

"But there is a baby being born," her new friend persisted. "The women are gathering in the mistress's chambers. It seems to take a lot of women for a baby to be born."

"It's much more fun to be here with you," Katherine said.

Robbie considered her for a long moment. "Ye do nae act much like a girl."

"That is because you are such a good teacher," Katherine informed him.

Robbie flashed her a grin before he gestured her after him. "Let's go down by the river and see if we can find some rabbits to hunt. The cook might even give us some treats if we bring back meat."

Katherine nodded and waited to tuck her skirts up until they were out of the castle. She longed to wear a kilt like Robbie, but didn't want to risk Ailis taking exception to her friendship with the boy. So it was better not to bring attention to herself. That was a lesson she had learned very young. Whenever someone noticed her, it was likely to be a very bad day for her.

Such as the day her noble father's wife had noticed her and put her out of the house. There had also been the day when Scottish men had noted her blue blood and taken her across the border to sell to the regent of Scotland. She recalled that day very well.

Yes, much better not to have anyone notice what she was about. Which was working out splendidly, because boys had ever so much more fun than girls. Robbie had shown her how to wrestle and use a dagger, and now he was sharing his lessons in archery.

"I bet if ye dressed like a lad, no one would notice ye're a lass," Robbie said as he watched her fight with her skirts. He laughed. "It would be fun, too."

"All right," Katherine agreed. In fact, it was better than all right; the idea sounded perfect to her. The sun couldn't rise soon enough. Everyone back in England would be disgusted by the Highlanders around her, even young Robbie. Savages. Barbarians. That was what the English labeled them.

Katherine saw them differently. They were strong and honorable. There were even bastards among them who did not live a life of scorned rejection. The truth was known, yet they took their places and lived peacefully. It made her wonder what the true meaning of *savage* was, because if the Highlanders surrounding her were in fact uncivilized, she wanted to dispense with such manners immediately.

So that was exactly what she would do.

A new day and a beginning to a new life for her.

"Are ye disappointed?"

Bhaic stared at his wife incredulously. "She is the most precious thing I have ever seen, except perhaps for ye."

He was holding his tiny daughter as carefully as an egg. Her little head was supported in one hand while he cupped her bottom in the other. "We'll name her Sorcha, and no' another word from ye, Ailis. Ye've given me a fine, healthy child and are here to celebrate that with me. That is all I prayed for."

He laid the infant gently in Ailis's arms and tucked back some of his wife's hair. "Be strong, me love. I know naught of raising a daughter, so ye must be here to see it done properly."

"I am fine," Ailis assured her husband, but she was sleepy. Her eyelids fluttered as she sighed.

"Is she truly well?" Bhaic asked Helen when she came to pick the baby up.

"I believe so."

He nodded, the worry in his eyes proving how deeply the couple loved each other. Helen felt her own feelings for Marcus stirring inside her. She had so much, and yet it was incomplete without a declaration from Marcus.

Damn her for a fool, for she longed for more in spite of all the reasons not to. Of course, Marcus had always defied logic. That was why she loved him.

❧

McLeod Castle

"Ye summoned me?" Janet Ross asked her husband.

He looked up from his desk and gestured her forward. "I would speak to me wife in private, lads."

The two retainers standing inside the door both reached up to tug on their caps before they turned and left, pulling the door shut behind them.

Janet ventured closer, so that their voices might be lowered.

"I've had a letter from Laird MacPherson. It seems…" Laird McLeod had trouble getting the words out. "It seems he intends to have his daughter returned home."

Janet's eyes rounded with horror. "He can nae. She is more my child than his. Me dear niece. She is me blood."

Her husband made a soothing motion with his hand. "I am sorry for that, Janet. Ye would have made a fine mother, and I know it is me failing that sees ye with only another man's daughter in yer arms. I do wish ye'd reconsider having a lover."

"I will no'," Janet declared in a hiss. "Fate dealt us both an unkind blow when that stallion trampled ye. Still, I shall no' be tempted to commit mortal sins because of it. I am yer wife, and I will no' be an adulteress."

Laird McLeod sighed. It was an old argument that he always lost because his wife was one of the finest women in the Highlands. Which was why he had to find a way to stop Laird MacPherson from recalling his daughter home.

"Laird MacPherson sent his son for Jocelyn, but the weather drove him back. Now that spring is spreading, I fear Marcus MacPherson will be upon our land within the month."

Janet's eyes glittered with unshed tears. "She detests her father."

"Aye, I know it well, and yet he is her sire."

Janet had wrapped her arms around herself, as if she were attempting to keep her heart from breaking. Laird McLeod didn't doubt that it was. Curse and rot the creature that had broken his member. The thing had never risen again, not since the first two weeks of his marriage to the fair Janet.

"We shall go to me sister's home in the Lowlands," Janet suddenly announced, hope brightening her features.

"For what reason?" Laird McLeod asked.

"There Jocelyn will have the opportunity to learn more about the world. Times are changing. A lady needs a proper education. Perhaps I will even take her to court," Janet assured him. "The roads are passable for us now. We shall leave before the ice thaws on MacPherson land."

"I want to tell ye nay," Laird McLeod said. "Her father is likely making a match for her."

"Well then, I shall just have to secure a grander one before the end of the summer. One that will keep my baby close to me."

Janet smiled at him, her eyes full of hope. She was already running names through her mind, weighing their merits.

"Yes, that is exactly what I shall do."

She lowered herself before she swirled around and left the room. He didn't deserve her devotion, and yet he could not truly bring himself to lament the fact that she would not consent to have a lover in order to conceive. Perhaps he could not be a true husband to her, but she held his heart, and he didn't think he would be able to hide his hurt if she welcomed another man into her bed as sweetly as she had him.

Curse Fate.

He sat up straight and pulled a fresh piece of parchment onto the desk. Janet adored Jocelyn MacPherson. Shamus MacPherson had two sons and a grandchild on the way. He would have to live without Jocelyn, because Janet had no child and had raised the girl.

Fate owed him that.

He dipped a quill into an inkwell and began to pen a note to his banker so Janet would have the funds she needed for an extended stay in the Lowlands.

⁓

"Plump and delicious…"

Marcus growled as he fingered the swells of Helen's breasts above the edge of her corset. She lowered herself onto his member, a small sound of delight escaping her lips.

"If I'd known how much I'd enjoy being on me back beneath ye, Wife," Marcus exclaimed, "I'd have snapped that Gunn's neck for putting his dagger in me shoulder. To think I've missed having ye ride me for the last few months."

"Mmmm…" Helen purred as she leaned down and moved faster. Pleasure was building inside her, but she didn't rush it now. In fact, she fought back the urgency, clinging to the moments she was able to be joined with him.

It ended in a burst, her body shuddering while

Marcus curled up and wrapped his arms around her
and erupted inside her. In spite of the cool night air,
they collapsed onto the bed, their bodies too warm to
touch for several moments. They lay near each other,
their panting the only sound in the chamber.

During the night, Marcus curled up along her back.
He seemed unable to sleep unless he was touching her.
It pleased her too, allowing her to rest so deeply that
she awoke feeling more alive than ever.

At least that was the way of it until the next day.

Marcus was stroking her as she awoke. The feeling
of his hands on her skin was wonderful and warm. She
let out a little sigh as she felt him move up behind her,
his member thick and swollen. She was smiling and
lifting her bottom when her belly suddenly intruded.
Nausea rolled through her in a thick wave as she
scrambled to grab the sheeting and pull herself from
the bed. Her bare feet slapped against the stone floor
as she ran toward the closet.

She got there just in time before she began heaving.
Her stomach wasn't content with merely sending its
contents up; the organ seemed intent on turning itself
inside out. Her dignity had deserted her as she retched
and finally collapsed in a quivering heap on the floor.
It was chilly and she stumbled to her feet, making a
clumsy entrance back into the bedchamber.

Only to find her husband in his shirt, offering her
his flask. She took it, but wrinkled her nose at the
scent and handed it back untasted.

"I'm fine," she offered, but he continued to consider her silently. "I said—"

"I heard ye, lass," Marcus informed her gently. Too

gently. The man never coddled her, and she liked it that way.

"And just what do ye mean by that?" She was suddenly hot, her skin feeling as though she'd been running through a meadow in the summer heat.

Marcus crossed his arms over his chest. "It means I'm waiting for ye to tell me."

"Tell ye what?"

He resumed silently contemplating her. In an abrupt shift, Helen discovered herself fighting back tears. It was humiliating, and she turned her back on her husband as she tried to scrape together her composure. She heard him let out a harsh breath.

"I must be doing this wrong." He wrapped his arms around her just as the tears stinging her eyes defied her order to remain unshed and trickled down her cheeks. "But I will nae go seek out me brother and ask him for advice while ye are shivering and weeping because of me."

He nuzzled at her hair, inhaling her scent and sighing as though she were the perfect woman. Her hot tears splattered on his arm where he had it wrapped around her.

"Christ, Helen," he said softly. "I can nae bear yer weeping. Does it make ye so unhappy to be carrying me child?"

"Ye know?" she asked as she turned and ducked under his arm. He might have kept her bound to him easily, but he let her go.

"Ye fascinate me." His eyes glowed with intensity. "From the moment ye came near me, ye've drawn me attention like naught else. Ye have nae bled, yer breasts are swollen, and now ye retch in the morning. For all that I am a man, I know a thing or two about how babes begin their entrance into life."

"Aye," she admitted as it dawned on her what he'd said. "Oh, ye were waiting for me to tell ye. That's what ye meant."

He nodded once, his expression becoming guarded. That drew her attention to him. "Why does it matter? If ye already know, there is little point in me telling ye."

He looked away. Helen let out a snort. "Why would ye be having trouble meeting me eyes, Marcus?"

He snapped his gaze back to hers, aiming the frustration he'd tried to hide straight at her.

"Ye are everything to me, Helen," he rasped out. "I've killed for ye and would nae hesitate to do so again if needed. I followed ye to court, a place I loathe, and yet ye stand here, miserable." He couldn't seem to remain in his position, pointing at her. "Why? Tell me, for God's sake, so I can have a fighting chance."

Marcus MacPherson, the man who never showed weakness, was looking at her with desperation flickering in his eyes. It edged his words, his tone breaking with the abundance of emotion. It struck her straight to the heart, making her feel like a wretch for causing him even a tingle of unhappiness.

"I love ye."

"As I love ye!" He threw his hands into the air but didn't look away. "Explain why ye weep."

He reached out and captured her wrist to hold her in place. "And tell me the truth, or I fear I will go mad from the need to see ye satisfied."

Instead, Helen felt her eyes welling up with fresh tears. They spilled over, and she didn't try to stop them. For the first time in her life, they were happy ones. Marcus looked at them, shaking his head as he tried to comprehend her.

"Ye never told me," she whispered. "I said 'I love ye' when ye rescued me, but ye never…said…"

He blinked several times while her words sank in. "Did nae say?" he said incredulously. "Christ, Helen, I am a War Chief. When I stripped away the evidence of who I was so I could enter Sutherland Castle and find ye, that was telling ye I love ye more than me own life."

"Ye might have been thinking it was yer duty."

He scoffed at her and pulled her against him. "It was, and yet that is no' why I went in there under the threat of being hanged as a spy."

He suddenly scooped her up and carried her back to his bed, working them both under the covers and pulling her close.

"I am no' a man of soft words. Ye'll have to be patient with me."

"I hope I shall be able to give ye forever, my love."

He buried his face in her hair. "And a day, vixen."

∽

Two months later, spring finally arrived in full force. The snow melted, and planting began. Merchants could once more take to the roads and sell what they had made during the winter months. Goods that had been stuck in harbor towns began to make their way into the Highlands.

It was also the time of year for raids, because storerooms were running low while everyone waited for the earth to provide new bounty. No one was happy to hear that the McTavishes were riding on MacPherson land. Marcus ordered the castle locked tight as he went out to meet them.

Rolfe McTavish pulled up when he spotted the MacPhersons. "There is the man I'm coming to see."

"Ye are either the most brazen puppy I've ever laid eyes upon or the biggest fool," Marcus informed Rolfe McTavish. "Perhaps both."

Rolfe grinned, arrogant and confident, as though he wasn't facing down a force equal to his own. "Well, at least ye will no' be thinking I would let something go unattended. Something important, that is."

Rolfe reached into his doublet and pulled out a parchment. "It seems me father thinks yer father needs to see this."

"I recall rather well what yer father sent me the last time he thought I needed something," Marcus growled.

Rolfe became serious for a moment. "Aye. I don't suppose ye'd believe me when I say he's seen the error of his ways?"

Marcus slowly shook his head. "That will take a bit more time, puppy."

Rolfe moved his horse forward so he could hand off the letter. "In that case, MacPherson, I'll be getting off yer land."

"Likely a good idea," Marcus told him.

Rolfe pointed at him. "Aye, but there's no fun in it, MacPherson, none at all."

Marcus chuckled at him. "Go home and grow up, lad. Ye can nae be more than twenty."

Rolfe sent him a grin before he turned his stallion around and rode through the center of his waiting men. They all turned and followed him. Last spring, Marcus would have envied the lad his freedom. Now he saw the merits of having a bed to retire to early and linger in. Like an old man? No, the young truly did not know of what they spoke. He was never more alive than when he was next to Helen.

Marcus arrived back at the castle in time for supper. His father and brother looked up as he came in. He sent his wife a smile as he stopped and tugged on the corner of his bonnet before climbing the stairs to the high ground.

"Laird McTavish has sent ye a letter." He offered the parchment to Shamus.

His father took it, but finished chewing and swallowing as Marcus went around to join Helen at the table. His belly was growling, but he kept his attention on his sire. Waiting, as all the captains at the table were, to see what was so important that Rolfe McTavish seemed to think it needed to be hand-delivered.

Shamus looked up, his expression one of frustration. "I do nae think I have ever heard of a couple who had a harder time staying wed."

He handed off the parchment. His captains clustered around it, some of them standing on their toes to stretch high enough to peer down on it. But it was Marcus who cursed. Long, low, and in Gaelic, and he shot Father Matthew Peter a look that made it clear he didn't care that the priest had heard.

"I am putting an end to this here and now," Marcus declared. He stood and pulled his dagger out of the scabbard on his belt. "Helen."

She looked up as he came around the front of the table. "That"—he pointed at the parchment—"is an annulment. One Laird McTavish arranged for." The hall went deathly still. "So."

"So…what?" she demanded as she pushed her chair back.

"So…" Marcus aimed his voice so everyone in the hall might hear it. "I want to know, do ye want it?"

"Ye know I do no'." Their morning together replayed across her memory. Doubt tried to needle her, but she refused to dance to its tune.

He nodded. "Nor do I. Since we can nae seem to stay wed because the world is being turned upside down by those fighting over the throne, I propose we fall back on tradition."

He used the dagger to cut his kilt and tore off a strip. Understanding flashed across the faces of many of the men seated at the high table, and Bhaic pushed his chair back, coming around to join them.

There was a half sound of protest from Father Matthew Peter. Marcus shot him a hard look. "I've wed her twice and been told the church does no' believe she is me wife as many times."

The priest closed his mouth and tucked his hands up into his sleeves. Perhaps it was not approval, but it was a lack of resistance. Marcus handed the dagger to Bhaic. His brother drew it across Marcus's wrist, cutting the skin. A thin line of fresh blood welled up. Helen offered Bhaic her own wrist. He cut her and then turned her hand so the two wounds met when Marcus clasped her hand and she closed her fingers around his forearm.

Bhaic bound them together with the length of plaid as Marcus clearly spoke the Gaelic words of a blood oath. She answered him, their voices filling the hall while their blood mingled.

⤜⤚

"Was that too barbaric for ye?" Marcus had barely closed the door to their chamber when he asked the question.

Helen had lifted her hand to observe the line marking her skin. She looked up and discovered her husband considering her. Only now, she knew he was concerned for her tender feelings.

"I think it far more savage to annul our vows in some distant place while we are merely trying to get on with living."

Marcus slowly smiled at her. "Aye. For all the good that is brought to us by the outside world, I have to question what those men of learning and exploration think they are doing by making mockery of a man's vows."

"So…" Helen began to finger the buttons going down the front of her doublet, a garment she'd started to wear because she knew he enjoyed her wearing long stays so much. "Since we are now a pagan Highlander couple…may I dispense with being an obedient wife?"

Marcus offered her a hopeful look as he dropped his kilt and she separated the fronts of her doublet to expose her cleavage. "I can nae wait…vixen."

⋞⋟

Young Robbie heard the strangest sounds coming
from the stairway. He got up from his spot on a bench
and went closer, cocking his head to the side to listen.
There was a thump and a scrape and a loud growl.

"Here now, lad," Finley called out. "Best to stay
down here."

Robbie's eyes widened as he heard a heavy thud.
"But there's something happening up there."

Finley laughed and elbowed Kam in the ribs, but
they didn't share whatever it was they found so amusing. "Just Marcus chasing that vixen he's wed to."

"Aye, naught to worry about." Kam gestured the
boy back.

"But—"

"Listen well, lad." Finley got up and shepherded
the lad back into the hall with a fatherly arm around
his shoulders. "Everything is very right."

"Even if it sounds as though she is killing him?"

Kam collapsed into a fit of laughter, lowering his
head to the table to rest on top of his crossed arms as
he chuckled.

"Believe me, lad, he'll die a happy man." Finley slapped
Kam on the shoulder as he joined him in laughing.

Another loud sound came bouncing down the
stairwell, but it was the last, which left Robbie trying
to puzzle the entire situation into something he
might understand.

Women sure were odd creatures. Between Helen
Grant becoming a high-standing member of the clan,
and the English girl wanting him to teach her how to
wrestle, he was very confused.

It was likely a good thing he didn't like girls all that much. They did tend to make his head hurt. When he wed, he'd make sure it was not to a vixen.

⤳

Depravity.

It had been a word used to instill obedience in her when she was young. Now, Brenda faced its true meaning and the ugliness of those who embraced it as a challenge.

The sun had not risen, and she half believed it was because of the shame that would be illuminated when it did. Around her, Brenda heard the snoring of Scotland's ambassador to England and England's ambassador to Scotland. There was a stench in the air from their excesses the night before.

She felt as though it was permeating her very soul.

But the sun would rise, and she would feel every ache they'd inflicted upon her flesh, so she rolled over and sat up, trying to ignore the pain that went through her passage. She didn't want to think about what was past.

It would replay across her dreams soon enough.

Morton had made good on his threat, making her his whore to be used at will, and the ambassadors had heard of her plight and decided to take advantage of Morton's generosity.

Indeed, she understood the meaning of the word *depravity* now.

There were scattered retainers in the room as well. They were all sleeping off the effects of the numerous bottles of French wine they had consumed during the course of the night. She picked her way through the limbs, escape from the chamber the only thing she might grant herself.

But she stopped when she realized how many of the retainers were inside the room. The horror of the night before had numbed her wits as to just how many men had been involved; now, she looked around and counted them in the predawn light. Her heart started to accelerate as she realized there was no one left outside the door. At least, no one belonging to the personal households of the ambassadors.

It was an opportunity she'd scarcely hoped for, and everything she needed was right there, within reach.

Suddenly, the aches in her body weren't so terrible, the welts down her back from the whip no longer excruciating. She was more focused on the clothing strewn about the chamber. She pulled a shirt up and put it on, wincing just a bit as the fabric landed on her back.

She didn't have time to dwell on the pain.

So she sat down and picked up a boot, lacing it in the low light and then pushing her other foot into a second one. When she got up, she spied a sword belt and a kilt lying forgotten on a table. She grabbed it and hastily pleated it. She had to use the dagger to work a new hole into the belt so it would fit her, but she got it fashioned and pulled on the doublet.

At last, she drew the dagger through her hair, shearing off two feet of it before she stuck a bonnet on her head and took a deep breath. The horizon wasn't really even pink yet. There was that lightening of darkness that happened right before dawn broke. Enough light to see, so the servants would be beginning their day.

Brenda crept toward the doors and pushed them open. Two men stood there, weary of their duty but still awake. She looked at the ground and heard one of them snicker at her, but he didn't stop her.

"Off to confession with ye, lad," the other said. "Best to gain forgiveness when ye'll be needing more soon enough."

Forgiveness. She didn't need it, and she certainly wouldn't be granting it either. But she was hearing the sound of her deliverance. The castle was opening its gates as dawn broke. She caught the scent of food as she walked through the passageways, but she didn't dare stop. No, Brenda Grant walked toward the yard and through the gates. No one stopped her, or at least the young lad she appeared to be. They thought her a messenger or a servant being sent on ahead of her master to prepare a welcome for him.

That made it simple to take a horse from the stable.

Simple? She was not sure if it was the correct word to use, but it did fit at the moment. She was suddenly on her way back to the Highlands, mile after mile falling behind her as the horse walked along.

Simple.

Perfect.

❧

Brenda Grant walked right into Grant Castle. Two burly retainers stepped into her path, but she pulled her bonnet off and sent them a solid stare. They immediately pulled on the corners of their caps and cleared her path.

She ignored the gnawing hunger in her belly and chose instead to climb the steps to the laird's

chamber. Her uncle was propped up on pillows, and
still he struggled to draw in breath. She stood at the
foot of his bed for a long moment, listening to the
sound of his manservant scurrying out of the chamber, no doubt to summon help in case she decided
to kill her uncle.

"Ye look…as though…ye have tasted…the harsher
side of life."

"I have," she confirmed. Truly she must be a sight,
filthy and bedraggled and wearing men's clothing.
Yet she had never felt so victorious in her life. It was
surging through her, awaking her spirit in a way she'd
never thought possible.

There was a soft step behind her, and she turned
to discover Symon reaching for her. He froze as he
caught sight of her face. "Brenda?"

"Aye," Laird Grant confirmed. "It seems…she
has…remedied…her situation…herself."

"I did," Brenda said. "So ye will no' be surprised
to hear that I will no' be honoring the arrangement ye
made for me."

Symon made a sound behind her, a moment before
he gently tugged the filthy collar of her doublet
down. She knew what he saw, the swollen red tracks
of the last lashing she'd received. The doublet was
bulky and large, allowing him a good view. The
cuts were infected now—she'd felt the burning start
several days past.

"And if I survive this fever, I will never answer to
a husband again."

That was the thing that had kept her going. The
need to speak her mind to her uncle. Now that it was

done, her strength was running out, but she would be damned if she were going to allow her knees to buckle now. Just a few more paces to a chamber she could call her own. She turned and shot Symon a hard look before she left.

She might die, but she was going to draw her last breath as a free woman, and that was enough contentment for her. She got to her chamber, where the furniture was covered in sheets, making it look shrouded. Perhaps it would be her tomb, perhaps not.

All that mattered was she was free, and that was the last thought she had strength for before she collapsed onto the bed.

◦≈◦

"I did nae do right by her."

It had been a long time since his father had spoken so clearly or without struggling for breath. Symon turned to stand by his side.

"Me brother failed her as well. Wedding her to that boy-lover." Laird Grant made a low sound of disgust. "And too young. A disgrace, it was."

He lifted his hand, "Bring me...me secretary."

His father waited while the man settled his small traveling writing desk on a table. Withdrawing a piece of parchment and uncorking a small inkwell, the secretary dipped the quill into it and waited for his laird to speak.

"Brenda is to have her mother's property." His father sent Symon a firm look. "Do nae begrudge her. Ye are better than her father and me."

"I will nae," Symon promised.

The secretary scratched away, filling the creamy length of paper with words that were shiny before the ink dried.

"She's to be her own woman."

Laird Grant was talking to Symon now, and he realized his father was making his peace, no longer fighting his death.

"I will no' force any match on her," Symon promised.

Laird Grant struggled to sit up. Symon had to help him, but the laird gestured to the secretary, who brought the document to him. His father signed it with a hand steadier than it had been in years, and then waited while the secretary melted wax from a stick with a candle so the laird might push his signet ring into it. His father read through the words one time before he nodded in satisfaction.

"Honor me words, Symon, as the fine man I have been blessed to see ye become. I'm righting a wrong here… Grant me the peace of knowing I'll no' carry this sin with me."

"I swear it to ye, Father."

His father reached up and placed his hand on top of Symon's. "Ye will be a good laird."

Symon watched as his father's eyes lit up and he seemed to stare into the distance. A rare smile curved his lips as he reached for something beyond the foot of the bed. Whatever it was, his father's spirit went to it. Symon felt a chill touch his spine as he noted the passing of life from his father's eyes. It felt as though the very chamber went cold.

The secretary looked at Symon for a long moment before offering him the parchment.

"It stands," Symon told the man.

The secretary nodded before he withdrew to his desk and put away the tools of his trade. Before long, the bells were ringing out his father's passing, leaving Symon to face his clan as the new laird.

∽

Brenda opened her eyes and found Symon sitting next to her bed.

"Have ye no' had enough of attending deathbeds?"

Symon offered her a smile. "Ye are nae dying."

"No' anymore, it would seem." She felt worn out, in spite of having been in bed for the last two weeks. But the fever was gone, even if it was still painful to move.

She started to say something, but stopped when she noted the three feathers on his bonnet. They were all pointing upward, instead of one being lowered.

"Aye, me father has died," Symon confirmed. He tapped something lying on the bedside table. "His last will was to make sure ye inherited yer mother's dowry property, and to extract a promise from me that I would no' make any match for ye that ye do not wish."

She reeked, and her back hurt every time she moved, but she got to her knees, clutching the bedding against her front to shield her bare body, and pulled the parchment closer. She read it twice, fixated on the seal for a long time.

"I'll send a bath up for ye."

Brenda looked at Symon. "I am sorry for yer loss."

"As I am for yer circumstances."

She hugged the parchment close to her heart. "Oh, me situation is very well. It pleases me greatly. For now ye are the one who must wed."

"Aye." Symon stood and reached up to tug on the corner of his bonnet. "I understand I should stay well away from the Earl of Morton."

Brenda snorted. "I plan to as well."

And the parchment clutched to her chest was the salvation she needed. Symon left her, and she smiled as she giggled like a girl.

It had been such a long time since she laughed.

She promised herself she would do it every day for the rest of her life.

❧

Four years later…

Helen stood on the steps of the keep, her son tugging on her skirts to get her to move down the steps. Rae was always in a hurry to see his father.

Well, she had to admit to having the same urge from time to time. The yard was full of the sound of boys training. She allowed Rae to tug her to where the main yard separated into the training one. There, she firmly pulled her young son to a stop. Marcus was standing on a small raised platform in the center of the yard. He was watching the boys, calling out corrections to some of them as they worked with wooden daggers.

To many, it might seem that Marcus didn't see her, but Helen knew better. Only a few moments later, he crossed through the boys and joined her. He scooped Rae up and tossed their son into the air, to the boy's delight.

"Me heart still stops when ye do that," she admitted as Marcus caught the boy and put his face on the little one's stomach, blowing out a long grumble that tickled him.

"Now, Helen"—Marcus looked over Rae's mop of blond curls—"I've told ye before. Ye'll just have to wait until I finish me duties before we can get on with how breathless I make ye."

Helen propped her hand on her hip, which made her belly stick out even further. "I know…" she muttered sweetly. "I know well ye need to work up yer courage to face me alone."

The training had slowed down, proving the boys were listening. Several turned astonished glances their way; Helen's lack of submission clearly shocked them. She suddenly looked beyond Marcus at a pair of older youths.

"Aye." Her husband followed her gaze, then lowered his tone and became serious. "I know, but they think I do no', so stop staring."

Helen tore her gaze from the sight and looked at her husband in shock. "Ye know Katherine is wearing a kilt and fighting?"

Marcus stepped close and rubbed her distended belly to make it look as though they were simply sharing a private, tender moment.

"She could be hurt, Marcus."

"As an English lass in the Scottish Highlands, it's for certain some might wish to harm her. Why do ye think I am allowing her to train?"

It was unconventional, to say the least. Helen snuck another quick look toward Katherine. She did indeed have a kilt on and a shirt as she tried to keep a dagger from being plunged into her neck by her partner. There was blood coming from her nose and a dark bruise on one side of her head, but she fought back with a skill Helen admitted she was envious of.

"Better hope Father Matthew Peter does no catch ye." Helen looked down at her belly. "This child will no' have a sibling for years if he does."

Marcus raised his eyebrows as a wicked glint entered his eyes. "But what would the man do to punish me?"

Helen let out a little grunt before she turned and left Rae perched on his father's shoulder. When she reached the top of the stairs, she turned back and watched the way Marcus held the boy with one hand, just as powerful as the first time she'd seen him.

Happiness.

Somehow, it had happened, and she had no intention of arguing with Fate.

None whatsoever.

*Keep reading for a sneak peek at the next book
in Mary Wine's Highland Weddings series*

HIGHLAND HELLION

1578

"YE'RE A FOOL," ROBERT MACPHERSON GRUMBLED.
"And likely to get us both lashed."

Katherine Carew didn't offer him even a hint of
remorse. She settled herself on top of her horse, confidence shining in her midnight-blue eyes. "I've trained
as hard and long as ye have."

"Yes, but ye're—" Robert clamped his lips shut
and took a hasty look around to make sure no one was
listening. "Ye're a woman now."

And Robert was a man. Katherine found the new
element in their relationship curious, and she didn't
care for the change. It threatened to upset the balance
of her life—an existence that she liked very much. So
she fixed him with a hard look, determined to change
his thinking. "You are the one who suggested I start
wearing a kilt in the first place."

Robert frowned. "I was young and a damned fool."

His eyes lowered to where she'd bound her breasts. His lips thinned and his jaw tightened, sending an unexpected sensation through her. It was slightly unsettling because Robert was her friend and compatriot. Yet he had taken to spending more time with the older men. She didn't dare venture too close when he was with them for fear they would realize her game. Dressing contrary to her gender was a sin, an argument against what God had decided she would be.

"We're going raiding," Robert insisted in a low voice. "It is no place for a…for ye."

"Ah, let the lad be," Bari spoke up from where he was securing his saddle. The burly MacPherson retainer peered over at them, his face covered by a thick beard. "If he pisses himself, he'll jump in the river before we return home, and he can share his whisky with us so we all don't tell the tale."

There was a round of laughter from the men close enough to listen in, proving that Katherine and Robert's words were very much in danger of being overheard. Robert went still in a way she'd never seen before. Katherine actually felt the bite of fear as she realized he was considering unmasking her.

He was her only friend, and the betrayal cut her deeply.

Well, she was going.

Katherine made sure the straps of her saddle were tight. She took a great deal of pleasure in the fact that she knew as much about preparing a horse for riding as every one of the men surrounding her. That would certainly not be the case if she'd been raised in England.

Her old life was only a memory now, hidden behind her adventures in the Highlands. She smiled as she recalled the many things she'd done at Robert's side while disguised as a boy. She gripped the side of the saddle, making ready to mount.

But a hard hand dug into the back of her jerkin and lifted her into the air.

"What?" Katherine was startled, or she wouldn't have spoken because her English accent persisted. More than one head turned in her direction as she landed and found herself looking up into the eyes of Marcus MacPherson, war chief of Clan MacPherson.

"I told her she should nae go." Robert was quick to assign blame to her.

Marcus had braced himself between her and the horse. The war chief was huge and stood considering her from a position she'd seen too many times to count while she trained under his command in the yard. Of course, he thought she was a boy, which made Robert's choice of words very bad.

Very, very bad.

"You clearly did nae tell her firmly enough." Marcus shifted his full attention to Robert. "There will be a reckoning owed when we return, sure enough."

Robert bristled as more men came to witness his chastisement. "She's the one who will no' listen to good sense."

"Agreed," Marcus said. "Which is why ye should have pulled her off her horse as I just did, since it was you who brought her into me training yard six years ago."

Katherine gasped. She hated the way the sound came

across her lips because it was so…well, so feminine. The men were frowning at her, clearly disapproving.

She shook her head and leveled her chin. "I have trained, and I am as good as many a man standing here."

"Ye are a woman," Marcus stated clearly. "And ye do nae belong riding out with us when we are going to needle the Gordons."

"It isn't a real raid," Katherine protested, but she kept her tone civil. She would always respect Marcus for teaching her to defend herself. "Just a bit of fun."

"Aye," Marcus agreed. "And yet, not as simple as that. Men get their blood up when they are testing one another's nerve. It is no place for a woman, even less so for a maiden."

"Ye see?" Robert said. "I told ye."

"But ye did nae make certain she could nae venture into danger. That's the difference between a lad and a man." Marcus spoke softly, which only gave his words more weight. "It's past time for ye"—he pointed at Robert—"to recognize that a little lass like Katherine has more to lose if our luck does nae hold. As a MacPherson retainer, I expect ye to make sure the women are taken care of. That's the real reason they respect us, no' simply for the sake of our gender."

Marcus shifted his attention back to her, and she felt the weight of his disapproval. "Ye could be raped and ruined."

"My reputation is already ruined because I am here," Katherine protested.

"That is no' the same thing at all," Marcus informed her in a steely voice. "And I hope to Christ ye never discover the truth of the matter. For tonight, ye'll take yerself back inside, and I will deal with ye when I return."

Marcus's word was law on MacPherson land. Only his father and his brother, Bhaic, could argue with him, and Katherine wasn't dense enough to think either of them would disagree. So she lowered her chin and bit her lip. It earned her a soft grunt from Marcus before he moved back toward his horse.

Then the muttering started.

"English chit…"

"More trouble than we need…"

"Damned English always think themselves better than Scots…"

Men she'd thought of as friends suddenly turned traitor, calling her "English" as though she had only recently arrived on their land.

She'd truly thought her feelings dead when it came to the subject of her blood. The rush of hurt flooding her proved her wrong.

Well, that was foolish.

And she would have none of it.

Her father's blue, noble blood was a curse, and she'd learned the burden of it by the time she was five. His legitimate wife detested her because of the cost of the tutors needed to educate her and the dowry she'd require. She'd been abducted because of that dowry and nearly wed at fourteen.

Marcus MacPherson had taken her into the Highlands instead. It had seemed to be the perfect solution. So far removed from England and her family, there was no one to tell her what she must be. She had been free.

Even from her gender.

Katherine lifted her chin because even after mounting, the MacPherson retainers were still considering her. She refused to crumble. Training among them as a lad, she'd learned to keep her tears hidden, and she'd be damned if she'd show them any now. A stable lad suddenly came up and tried to take her horse.

"I'll tend to my own mount," she informed him, making sure her voice carried. "As I always have."

Katherine didn't wait to see what those watching made of her words. She reached up and ran a confident hand along the muzzle of her horse before she turned and started to lead it toward the stable.

Indeed, she took care of herself, and that brought her much-needed relief from the sting of her bruised emotions.

❦

"What do ye mean by that?" Helen Grant demanded.

Marcus eyed his wife, crossing his arms over his chest and facing her down, as was his fashion. Helen's eyes narrowed. "Ye heard me clearly, Wife."

Helen scoffed and settled her newest babe into its cradle before she turned on him while pulling the laces on her dress tight. "What I heard was that ye seem to think what a woman does with her day is easier to learn than a man's lot."

Marcus frowned. "Do nae go twisting me words."

"I should have had charge of her years ago if ye wanted her trained properly in the running of a house," Helen continued. "Ye are the one who allowed her to be a lad."

"And for good reason," Marcus answered back. "She's English. Ye know how often ye have heard curses against her kin, and I assure ye, I have heard three times as much because the men do tend to mind their tongues in the hall."

Helen had finished closing her dress and settled her hands on her hips. "As I said, I do nae know what ye expect me to do with her now that ye've let her run wild for the past six years. She's twenty now."

"I know." Marcus's control slipped, allowing his exasperation to bleed through into his tone. "She's a woman, and yet she was intent on riding out with us last evening."

"It wouldn't be the first time," Helen replied. "Why is it a concern now?"

Marcus's jaw tightened, and his wife read his expression like a book. There was no point in trying to keep the matter to himself. He let out a soft word of Gaelic.

"We went out and lifted some of the Gordons' cattle."

His wife stiffened. The Gordons hated the MacPhersons and would spill blood if they could. Old Laird Colum Gordon wanted vengeance for the death of his son, Lye Rob, and the old man didn't seem to care that Bhaic MacPherson had killed Lye Rob with good reason. Lye Rob had stolen Bhaic's new wife, Ailis, and no Highlander worth his name was going to let a man get away with that. Nothing seemed to matter to the old laird of the Gordons except vengeance.

Marcus knew he was playing with fire by going

anywhere near Gordon land. Needling the local clans was one matter; going onto Gordon land was another altogether because it might get him killed. His wife was going to tear a strip off his back for chancing it.

"Damn ye, Marcus," Helen berated him. "So, ye are still acting like a child?" She pointed at their son. "And what will become of the children I bear ye if ye get yer throat slit?"

Marcus only lifted one shoulder in a shrug. "Ye know it will nae come to that. The Grants took some of ours last month. It's just a bit of fun."

Helen made a soft sound. "With the Gordons, it is very different. Which is why ye do nae want Katherine along. Do nae think to pull the wool over me eyes."

Marcus opened his arms in exasperation. "Aye!" He snorted. "There, I've agreed with ye. And ye would have a place if I were to pay for me choices in blood, so do nae insult me by asking such a question. Now tell me ye will take her in hand." He made a motion with his hand. "And teach her…what a woman should be doing with her time."

Helen wasn't pleased, and as she looked at her baby, worry creases appeared at the corners of her eyes.

"I love ye, Helen, but ye know full well what manner of man I am." He pulled her close, wrapping her in his embrace. She settled for just a moment, inhaling the scent of his skin before she pushed against his chest and he released her.

"Aye, well," Helen said softly. "At twenty years of age, Katherine has decided what sort of woman she is as well. Something ye have allowed. Now ye expect me to be the one to destroy her world?"

Marcus's expression tightened as he crossed his arms over his chest. "I'll have words with her."

∽

"The laird is asking to see ye, mistress."

Katherine had been expecting the summons. It was a relief, in a way, to have the matter at hand, and yet she felt her belly twisting as she rose and followed Cam through the passageways toward the laird's private solar. For all that Cam had spoken softly, there were plenty in the great hall who noted what was happening.

From the moment the sun rose, Katherine had felt the weight of everyone's judgment. She'd seen such treatment before and realized it had its uses because it maintained order inside the clan. Those who transgressed learned it would not be tolerated, and being shunned was their fate until they made recompense.

Justice.

It was something they all relied upon the laird for, and she was expected to comply as well.

At least that idea restored some of her composure. The MacPherson clan still viewed her as their own, or something close. She truly didn't want to think about any alternative, so she followed Cam willingly enough. The laird of the MacPherson clan was waiting for her behind a desk. Shamus had a full head of gray hair and a beard to match. A portrait hung behind him, depicting him several decades before when his hair had been as dark as his son Bhaic's.

"Aye, I was a young man once." Shamus proved that his eyesight wasn't failing by noting her interest.

Katherine lowered herself and straightened back

up while the laird contemplated her. He was tapping a finger on the top of his desk. Marcus and Bhaic framed him on either side, proving the gravity of the moment.

"As foolish too," Shamus concluded in a voice crackled with age.

"Hardly foolish to learn to defend myself." In the back of Katherine's mind was the memory of a time when she'd been taught to hold her tongue in the presence of men and her betters. It was too dim to hold back her impulse, though.

Shamus snorted and slapped the tabletop. "From a lad, I'd no' have to take exception to that comment."

"I don't see why it matters that I am a female." Katherine shifted her focus to Marcus. "I can best half the boys with a rapier."

"But ye can nae carry one or risk reprisal from the Church," Shamus said gravely. "A fact ye surely know, lass or ye're daft."

Katherine closed her mouth and nodded a single time.

"Me son, Marcus, trained ye because he thought it best, considering yer circumstances," Shamus said.

He made it sound like she was to be pitied, and that stirred her temper. Katherine lifted her chin in defiance. "I find my circumstances very well."

Shamus offered her a grunt of approval. "Aye, that pleases me, and yet ye are, as both me sons have noted, a woman grown now. The Church might overlook a fair number of things when youth is involved. They are not so lenient when it comes to adults."

Katherine didn't care for the feeling that a noose

was being slipped over her neck. She recalled that feeling from when she was young and living in England. What she detested was the way tears stung her eyes.

She did not cry.

And hadn't since the day the Earl of Morton had looked at her like a creature to be bartered. She'd realized growing strong was her only way to avoid becoming exactly what he saw her as. She would be more than a thing.

"Well…" Shamus resumed tapping the top of his desk. "I'm glad to see that ye agree with me, lass."

"You have yet to tell me what you wish of me."

"Aye." Shamus made a motion with his hand. "Ye'll need to keep company with the women. Helen will instruct ye on the running of a house."

"And ye will keep a skirt on," Marcus added sternly. "No more kilts."

She knew that voice. Had trained under it and learned to respect it because Marcus was preparing the youths of the clan for the realities of life, where his training would mean the difference between surviving and an early grave.

Arguing with him felt wrong because he'd given her so many years of joy, and yet she felt cut to the bone by his order. So she lowered herself and left.

She hadn't been dismissed, but Shamus didn't call after her. She needed fresh air, feeling like a stone was crushing her chest.

But relief wasn't hers just yet. Robert appeared next to her, clearly having been waiting for her meeting with the laird to be finished.

"It's for the best," Robert began, his soft tone grating against her frayed nerves.

"Don't you dare speak to me in that fashion." She turned on him.

His eyes widened.

"Like you do to a child," Katherine clarified.

Robert stiffened. Somehow, she'd failed to notice his shoulders had widened and his chin was covered in a full growth of hair now.

"I'm no talking to ye like ye're a child," Robert said, defending himself. "Just—"

"Like a woman?" she demanded. "Go take the hand of Satan and walk yourself to hell."

His cheeks darkened. "Ye have to stop talking like that too. Women do nae curse."

"Easily accomplished," she informed him. "For I will not be speaking to you anymore."

She turned to leave, but Robert reached out and caught her wrist. The bit of strength was there, one she knew and detested because it proved that time was going to destroy the life she had thought she'd built.

"Kat," he said. "Do nae be cross with me. Ye are a woman, and they are right. The bloody Gordons will no' rape me. Ye need to keep to yer place. Do ye want to be known as a hellion? No man will ever have ye if that happens."

"And so my entire worth should be measured by what a man wants me?" She scoffed at him. "My prospects for a good match died when I was abducted by the Earl of Morton."

Robert didn't disagree. He wanted to, opening

his mouth but shutting it when he couldn't form an argument.

"Keep yer hands off me," she declared before she twisted and stepped to the side, breaking his grip. "And do not follow me to speak to me alone. It is improper."

She turned her back on him and found Marcus considering them. She lifted her chin and shot him a hard look.

Wasn't that what they all wanted? Her acting like a woman?

Well, she'd certainly not be apologizing.

Even though she ached to, for Robert was her only true friend.

And now, she was forbidden that comfort.

Why had Fate cursed her with being a female?

About the Author

Mary Wine is a multi-published author in romantic suspense, fantasy, and Western romance. Her interest in historical reenactment and costuming also inspired her to turn her pen to historical romance with her popular Highlander series. She lives with her husband and sons in Southern California, where the whole family enjoys participating in historical reenactment.

My Highland Rebel

Highland Trouble

by Amanda Forester

❧

A Conquering Hero

Cormac MacLean would rather read than rampage, but his fearsome warlord father demands that he prove himself in war. Cormac chooses what he thinks is an easy target, only to encounter a fiery Highland lass leading a doomed rebellion and swearing revenge on him.

Meets an Unconquerable Heroine

Jyne Campbell is not about to give up her castle without a fight, even though her forces are far outnumbered. She's proud and determined, and Cormac can't help but be impressed by her devious plots to force him to leave. Soon, his allegiances are as confused as his feelings for the fair Jyne—though he may have captured the castle, it is she who captures his heart.

❧

Praise for *The Highlander's Bride*:

"Another winner from Forester!"
—*RT Book Reviews*, 4.5 Stars

"A super romantic tale…heart, laughter, and adventure."
—*Harlequin Junkies*

For more Amanda Forester, visit:

www.sourcebooks.com

Every Time with a Highlander

Sirens of the Scottish Borderlands

by Gwyn Cready

New York Times bestselling author

She Can Work Her Magic on Any Man

In a quest to bring peace to her beloved Scottish borderlands, fortune-teller and spy Undine Douglas agrees to marry a savage English colonel. Desperate to delay the wedding long enough to undermine the army's plans, Undine casts a spell to summon help and unexpectedly finds herself under the imperious gaze of the handsome and talented Michael Kent, a twenty-first-century British theater director.

But in this Production, He Commands the Action

Though he abandoned acting years ago, Michael will play whatever part it takes to guard Undine's safety—he's used to managing London's egocentric actors and high-handed patrons, after all. But not even Shakespeare could have foreseen the sparks that fly when the colonel's plans force Undine and Michael into the roles of their lifetimes.

Praise for *First Time with a Highlander*:

"Another charmer...guaranteed to set off the kind of sexy fireworks Cready's fans expect."
—*RT Book Reviews*, 4 Stars

For more Gwyn Cready, visit:

www.sourcebooks.com

How to Train Your Highlander

Broadswords and Ballrooms

by Christy English

❧∞❧

She's the Hellion of Hyde Park...

Wild Highlander Mary Elizabeth Waters is living on borrowed time. She's managed to dodge the marriage banns up to now, but even Englishmen can only be put off for so long...and there's one in particular who has her in his sights.

Harold Percy, Duke of Northumberland, is taken by the beautiful hellion who outrides every man on his estate and dances Scottish reels while the ton looks on in horror. The more he sees Mary, the more he knows he has to have her, tradition and good sense be damned. But what's a powerful man to do when the Highland spitfire of his dreams has no desire to be tamed...

❧∞❧

Praise for *How to Wed a Warrior*:

"Fans of Grace Burrowes and Amanda Quick should be introduced to English." —*Booklist*

"Irresistibly charming."
—*Night Owl Reviews* Top Pick

For more Christy English, visit:

www.sourcebooks.com

Kill or Be Kilt

Highland Spies Series

by Victoria Roberts

— ✑ —

It's been three years since Lady Elizabeth Walsingham ended her childish crush on Laird Ian Munro, the fierce Highlander who scared everyone but her. She's a grown woman now, heading to London to find a proper English gentleman. But when the wild Highland laird walks through the door, she's that breathless youth all over again.

Ian tries hard to avoid the young lass who's confounded him for years. But now that they're attending court, he must keep watch on her night and day. Danger is at every turn and advisors to the Crown are being murdered. Ian soon realizes the girl he's been protecting is a beautiful lady who needs his help, almost as much as he needs her.

— ✑ —

Praise for *My Highland Spy*:

"An exciting Highland tale of intrigue, betrayal, and love." —Hannah Howell, *New York Times* bestselling author

"This book begs to be read and reread." —*RT Book Reviews*, 4.5 Stars

For more Victoria Roberts, visit:

www.sourcebooks.com